A DARK Iris

Elizabeth J. Jones

D0981606

Blouse & Skirt Books
KINGSTON AND NEW JERSEY

© Elizabeth J Jones 2019

First published by Blouse & Skirt Books, 2019

Blouse & Skirt Books is an imprint of Blue Banyan Books Ltd.

This is a work of fiction. All names, characters, and incidents are the product of the author's imagination.

A CIP catalogue record of this book is available from the National Library of Jamaica

ISBN 978-976-8267-25-2

Cover and book design by Ion Communications

Blue Banyan Books
PO Box 5464
Liguanea PO
Kingston 6, Jamaica

www.bluebanyanbooks.com

Thanks are due to CODE, The Burt Award for Caribbean Young Adult Literature and the Bocas Literary Festival

Acknowledgements

My deep appreciation and thanks go to:

Tanya Batson-Savage and Joanne Hillhouse for their insightful and meticulous edits.

Mike Jones for his love, support, encouragement, for everything.

Doug Jones – for being my best critic.

Dr. Kim Dismont Robinson for her constant support and promotion of Bermuda writers and for organising writing workshops led by prominent Caribbean writers.

Lynn Joseph whose workshop on Young Adult Fiction held in Bermuda in 2011 helped me to improve early drafts.

Members of a Bermuda writing group for their generous support at the time of writing: Lisa Brewster, Julie Farnsworth, Mike Jones, Florenz Webbe Maxwell, Andrea Ottley, Dr. Kim Dismont Robinson and Alan Smith.

Dr. Olivia Judson who encouraged me to start writing A Dark Iris and who has been a constant support.

Friend and former Bermuda College colleague, Alison Masters, who has been a stalwart supporter and critic throughout every stage of the novel.

Artist and educator Sharon Wilson who introduced me to pastels and whose artistic technique was a major inspiration for the novel.

Historian Dr. Clarence Maxwell for information about Sally Bassett.

Christie Owen whose enthusiasm for an early draft of my novel encouraged me to continue when I was ready to give up.

Former staff and students at the Berkeley Institute between 1973 and 1974 who gave me a Bermuda education. Staff included: Marva Allen, Jolene Bean, Joan Blades, Pamela Maxwell, Frances Furbert, Robert Horton, Ronald Lightbourne, and Gary Philips.

For my Lovely Family

Mike
Doug and Sam
Ariel and Milo

Chapter

1

"What are you drawing, Rebekah?"

"Just a girl, Mama. Someone I saw."

Rebekah had been sitting at the kitchen counter, attempting yet another sketch of that strange child she had seen on the rocks at Hog Bay.

"But the drawing's not very good."

"Let me see."

It's funny Mama's so interested in my drawing now my daddy has left, Rebekah thought. *She never was much before.* It was always "Do your homework, Rebekah". Or "For heaven's sake, do something useful." Why there was even that time Rebekah's grades were so bad her mama confiscated all her pencils and crayons for a whole month. It had seemed the longest month of Rebekah's life. But now her mama was asking about her drawings? *Maybe she's changed. Maybe if Daddy came back now it would be all right and we could all be happy. Maybe . . .*

"Rebekah?"

Sighing, she tore the page from her pad and handed it to her mama.

"That's lovely, Rebekah – it looks just like you."

"Me, Mama? It's not me. It's someone much younger." Rebekah took the drawing back and looked at it again. "But I can't get her features right."

"When did you see her?"

Rebekah knew the exact date – six weeks ago, the 2 June 1972. The day she and her friend Wanda Lambert had taken the entrance exam to the Meridian Institute, the most prestigious high school in Bermuda. After the daylong exam was over, the two girls had walked home together along the North Shore Road, lined with an assortment of pastel coloured houses and apartments. Rebekah noticed none of them, terrified she had failed.

"Bekah, don't even worry with it," Wanda had said when

Rebekah had muttered she'd got two questions wrong in the exam. "It's over. It's history. Who cares?"

"My mama," Rebekah had said, her mother's voice still nagging in her ears. "You have to have top grades in the exam, Rebekah. You have to get in if you want to make something of your life."

"That's because she's a teacher," Wanda had pointed out. "She can't help it."

As they approached their apartments, which were attached to houses opposite each other down a narrow lane, Rebekah had noticed her daddy's grey Mobylette parked next to their car. *Good, my daddy's home early,* she'd thought. *When Mama starts interrogating me, I can count on him to change the subject.*

It hadn't occurred to her that his coming home early was ominous. All she could think about was how to explain she had probably failed her exam. But when Rebekah walked through the front door her stomach lurched as she heard her mama shouting at the top of her voice in the kitchen.

"You've never earned enough cos you never sell any houses! Gabriel says so. It's your hair. How can you sell houses with your hair like that?"

Rebekah had sighed inwardly. Her daddy's hair was a constant source of argument between her parents. For some reason he was growing locks. It seemed to her the longer the locks grew, the shorter her mama's temper became. *I don't like his hair much, myself,* she'd thought. *It's not very respectable. But Mama needn't be mad at him all the time.*

"I don't want to sell houses!" He was actually shouting; he never did that. "I want to..." Then his voice had dropped and Rebekah hadn't been able to hear what he wanted to do.

"The very least you could do, Jonah Eve," her mama had started yelling again, "the very least, is sell your share of Papa Malachi's land. Or build on it."

"Patricia!" her daddy had yelled back. "I'm not going to do that – you hear me? I'm *never* going to do that." Then his voice had dropped again.

"How could you," her mama had screamed. "How could you just walk out?"

While her parents had been arguing, Rebekah had run upstairs to her bedroom and held her hands over her ears. Then, what seemed like hours later, her daddy had come up and tapped on her door.

"Bek? You all right?" He always called her Bek, or Bekah which sometimes annoyed her mama because she thought shortened names didn't give you respect. "Nobody will *ever* call me Pat. Or Trish. My name is Patricia."

But Rebekah liked it when her daddy called her Bek – it was his special name for her – nobody else used it.

"I'll take you fishing, Bek, but first I wanna show you the field in Somerset."

Her heart had lifted. Papa Malachi, her grandfather on her daddy's side, had a field he used to farm in Somerset. He had given it to her daddy. *Maybe Daddy's gonna show me where he'll build a house*, she'd thought. *And then Mama will feel better.*

"Bekah, you're not listening," her mama said now as she finished washing the dishes. "I asked you when you saw this girl. And where were you?"

"In Somerset, at Hog Bay, with Daddy."

"Oh."

Rebekah could see on her mama's face that she didn't want to think about her daddy. Rebekah didn't want to think about that day either, but she couldn't forget it. They had parked the car and walked along Hog Lane, carrying buckets, fishing lines, and bait until they reached the field. The land stretched up to the top of a hillside lined with trees – casuarinas with feathery, green leaves and pinkish brown fiddlewoods. She remembered seeing faint ploughed furrows but most of the dry, red earth was covered with weeds, wild flowers, and grasses – tufts of minute blue and magenta flowers.

"That's vetch," her daddy had said, walking next to her along the dips. "It's good for the soil – it puts nitrogen into the earth. You'll learn about that when you start chemistry in high school."

But she hadn't been interested, thinking instead about where her daddy would build the house. *If he builds a nice house like Uncle Gabriel's, maybe Mama won't be mad with him all the time.* Her eyes took in the whole field and for a moment she thought she saw dim figures – bent double, pulling stuff out of the ground. She wasn't sure what. Carrots maybe. Then the figures slipped out of vision.

"What do you think, Bek?"

The words had rushed out of her. "Mama will be most disappointed, you know. Because you can't see the water. She wants a water view. Where you gonna put the house? On top of the hill?"

There was a silence interrupted by the shrill, scratchy cries of the kiskadee birds. Then her daddy had dropped his bombshell.

"There's not going to be a house. I'm going to follow in your papa's footsteps. I'm going to farm this and the other fields he gave me, too."

No wonder Mama's so angry, Rebekah had thought miserably. *No wonder.*

Papa Malachi and Grandma Kezia lived just outside St. George's, the old town on the eastern end of Bermuda, where they had a small farm with livestock. But Papa Malachi also had fields all over the island. Some he rented and some he owned. The ones he owned were the reason her mama and daddy argued so often. Because Papa was too old to cope with so much land, he had given some of his plots on the North Shore to his eldest son, Uncle Gabriel, and some in St. George's and Somerset to her daddy. Uncle Gabriel had used part of his share to build a fabulous house with a stunning view of the North Shore and a swimming pool. The rest he had sold to open a real estate office in Hamilton where her daddy worked as well.

"What about at Uncle Gabriel's? You still gonna sell houses?"

"No, Bek. I've quit."

His bluntness shocked her. Then her mama's outraged voice came back into her head. *So that's what Mama meant.* "Mama won't like that," she said in a small voice.

"Well, no, she doesn't but, Bek–"

"What about Uncle Gabriel? Won't he mind?"

"No – he understands me. We're brothers but we're different. We've always been different. He knows that. I'm going to grow vegetables. And maybe start up a farmers' market like they had in the old days."

Rebekah started to feel cold inside.

"Mama will mind. Mama will be *most* upset. She wants houses. She thinks farming is – she says it's demeaning. She says if you want to get some place, you've gotta be a lawyer – some position like that – with things nice – a nice house, nice stuff. That's what she says."

"Bek," her daddy had said. "Where does your food come from? It grows, Bek. Where do you think it grows? In the supermarkets?"

She wanted to finish telling him what she knew her mama thought. Anyone can be a farmer. Her daddy could be something better. He was a real good student in school, he … But she knew she couldn't carry on the conversation. His eyes, usually so calm, shone with determination that day.

"You still want to go fishing?" her daddy had asked. "It's not far."

She'd nodded. They'd gone back to the lane to pick up the gear, strolling past the field and then down again, until they reached the water. Near to the shoreline was a blighted cedar thicket, with smooth weathered silver trunks and silver branches, sticking out like the arms of scarecrows waiting for coat sleeves. She had taken off her shoes and sat on a flat piece of rock that protruded from the middle of the cove. The colours all came back to her – the violets and the ochres of the limestone in the sun and the rich turquoise of the shining sea. She remembered wishing she had brought her sketch book, charcoal, pencils, and crayons to capture the dancing light on the water, emerald rather than turquoise now because the light was always shifting, and the boats moored in the cove, one old and wooden and somehow appealing. One side of it was cast in shade so she couldn't see the engine. But it was a simple boat with simple lines – a boat for doing stuff, not for showing off. She had liked the way the shadows played on the peeling green paint and the dull metal of the steering wheel.

Her daddy had sat next to her. "It's nice, Bek." She had nodded, feasting on the colours around her, wishing she could produce them somehow. But even if she had remembered to bring her crayons, their waxiness wasn't right. She wanted pastels and paint.

"I can't work in an office, Bek. I can't. I have to breathe. I can't breathe in an office. You love drawing and painting, right?"

She nodded. "Course I do."

"Well, I love working with the earth, I have all my life. When I was your age, I worked with Papa Malachi. All of us children did. But I was the one that loved it. It's spiritual – you reap what you grow. You know what I mean? You work with nature."

He took a deep breath. "I've got to do this, Bek." Then he told her he was moving out to stay with Papa Malachi and Grandma Kezia. He held her hand as she tried not to cry. "Your mama and I both love you, Bek, you've got to believe that. But we've grown into two different people – she wants things I don't care about."

She wished it wasn't true but knew that it was.

"Whatever happens, you remember, you're my number one, you hear me?" Her daddy held her close, then let her go too soon. For the first time ever, his hug was no comfort at all. "Now let's do some fishing before it gets dark."

But they had left the hooks in the car. "I'll get them, Bek. I won't be long." He strode back up the hill.

Suddenly her face and arms had felt clammy though the sun was still high. She'd turned towards the cedars and gasped. They weren't dead anymore, they weren't silver! Dusky green, feathery leaves clothed the branches. The air fell silent. A chill had run through Rebekah, clenching her heart. She'd turned again to look at the bay and gasped once more. The green boat in the cove had disappeared and so had the others except for one small unpainted rowing boat she had not noticed before. It was tied with rope to a spike hammered into a rock near the shoreline. The rope looked strange – not as white as the rope Papa Malachi used; it looked as if it had been made out of twisted and plaited palmetto leaves.

That was when she had seen the child.

A small girl darted out from the trees, made her way barefoot to the bay and then clambered onto the jagged rocks as easily as if she was wearing shoes. Rebekah could see her face quite clearly, an elfin face. She had a light coffee complexion and almond-shaped, green eyes. *What a pretty child, but kind of strange, too.* Her hair was a tumble of tight curls tucked under a turban cap. And her dress – Rebekah had never seen anything like it. It was a roughly made, white, grubby shift. The child's head was tilted to one side and she was smiling at something she could see in the water – a fish, an angel fish perhaps. Her lips had parted, and Rebekah thought she could just see the child's front teeth

– one baby tooth next to a larger one. Then the girl had turned towards Rebekah, looked straight into her eyes. But said not a word. The silence was so deep that Rebekah had not dared break it. It would have been like breaking a spell. But how she wished she had brought her pad and charcoal so that she could draw the child. *I have to remember what she looks like. I have to.*

The child had turned her face away from Rebekah's and gazed out to sea. Then she'd slithered down from the rocks, splashing her way into the water.

"Bek, I've got the hooks," her daddy had called. And Rebekah had swivelled towards the direction of his voice. He was waving and walking towards her, past the cedars, now their normal naked selves. She had looked back at the bay. The green boat was there again. The one with the palmetto rope had disappeared. And so had the child.

"My, you're in a funny mood, Rebekah." Her mama's voice jerked her back to the kitchen. Rebekah watched her place the drawing on the counter. "Why aren't you answering me? What made you draw the child? Did you talk to her?"

"No, I just saw her."

"Oh," said Mama. "Well, I still think she looks like you. It's a good drawing, but I wish you wouldn't make yourself look so sad."

"It's not me, Mama, I'm telling you. And she didn't look sad. She looked..." Rebekah stopped to think about it. *Had the girl looked sad? I wish I'd looked at her properly. I wish I'd had my sketchbook.* "Well, I'm not sure how she looked except she was cute."

"Oh," Mama said, taking dishes to the sink and starting to wash them up. "Well, little girl, try not to look so sad."

Great, Rebekah thought. *What am I supposed to look like? Cheerful? My daddy's not here. I can't really talk to him on the phone cos Mama's listening and I feel embarrassed. I can't even tell Wanda because what she'll say, I don't know. There's no way her daddy would leave her. Cheerful? Forget it.*

The phone rang.

"Rebekah, you answer it."

She went to the living room to pick it up and heard Wanda, madly excited. "I've got into the Meridian, Bekah. I got an 8/8 stanine. An 8 for Math! I can't believe it."

Rebekah's heart started to thud. What if her marks weren't good enough? What if Wanda went to the Meridian and she didn't? She'd been best friends with Wanda since they'd both been to preschool. They'd swum together, acted in school plays. They'd done everything together. The thought of high school without Wanda was unbearable. Besides, her pride was at stake. Wanda was nearly a year older, but it was Rebekah who was always top of her class – well, nearly always. What would her mama say if her stanines weren't good enough for the Meridian? If they weren't as good as Wanda's?

"Congratulations," she said, feeling distinctly queasy. "How do you know the result, Wanda?"

"It came in the mail. Have you checked your mail?"

"I don't think so. I'll call you back."

Back with her mama, she asked in as casual a tone as she could muster, "Have you checked the mail?"

"Not yet. Who was that?"

But Rebekah was out the door before she could answer. She lifted the lid of the mail box and saw a thin envelope with the Meridian's logo on it. It was addressed to her parents. She dashed into the kitchen where her mama was wiping down the counters. Outside, the kiskadees were screeching their usual conversations. Mama seemed to be taking forever with the dishcloth. She looked up and must have seen the tension in Rebekah's face. "Are you all right, Rebekah?"

Wordlessly, she handed the envelope to her mama.

"What's this? Oh!" She tore open the envelope and her whole face relaxed into a beaming smile. "You got a 9/9, Rebekah. Perfect score. Congratulations!"

Rebekah felt her heart beat slow down and her stomach relax. *I've got in. And Wanda didn't beat me. Thank you, Lord, thank you.*

"I'm so proud of you, girl." Her mama hugged her so tightly Rebekah felt her feet rise from the floor. "Oh, Rebekah, you have your whole life ahead of you now. If you work hard at the Meridian, you can be anything you want, you know."

Here we go. She's going to go on and on about how all the important people in Bermuda went to the Meridian and got to be lawyers and doctors and goodness knows what else. Thank heavens Wanda's got in! Or it might not be any fun at all.

But her mama surprised her. "Wait a minute," she said. "I have something for you. It's in the bedroom."

Alone in the kitchen, Rebekah picked up the drawing from the counter. *It's no good*, she thought, *it's not how the child was.* And for a minute, in spite of the relief the letter had brought, she felt sick, as if she had lost the memory of something very important. Scrunching the drawing up, she threw it into the waste paper basket just as her mother came back, a small box in her hand.

"Here you go, Rebekah. I want you to have these. After all, now you're going to high school, you're nearly an adult."

When Rebekah opened the box, she found a pair of hooped gold earrings nestling in velvet. "Thank you, Mama. They're beautiful." They were, too; the first pair of earrings she'd ever had other than her studs. She had always felt envious of Wanda, who had several pairs of fashionable earrings.

"You won't be able to wear them at the Meridian, of course. But you can wear them at church and for best."

Her mama looked so happy. Rebekah took another piece of paper and started to draw with her charcoal. "You look pretty when you smile like that, Mama," she said when she finished, showing her mama the drawing – her mother's eyes alight and her lips happily apart, her teeth pearly white. "See?"

"My hair looks pretty," her mama said, pleased.

Rebekah had drawn it straight, framing her face. Mama's hair was always as straight as chemicals could make it, and sometimes when Rebekah drew it, it emerged from the charcoal stiff and tight. This time it looked softer and more natural.

"It does look pretty," Rebekah said.

Mama touched Rebekah's soft waves that fell to her shoulders. "But yours is prettier, girl. You've got good hair."

Chapter
2

Come September, everybody was talking about how the British police commissioner had been shot and killed in his house near the North Shore, and how his daughter was shot and wounded, too, though people were saying she would be all right. Wanda's mama said it was a terrible thing for the country. She said if the tourists were too frightened to come for a vacation she could lose her housekeeping job in the Oleander Guesthouse and Wanda's daddy would lose his job too because he worked in a bar.

But though the murder happened just down the road from where they lived, the two girls didn't have time to think about it. Their first week at the Meridian School was so daunting. They weren't used to having so many teachers for so many different subjects or so many teachers from different countries all over the world. It was very confusing. And there were so many students, too. The ones in the higher years were so tall, so much older, and they all knew where to go and what to do. Rebekah felt too shy to say much to them. Wanda, on the other hand, had no such inhibition and asked lots of questions. As a result, of the two of them, she was more able to quickly figure out how the school worked. So, it was Wanda who made sure they both had the best window seats in their form room and always had textbooks, even when the supplies ran out and other children were left short. She also made sure she was chosen to read aloud in class, because she was naturally dramatic.

"I want to be an actress when I grow up," she'd announce to anyone who would listen. "Rebekah's going to be an artist. Aren't you, Bekah?" And she would show off Rebekah's sketches of the teachers to the other students, much to Rebekah's outward embarrassment but secret delight. *At least I'm still good at something,* Rebekah thought. *All the different subjects we have to do at high school are really hard.*

Then there were the classrooms. They were enormous and there were so many of them, Rebekah kept getting lost. But there was one room that was familiar to her – at least from the outside. That was the school's turreted square tower that she'd often passed when walking or taking the bus into Hamilton. It had always intrigued her. Her daddy, who, along with her mama had studied at the Meridian, said the tower was the only place you could get some peace and quiet, other than in class. "The library's there," he had once explained. "Always has been. You can't miss it – you go up a long flight of stone steps near the office and there it is. As far as we know it's the only room in the tower."

"What do you mean, 'As far as we know'?"

"You're quick, aren't you, Bek? Some say there's a door in the library that leads to another room above the assembly hall. They say the Lady of the Library lives there."

"Who's the Lady of the Library?"

Her mama had sniffed. "She was a teacher – she started at the Meridian long before we were in the first year. She can't possibly be living there. It's just a silly rumour. She must have died years ago."

"You're probably right," Daddy had said to keep the peace. "But I wouldn't put anything past her. If anyone lives to a hundred, she will. And she always loved the Meridian."

Rebekah couldn't get the thought of the hidden lady out of her head. "Have you heard of the Lady of the Library?" she'd asked Wanda a few days later. Wanda immediately nodded. "Oh yes. Roger Peterson's brother told Roger she's an old woman who's supposed to live in the school library, but nobody's ever seen her. Not for years and years. If she is still there, she must be real ugly."

One lunch time towards the end of her first week at school and after a disastrous first art lesson with a horrible man called Mr. Fenwick, Rebekah decided to check out the library to cheer herself up and satisfy her curiosity. Climbing the stairs that led to the tower, she found a large room with a high ceiling, long narrow windows, and walls lined with books. There were also two inside doors. One was open and led to a stock cupboard full of new books and invoices. The other one was closed. The closed door was panelled, painted maroon red, and had a silver knocker. At the bottom of the knocker were two embossed African elephants, in profile, their trunks meeting. Rebekah had never seen a knocker before, except in story books. Everyone she knew, including her family, had a door bell. *If the Lady of the Library is still alive, I bet this is where she stays*, she said to herself. *Because only somebody old would have a door knocker like that.* She stood looking at the door in case someone came out or someone went in. But then the lady at the main desk looked up and Rebekah thought she had better move. She knew the woman couldn't be the Lady of the Library since she was far too young, much younger than her mama.

Rebekah sat down at one of the student tables and proceeded to sketch the lady at the desk because she thought she was so lovely. When Rebekah had finished, the lady came over to talk to her. "My name is Mrs. Chatterjee, and I'm the school librarian. What's your name, child?"

"Rebekah Eve."

"You like drawing, Rebekah? May I see what you've drawn?"

Nodding, Rebekah handed over her sketch. A head and

shoulders portrait of Mrs. Chatterjee with her cap of black shining hair, her lilting smile, and her eyes – alight with interest.

"You've drawn *me*? My goodness, you're so artistic. Mr. Fenwick will be happy to have you in his class. He's a new teacher from England this year. He has a very good reputation because his art commands very high prices."

Rebekah's heart sank as she remembered how disappointing her art lesson had been that morning.

"He's so rude," Wanda had commented loudly when Mr. Fenwick marched into the classroom and, without any introduction, asked the children to draw and paint a tube of Polo mints. Nobody had known what he was talking about.

"The mint with the hole in the middle," he'd barked in his English accent, his mottled face becoming more mottled by the minute.

"Life Saver?" Wanda had asked, holding up a tube.

"Well, I suppose that will have to do."

Rebekah couldn't understand the point of drawing a stupid cylinder and then painting it with poster paint when she could be learning to use different paints and media. *Childish*, she'd thought. *Why can't we have watercolours or oils? Or best of all, pastels?* She'd made a rudimentary sketch of the tube and then focussed on the kids in class who had been in junior school with her. Roger Peterson, the junior school tease, had come to life on her paper as she made her charcoal work, framing his short Afro around his mischievous face. And Juan Symonds, often the object of Roger's teasing, had appeared next, on another piece of paper. He had an Afro too but a much thinner face, owlish spectacles, and a serious expression. Engrossed in her work, she'd all but jumped out of her chair when Mr. Fenwick came up to her and, looking at the drawings, snarled, "We're focussing on still life today, not life drawing. You will please draw and then paint a tube of Polo mints."

Rebekah had shown him her attempt at the candy.

"You haven't painted it! I'll thank you to follow my instructions. Or I will be forced to give you detention." And he'd stormed off.

"I'm sure you'll do very well in art," Mrs. Chatterjee was saying. "Why don't I show you our library's art section? Would you like that?"

"Yes, please."

Rebekah spent some time browsing through the books and then a thought occurred to her. She went to Mrs. Chatterjee's desk. "Are there any books with paintings by black people?" she asked.

Just as she asked the question, she could swear she saw the red door open slightly. But when she looked again, it was tightly shut.

"That's a good question," Mrs. Chatterjee said, drawing Rebekah's attention away from the door. "I don't know as much about art as you do. But I do know the art department has some spare money in the book budget. I shall ask Mr. Fenwick about buying more books about black artists."

Well, that's not going to happen, Rebekah thought.

So she was amazed when the next day Mrs. Chatterjee presented her with four well-thumbed books about Aaron Douglas, Laura Wheeler, Henry Ossawa Tanner, and Horace Pippin. "But they're not library books," Rebekah said when she opened one. "See? There isn't any library card."

"I know," said Mrs. Chatterjee. "It's strange. I found them on my desk this morning. So I think you are meant to borrow them. Why don't you choose one to start with?"

Rebekah chose the volume called *The Paintings of Henry Ossawa Tanner* and flipped through the pages until she came to a picture called *The Banjo Lesson*. Her mouth dropped open. An old man in the painting was teaching a young boy to play the banjo. *He's a grandfather,* Rebekah decided, *teaching his grandson.* He reminded her so much of Papa Malachi – the same serious, watchful and yet kind expression, the same dark skin tones. He reminded her, too, of her daddy and all the things he had taught her like fishing and looking at plants and reading an encyclopaedia. She looked at the boy, half leaning against his teacher, and at the room itself which was poor in one way – a bare wooden floor, a pan, a pitcher, a jug and a plate – but so rich in another because of the light glowing from the plain wall onto the cloth on the cabinet behind them and the lustrous browns of the floor.

"Let me see," said Mrs. Chatterjee and Rebekah showed her the man and boy. Mrs. Chattergee was silent for a minute. Then she said, "Do you like that painting, Rebekah?"

"Oh yes. How could anyone not like it? Besides..."

"Yes?"

"It's the first time I've seen any black people in a proper painting, you know."

"That's very important," agreed Mrs. Chatterjee.

Rebekah nodded. *I don't care about Mr. Fenwick and his stupid mints,* she told herself. *I'm going to paint like that, just like that.*

Chapter 3

Rebekah watched hypnotised as three drops of water trickled down the outside of the classroom window pane next to her. *It's peculiar how whenever Miss Spruce teaches us, it rains,* she thought. *Typical, somehow.* She could hear the teacher's voice droning on and on about history. But she thought instead about the weekend and how nothing much had happened. Wanda had been busy looking after her little twin brothers, Trey and Troy, so they couldn't spend time together. Rebekah had stayed at home doing her homework and drawing. On Sunday morning she'd gone to church with her mama and, after the service, people had still been talking about how the Police Commissioner had been shot in his home.

"It's a bad day for Bermuda that it's come to this," one person had said, "but it's time we got to grips with the problem …"

"What problem?" Rebekah had asked.

"Hush. This is grown up conversation," she was told. Why was it that anything interesting was grown up conversation?

As she sat in the classroom, her elbows propped up on the desk and her hands almost covering her ears, questions whirled around her head. *I wonder what a police commissioner does. Why would someone want to shoot him? And what is the problem they're talking about?*

The rain kept dripping, and Miss Spruce's voice droned on.

"Now, class, I want you to think about why the past is very important and about what you think we can learn from it. Perhaps you can think of an event that happened in your family's past and the difference it made to your lives."

Wanda jabbed Rebekah in the elbow.

"Can you smell her smoke?" she whispered. "I can. Roger says his brother says she's always in the Starry Night Club smoking and drinking. And look at her skirt. It doesn't go with her top – her colour combination really makes me laugh."

Rebekah half smiled but she wasn't really listening. *Who cares about what Miss Spruce looks like?* she thought. *She's so boring. It's too bad we have her so often.* Miss. Spruce was Rebekah's English, history, and form teacher. She could hear her asking again, "Come on students, can you think of a reason for the past being important?"

Rebekah sighed inwardly. *What's the point of history when it's over already?* Somehow that made her think of her mama and daddy and how her daddy wasn't living with them anymore. She traced the rain drops on the pane with her fingers. If only her daddy would phone her more often. He hadn't called for days. She'd tried phoning him, but he was always out.

"He's busy," Grandma Kezia had told her. "He's busy ploughing the fields and planting because it's planting season, you know. By the time he gets home it's late. But he'll call you. Just be patient, child."

But it was hard to be patient. There were so many things she wanted to tell him. That she missed him. That school was so tiring and art class was horrible because of Mr. Fenwick. And the other subjects weren't much better. She couldn't concentrate. And then there were the children in her class – Luanne Butterfield who sucked her teeth and rolled her eyes and thought she knew everything. Trina Tucker who was nice but was always asking her to draw pictures when she didn't feel like it. And Roger Peterson from junior school who was his usual nasty self. And worst of all, there was Wanda who was changing every day and Rebekah didn't appreciate it. Perhaps even if her daddy did visit her, she wouldn't tell him about Wanda because it would be disloyal. But she could show him. These days when she drew Wanda, she saw that her body shape was different. Her bust was filling out. She walked differently too, with a wiggle in her rear end. She didn't wear her hair in a top knot any more either or braid it. Instead, she wore it in an Afro and she was always fussing with it with her Afro pick. She was still Rebekah's best friend, of course – that would never change. But sometimes Wanda wasn't as much fun anymore. Sometimes not very nice either. At junior school, they had both agreed Roger Peterson was the meanest boy in the school and that he shouldn't tease Juan Symonds for not having a father. Not for stuttering either. It wasn't Juan's fault. But lately Wanda seemed to like Roger. She kept eyeing him and every time he cracked a joke at Juan's expense, she'd laugh loudly.

Rebekah was glad she had never told Wanda about her daddy leaving. If Wanda could laugh when Roger teased Juan for not having a father, what would she say if she knew Rebekah's daddy had left?

Thinking of her daddy brought the picture of the strange child she'd seen in Somerset into her mind. *Maybe this time I can get her face right*, she told herself, remembering the moment when they had stared at each other. *We did stare at each other, didn't we? I didn't imagine it?* Picking up her pencil she started to draw in the middle of her new exercise book.

"Rebekah! You haven't been listening, have you?" Miss Spruce's voice jerked her back to the class. "What did I just ask?"

She strode up to Rebekah's desk and saw her drawing of

the child sitting on the jagged rocks. "Rebekah, you're always drawing!"

"She can't stop herself," Wanda said helpfully. "She's an artist, you know."

Miss Spruce's mouth twitched. "I'm glad to know that, Wanda. But Rebekah, you need to concentrate in my class." She picked up the exercise book and ripped out the drawing. "I'm sorry," she said in reaction to Rebekah's furious expression. "I don't want you drawing in my class. And not in your history book, either. Not unless I tell you to. Now, Rebekah, can you think of an event in the past that has made a difference to you?"

Rebekah's mind went totally blank.

"No, Miss Spruce, I can't. I'm sorry."

"Well, Rebekah, I'm sorry, too." Walking back to her desk, Miss Spruce filled out a slip of paper and gave it to Rebekah.

Wanda's eyes went round. "Oh dear, Rebekah, that's a parent/teacher request."

"Yes," said Miss Spruce. "I am going to ask the headmistress to call your parents to meet with your teachers."

"That's not fair, Miss Spruce,' Rebekah said. "I'm not the only one in the class not to answer."

"No, but you are the only one to draw in class. And as your form teacher, I've noticed your other grades are not as high as your exam result led us to expect. So we'll have no more argument about it."

Rebekah dreaded bringing the note home. But when her mama saw it, she was not angry. Instead, her eyes filled with tears which made Rebekah feel far worse.

"Mrs Drinkwater called me," her mama said. "You have to keep your grades up. You don't want to be like Grandma, do you?"

"Grandma Kezia?"

"No – you have two grandmas, you know. Though sometimes you mightn't know it," Mama said with a touch of acid in her voice. "Grandma Violet."

Grandma Violet, her mama's mama, lived in the back of Hamilton in three small, cramped rooms. Sometimes they would go visit her, but Grandma Violet was always so quiet and sad, Rebekah never enjoyed the visits. Grandma would just sit and stare out of the window while Mama talked.

"She cleaned houses all of her life because she didn't have an education. You don't want to clean houses all your life, do you?"

"No, Mama."

But I wouldn't mind really, Rebekah thought. *It would be better than sitting in a classroom being bored to death. At least it would be doing something. Besides, what's wrong with cleaning houses? Someone has to do it.*

"You have to do well in school." Her mama's eyes glittered with intensity. "You have to, you hear me? Because, trust me, you wouldn't like to be like Grandma Violet."

She had to admit she wouldn't, but she couldn't really see the connection. She was a completely different person from Grandma Violet.

"What's Grandma Violet got to do with it anyway, Mama?"

"It wasn't easy when I was young, Rebekah. We were poor and the children at school let me know it, I can tell you. I didn't have nice clothes the way you do. I knew it was up to me to climb out of poverty. I worked very hard so I could go to college and become a teacher. I knew education was the only thing to help me."

Rebekah sighed. The very sound of the word 'education' made her feel tired. Then a thought occurred to her. "What about your daddy, Mama? What did he do?"

"I never knew him," she said. "He died when I was very young."

Rebekah could see her mama wanted to change the subject. Then she thought of her own daddy not living with them anymore and tears filled her eyes.

Her mama reached out to hold her hand. "You can do better, you know that you can."

"I miss my daddy."

"I know you've been missing him, but you've got to be strong, Rebekah. You mustn't get into trouble like this."

"Are you going to tell Daddy?"

"No," she said, frowning. "He's too busy anyway."

Mrs. Drinkwater sat at her desk in her office. Empty chairs were arranged in a circle facing her.

"Good morning, Mrs. Eve, good morning, Rebekah." The good morning ceremony over, Mrs. Drinkwater got down to business. "Do sit down, Mrs. Eve. Rebekah, I want you to stand there, against the wall. Your teachers will be arriving shortly and will be reporting on your grades."

It was agonising waiting for them, knowing she would hear nothing but criticism. The teachers started to file in. Rebekah distracted herself by reflecting on the drawings she had done of the various teachers.

Mr. Enfield, who taught chemistry, took a seat first. He was wearing his normal nasty looking yellow suit. "Have you noticed," Wanda had said once, "how teachers from England don't look sharp? It's cos they don't know how to dress. Miss Spruce is bad but Mr. Enfield!" She had laughed at how Rebekah had caught on paper his lumpy, red nose, lopsided glasses, and rumpled suit.

Then came Monsieur Bellamy, who was from Martinique and taught French. It was funny how he always looked so dapper in his perfectly cut blue suits and yet so worried. Rebekah had given him a furrowed frown.

One by one her teachers took their seats, Rebekah standing all the while.

"We are here to discuss Rebekah's academic standing," Mrs. Drinkwater explained. "I would like for all the teachers to give a short report on her progress."

Just as Mr. Enfield stood up to begin, there was a knock on the door.

"Come in," said Mrs. Drinkwater and there, to Rebekah's horror, was her daddy. *Mama called him after all?*

"Good morning, Mrs. Drinkwater."

He refused her offer of a seat and stood against the wall opposite Rebekah. She could not bear to look directly at him but when he looked at the teachers, her eyes took in the fact that his locks were much longer and that his hands – large palmed, long fingered, and so like her own – were calloused and scratched.

She felt sick at heart. For days, she had been longing to see him and now the one time she saw him again was on her morning of disgrace. Mr. Enfield began his report. "Rebekah isn't working hard enough; she's wasting far too much time drawing."

"She has no sense of history," Miss Spruce continued. "She keeps drawing in class."

One after the other, the teachers told how she was slipping below the class standard because of her drawing. Her mother's mouth tightened as she listened. Rebekah had a flash of insight. *It's not just about me. It's about her as well. I bet if I wasn't a teacher's child, I wouldn't be here. Wanda doesn't work nearly as hard as I do, and she isn't punished.*

Finally, Mr. Fenwick rose to his feet and stood next to her against the wall to make sure her mama and daddy would hear every word.

"The word progress is not relevant since Rebekah appears to have made no progress whatsoever. I understand Rebekah is spending time drawing in other people's classes. I wish she would spend more time drawing what I ask her to draw in mine. Her work is in no way up to the standard I require in my..."

Rebekah saw this was too much for her daddy. Before Mr. Fenwick could finish, he shot across the room towards Rebekah, his hand raised in anger. She felt nauseated. He was going to hit her – her daddy who had never hit her in his life. But at the very second she thought his hand would reach her, he swerved slightly and his hand stopped in front of the art teacher, inches away from his nose.

"How dare you disrespect my daughter's talent? How dare you? Have you seen the drawings she does? The pictures?"

"Jonah," her mama called out. "Stop this. It's not helping. Rebekah has no business drawing in all her classes."

"I'd like to see your standard," her daddy continued, his voice still soft but furious. "Can you draw a person's story, a person's very soul? Because Rebekah can."

Rebekah thought her knees would buckle. Her daddy wasn't angry with her. And he hadn't forgotten her drawing. He was on her side even though she was in trouble. She wanted to rush into his hug, the two of them against the world.

"Jonah," her mama called out again. "You mustn't ..."

"Rebekah," Mrs. Drinkwater said sharply, "I think you have heard enough. We will have further discussion without you. I want you to go to the library and wait there. Someone will come and get you when we have finished. Do you understand?"

Rebekah nodded and, carefully not looking at anyone in the room, she picked up her bag and left the office.

The library was completely empty. Rebekah noted that the red door with the silver knocker was closed tight. *I wonder if the Lady of the Library did leave me the art books*, she thought. *It can't have been Mr. Fenwick. Maybe, maybe if I'm really quiet, she'll come out. Or maybe I could try turning the door handle. But if Mrs. Drinkwater comes back and catches me, I might be in even more trouble.* So, she decided against it.

Resting her bag on one of the tables, she sat down,

exhausted. She wondered what they were all saying to her parents. And what Mr. Fenwick would do to her the next time she went to art class. Because one thing was for sure, he'd be vexed after what her daddy had said to him.

Rebekah pulled out a pencil and her pad from her school bag and thought she would doodle to help her calm down. As she drew, a male figure began to emerge. First the head and face – short clipped hair; large eyes, though one eyelid drooped a little; a wide, slightly crooked, nose; lines carving the curved brown cheeks and then delineating the broad, broad smile. Then the jacket – red and yellow plaid, she envisioned, but she could only draw in the lines and the shading; and navy Bermuda shorts with bright yellow knee socks. If only she had the colours. The hands were tricky, because they should definitely be large, much larger than her daddy's. She drew them in with long, wide fingers. Just as she was contemplating what shoes to put on him, the library door opened and in walked Mrs. Drinkwater with her father. Rebekah put her pencil down and rose to her feet. She could see her daddy was trying not to smile.

"Drawing again, Rebekah?" said Mrs. Drinkwater. "Now I want you to promise me you'll pay attention in your classes. We don't want to see your grades slipping, do we?"

"No, Mrs. Drinkwater."

"Good. In the meantime, let me see your drawing."

Rebekah handed it to her and, studying it, Mrs. Drinkwater and her daddy both looked stunned.

"I didn't know you knew this gentleman, Rebekah," Mrs. Drinkwater said at last.

"She doesn't," said her daddy. "Do you, Bek?"

She shook her head, feeling shy. "He's not real, you know. I made him up."

The two grown-ups looked at each other.

"And what are you going to call the drawing, Rebekah?"

asked Mrs. Drinkwater.

She hadn't thought of that but suddenly she could see the title clearly.

"The Art Teacher," she said. "By Rebekah Eve."

"Oh my goodness, Lord, have mercy." Mrs. Drinkwater gasped. "I think I'd better sit down."

"Me too," said her daddy.

Rebekah thought she should sit down too. "What's the matter?"

"You have to have told her about him, Mr. Eve. Shown her a picture. You *have* to have done. It's an exact likeness."

"You're right. But I don't remember telling her."

"Telling me about who?" Rebekah asked

"Whom, Rebekah, whom," Mrs. Drinkwater corrected her.

"Mr. Stowe," her daddy said. "Mr. Everard Leopold Stowe."

"Who was he?"

"My art teacher. The best art teacher the Meridian ever had. And the best artist Bermuda has ever had."

"Is he dead?"

"Certainly not." Mrs. Drinkwater was starting to recover and return to her usual stern self.

But Rebekah felt stern, too. "Then how come he's not teaching us?"

There was a silence. And then she could have sworn she heard a cough from behind the red door. But the lunch bell sounded, drowning it out.

"I'm picking you up after school, Bek," her daddy said once Mrs. Drinkwater had gone.

"You are? Does Mama know?"

"Sure she knows. She's going to pack you some clothes because this weekend you're going to stay with me, and Papa Malachi and Grandma Kezia."

Rebekah's face lit up. How could a morning start so horribly and end so sweetly?

At the bottom of the stairs, she bumped into Wanda who immediately took her by the arm. "Hey, girl. How did it go?"

Rebekah thought about it. "Mr. Fenwick was rude to me."

"Embarrassed."

Rebekah smiled. Sometimes Wanda wasn't so changed after all. Sometimes she was the best friend she'd always been. The two walked, arms linked, out of the veranda and headed for one of the classrooms that were detached from the main building.

Mr. Fenwick came towards them. "Good afternoon, Mr. Fenwick," Wanda called out. "Your fly's undone!" He gave a half snarl as he looked down and saw it was true. And both girls collapsed into laughter.

Chapter 6

Rebekah's daddy was waiting for her in the school car park after the last bell. She saw her suitcase in the back of Papa Malachi's truck, together with a large box wrapped in brown paper and covered in stamps. "What's that, Daddy?"

"Never you mind; you'll see later. Now let's get started."

Going to Papa Malachi and Grandma Kezia's was always a treat. They lived far away in St. George's Parish which was on the eastern end of the island. Because that part of the island was different from the rest of Bermuda, once Rebekah crossed the Swing Bridge and entered the Town of St. George she always felt as if she were on holiday in another country. The town, which most people also referred to as St. George's, was so old and quaint with its white-stepped rooftops and shuttered pastel cottages, its narrow alleyways and walled gardens, it was as if it hadn't noticed the 20th century was well on its way. Sometimes Papa Malachi would take her to St. Peter's Church because he loved to show her the cedar workmanship inside. Then they'd wander around the cemetery to the unmarked graves of people who had died enslaved.

Papa Malachi and Grandma Kezia did not live in St. George's itself. Their house was on the other side of the town, past a couple of old forts and Buildings Bay. Papa Malachi and Grandma Kezia's house was on a hillside, overlooking another fort called St. Catherine's which sat atop a much higher hill. Rebekah remembered Papa Malachi had taken her there once. You had to pay to go in but, once there, you could see some replicas of jewels belonging to the Queen. You could see the fort ghost as well. That wasn't real either. It was Papa's friend who got paid to chant in a spooky way to entertain the tourists.

As the fort loomed into view, Rebekah and her father turned left and drew up into the dirt driveway leading to her grandparents' house. It was different from her home. For one thing, it stood alone and there were no houses next to it. Instead, there was a large yard and, next to that, fenced enclosures where Papa Malachi kept a few goats, pigs, chickens, and turkeys. Many a time Rebekah had drawn the chickens because their colourful plumage fascinated her. She used her wax crayons to capture the glorious green, red, and yellow feathers of the rooster. She often tried drawing Marmalade the cat when he was asleep but that was impossible. Every time Rebekah started to draw him, he'd instantly wake and leap off. The goats were easier and sometimes she'd sketch the one with long brown and cream, silky ears and shrewd looking eyes. She was glad Papa Malachi didn't keep cows anymore. In the days when he had kept them, she had been too petrified to stand anywhere near them. Her grandfather had laughed at her. "Look how mild they are. They wouldn't hurt you."

But their eyes had frightened her because when she looked into them – they were empty, empty of any emotion she could recognise. And that was also true of the bull that Papa had admitted was dangerous and to be avoided. She could see its aggression in the set of its body and the lowering of its horns but in its eyes she saw nothing at all. It was a good thing, she thought, Papa Malachi never kept dogs. His philosophy was to keep animals that could feed a person – that was only good economics. So from time to time, there'd be a chicken for dinner or a piece of turkey or a goat curry. What was the point of keeping a dog when at the end of the day you couldn't eat it? Rebekah didn't like dogs any more than she liked the cows. They made her feel uncomfortable, especially if they took a liking to her and wouldn't leave her alone. She hated the way they sniffed around her and tried to lick her hand. Their saliva disgusted her and when they bared their teeth, they were terrifying.

Her mama didn't like the animals either because of their messiness. In fact, her mama didn't like the Eve homestead at all. Her own yard being immaculate, she could not bear what she called the junk – the metal plough, trailers and harvesters, and buckets that filled the surroundings of the house. Rebekah disagreed. She was really interested in people's tools. She liked to sketch the equipment and, best of all, her grandfather on his tractor. She liked to draw Grandma's kitchen garden, too, with its neat rows of herbs, onions, chives, and tomatoes.

"You go and say good afternoon to your grandma, and I'll bring in your case," her daddy said as she got out of the truck. "She's in the kitchen."

Rebekah felt a stab of anxiety at the realisation that she hadn't seen her grandparents in at least three months.

"Off you go, Bek. She's waiting for you."

She made her way to the kitchen that she had always loved because, apart from the stove and fridge and the washer and dryer, it was so old fashioned and homey. The familiar open shelves lining the whitewashed walls were painted an old-fashioned, pale green and were filled with her grandma's china and glasses. A huge wooden table, covered with an oil cloth that Grandma changed every year in time for Christmas, was in the centre of the kitchen. Grandma Kezia stood next to it, taking laundry from the dryer. She looked up as soon as she heard Rebekah's step and her face lit up with a warm smile.

Grandma looks glad to see me, Rebekah thought. *She hasn't changed at all. Thank goodness for that.* They hugged and then laughed because Rebekah was now taller than her grandmother. "Why, you're a young lady now – not a little girl at all."

"I'm thirteen, you know!"

"A teenager," Grandma smiled. "Go change your clothes now, and then we'll talk."

Rebekah went into the bedroom where she always slept and found her suitcase on her bed. She opened it to find an envelope on top of her clothes. It was from her mother. Inside were her gold hooped earrings and a note. "Rebekah, I know you will work harder and get your grades up. I have faith in you. I thought you might want to wear your earrings in church. Telephone me this evening. I love you. Mama."

Rebekah held the earrings in her hand and felt tearful. She wanted to please her mother – she knew that. She wanted to do well. But working harder wasn't as easy as grownups made out. As if she could just take hold of her mind and tell it what to do. It was all over the place, like a cat she couldn't pin down, sneaking her into all sorts of places that had nothing to do with school grades.

"Bek!"

She heard her daddy calling her and quickly replaced her studs with the hoops, then changed out of her uniform into a white, cotton top and a flowing, blue skirt before going back into the kitchen. On the table was the box she had seen in the car. "It's a present for you," he said smiling.

"It's not my birthday, daddy."

"Course, I know that. It's a present for getting into the Meridian. You should have had it weeks ago, but it's only just arrived. The post office is something else. Come on, open it."

She tore off the paper while Grandma Kezia, still sorting the laundry, looked on out of the corner of her eye. Ripping open the cardboard box, Rebekah found inside a wooden chest with six drawers and a lid. Carefully, she lifted the chest out and set it on the table.

"What is it, Daddy? A jewellery box?"

But how could it be? Nobody but a princess could own enough jewellery to go in a box that big.

"Open one of the drawers and find out."

She pulled one of the knobs and slid out a drawer. Her mouth dropped open. Inside was a double row of pastel sticks.

"Oh," she gasped. "Oh, *Daddy.*"

"It's at least 500 colours in all," he said. "So, you should have enough to paint. He stopped to think for a moment. "Do you paint with pastels, Bek? Or draw?"

"Both," she said opening each drawer and feasting on the fantastic mix of colours. There were so many shades, from the palest blue of an egg shell to the vibrant deep violet of the night sky. And the ochres and greens! Not to mention the earth colours and the mad variety of pinks and reds.

"Oh Daddy, I can't believe it. I never thought I'd ever have a pastel set like this."

He couldn't stop smiling at her excitement. "Open the lid, Bek. Go on." She did. Inside were brushes, palette knives, erasers, charcoals and all kinds of pencils. There was also a smaller empty box.

"That's for you to take a selection of pastels when you go outside to paint. You can't take them all, can you? You pleased, Bek?"

"Pleased, Daddy? Are you kidding?" She threw her arms around him. "Thank you. Thank you so much."

"They look expensive," Grandma Kezia said.

"A good craftsman needs good tools," said Papa Malachi who had just come in from his office – the covered shed outside so full of papers, and catalogues and old metal cabinets, and seeds and sacks, nobody could understand how he could possibly do any work in it. "That's what my father always used to say. And he knew what he was talking about being that he was a fine cabinet maker." Papa went up to Rebekah and hugged her hard. "How's my little girl?"

Rebekah hugged him back "Fine."

"She's not so little anymore," Grandma said. "She's taller than I am."

But Papa was looking at the chest and all the colours.

"So you've got a lot of painting to do, huh? What are you going to paint next?"

"I dunno. You, Papa?"

"Why don't you paint a self-portrait?" asked Grandma Kezia. "Rembrandt painted himself all the time."

"Well, excuse me, Mama. What's all this about Rembrandt? I don't even know about Rembrandt. You best listen to your grandma, Bek!" Her daddy couldn't contain himself, he was laughing so hard.

"I know way more than you think I do, so you behave, Jonah."

Chapter 5

That evening they ate dinner out on the porch overlooking the water. Papa Malachi reminded Rebekah about all the cedar furniture his father had made – the table and six chairs and the large sideboard in the dining room that only got used on Christmas Day. Rebekah had heard it all before, so she smiled politely while letting her mind tune out and concentrate on her gorgeous pastels.

The conversation switched to farming, to planting potatoes in time for Christmas. Papa Malachi looked directly at her. "Underground vegetables always do better when planted during a full moon," he said. "So that's why we're gonna plant them tomorrow, Bekah."

Why should I care? Rebekah couldn't help the thought. *I mean really, who cares about the moon and vegetables?* But she loved Papa Malachi, so she said "Why? What difference does the moon make?" to make him feel she was paying attention.

"The moon always makes a difference to root vegetables – the potatoes will grow better."

"Oh. I thought it was the sun that made a difference."

"You're right. The sun makes a difference as well. No point planting on a Sally Bassett day."

"A Sally Bassett Day?" Now she was intrigued. "What's a Sally Bassett day, Papa?"

"Don't you know your Bermudian history, girl?"

"I don't like history, Papa."

"You don't?"

"I like stories though. Who was Sally Bassett?"

"That's what history means, child. A story. You didn't know that? Well now, Sally Bassett was a slave and she was burned at the stake at Crow Lane, just outside where Hamilton is today. The day she burned was so hot, most folks call a real hot day a regular Sally Bassett day."

"How come they burned her?"

Grandma Kezia grimaced. "They say Sally Bassett told her granddaughter to poison her owners and another slave working in the same house."

"Did the people get poisoned?"

"The owner and his wife fell sick, that's for sure. And so did the slave."

"*Did* the granddaughter poison them?" Rebekah asked, her voice rising. Unaccountably, she was really worried that the granddaughter had done such a horrible thing; though why it should bother her that much, she didn't know.

"Maybe the granddaughter did it, maybe Sally did it by herself," Grandma said. "Nobody knows for certain. But the granddaughter lived in the house, so she had more opportunity."

"One thing is for certain," said Papa Malachi. "Sally Bassett got burnt to death for it. Guess what they found growing in her ashes?"

"What, Papa?"

"A Bermudiana iris. Some say that's when it first grew in Bermuda."

Rebekah knew all about Bermudianas – the little purple flowers with tiny yellow centres that came into blossom all over the island in the springtime. She'd picked some once but they drooped so quickly, she never did it again.

Just then the telephone in the kitchen blasted into the evening air and Grandma got up, sighing, to answer it. She hated being interrupted at mealtimes.

Minutes later she was back. "It was your mama, Rebekah. She wants to talk to you." Rebekah saw her daddy and Papa Malachi exchange looks. She rose to her feet, but Grandma shook her head. "I told her you'd call her after we've finished dinner."

"Is she all right, Grandma?"

"Of course, she's all right. Nothing that won't keep until you've eaten."

Rebekah could see that she was annoyed. One of the arguments she had overheard between her parents came back to her. "Your parents have never liked me," her mother had yelled. "Specially Kezia. She thinks her family is better than mine just because my mother is poor."

"That's just foolish," her daddy had said. "If anybody thinks that, it's you."

But now Rebekah wondered whether her mama was right. *Maybe Grandma never liked my mama. Supposing Grandma Kezia doesn't like me anymore because she never liked Mama and now Mama isn't family anymore? Supposing...*

"Would you like some more fish, Rebekah?"

Her stomach full of knots, Rebekah said, "No thank you, Grandma."

Later, she helped wash the dishes. She wanted to ask her grandma for permission to use the phone to call her mama but somehow, she couldn't in case Grandma said no. *If it's really important, Mama will phone back.*

After the dishes were done, she couldn't help going to her pastels box to make sure it was still there. She stroked the wood tenderly and slid the drawers open and shut.

"I should have bought you paper, Bek. I don't know why I didn't," said her daddy, watching her.

"I've brought my sketch book, Daddy. I always have my sketch book."

"Then why don't you go down to the cove? There's still some light. You could paint the sunset."

After grabbing her sketch book, Rebekah carefully chose charcoal, pencils, and pastels for her portable box and slipped out of the back door into the yard and down towards the gate. The narrow driveway was more of a lane edged with the fronds of stumpy palmetto trees. Rebekah walked through the gate, down to the road, then crossed over and turned left, following the road until she came to a little cove tucked between rocks. Sitting on a grassy slope, she gazed at the glassiness of the water and the roots of mangroves pushing upwards and edging the sand. To her left, a frangipani with creamy flowers filled the air with fragrance. She thought of painting the frangipani, but she had brought the wrong colours. How impossible it was to decide in advance which colours out of 500 would work and how wonderful to have that problem.

She took out a charcoal and quickly sketched the curve of the mangroves around the bay, the hillside in the distance, topped with casuarinas, the jetty on the left. Then she tried blues and pinks for the water, greens and ochres for the foliage. How could she capture the mysterious lights in the entangled roots of the mangroves? And the frangipani. She decided to sketch it in after all but as she did, it seemed to fade out of the light until there was almost nothing there at all. The casuarinas on top of the hill faded out as well, replaced by a few spindly cedars. But the mangroves remained, thicker and lusher. *What's happening?* She looked up and caught her breath. The casuarinas really had gone. And the frangipani. Even the scent had faded from the air.

She looked towards the jetty and saw a small figure stand

there, then jump onto the narrow strip of sand. The figure came closer so that Rebekah could see it was a girl. *The* girl. The same child she had seen at Hog Bay when her daddy went to get the hooks. Rebekah's heart leapt. The child darted towards her, running to the top of the slope. Then she sat next to Rebekah, right next to her.

"Well, hello, little girl," Rebekah said after only a slight hesitation. The girl looked at her with such trust, Rebekah wanted to hug her. But, no, that would be too forward. This was already strange enough.

The child was older now. Her front teeth had grown through. And somehow her face had lengthened a little, losing its elfin quality. Her chest was more developed; she had breasts, tiny but breasts all the same. She was smiling and her eyes, the colour of seaweed, had an innocent expression. *This time I mustn't forget what she looks like*, Rebekah told herself. *I must learn her face by heart. I must draw her.*

But then the child surprised her. She pointed a slim brown finger at Rebekah's drawing of the cove.

"Don't touch please. You could spoil the pastel."

But the child shook her head and put her finger firmly on the page, followed the contour of the shore line. She left no mark.

Then the little girl, not so little now, turned to Rebekah. She touched one of her earrings, then the other, her eyes seemingly entranced by the brightness of the gold.

Her finger is so light, Rebekah thought. *Like a feather*. She noticed the girl's ears were not pierced.

"You don't have any earrings?"

Once again, the child shook her head. Her lips parted and she said softly, so softly, her words were fluttering breaths, "No finery. No finery."

The words sounded so odd to Rebekah's ears, she thought she'd imagined them. But then she heard them again floating on

the air. "No finery." What could that mean? The words filled her
with unease.

"What's your name little girl? Who are you?" Her voice
sounded unnaturally loud, almost impolite. Rebekah never liked
to be impolite but, after all, it wasn't good manners to touch
someone's painting without asking. The child ignored the question.
Instead, she pointed again to the sketch book and Rebekah could
have sworn she heard the whisper, "Draw me, draw me."

I'm imagining it, Rebekah thought. *But even if I'm not, I want
to draw her anyway. That's what I should have done in Somerset.* She
tore out her drawing of the cove and started a new page. The girl
went to her box, picked out a charcoal and handed it to Rebekah.
She put her finger on the dazzling white page leaving no print, no
mark at all. Then she looked up at Rebekah, her eyes begging her
to begin. Rebekah obediently worked the charcoal onto the page,
and soon the child's cap, face, and frame emerged. Her skirt was
the same as before, but it was shorter, Rebekah realised, because
her legs were longer. The child's eyes grew round, spellbound by
the magic of the creation.

She's really beautiful, Rebekah thought. *But who is she? Where
has she come from?*

"What's your name, little girl?" Rebekah asked again after
she had signed the drawing in the bottom left hand corner. "I'm
going to write it on the drawing so everybody will know it's you."
But the child seemed no longer interested now that the drawing
was finished. She jumped to her feet.

"Why don't you tell me your name? See, my name is
Rebekah Eve," she said pointing to her signature. "What's yours?"

The little girl turned away and started to run towards where
the frangipani had been. Then she stopped, turned her head and
waved. Rebekah thought she could hear her calling out, "Bek,
Bek." The frangipani drifted back into view and then sank into
silhouette, its perfume once again lingering on the night air. The

child disappeared altogether.

Nervy, Rebekah thought, *calling me that. Nobody calls me Bek. Nobody except for my daddy.* Without knowing why, she felt tearful again and then vexed with herself. Until recently she was rarely one to cry, not even when she hurt herself. There was the time Roger Peterson had pushed her into a prickly pear patch and she'd been pierced all over with thorns. Even then she hadn't complained – never told who'd done it either. And there was the time she'd gashed her knee badly on a reef and the doctor in Emergency at the hospital had to gouge the slivers of coral out with a knife. The pain was terrible, but she hadn't cried then either. Yet lately, with little reason, and now, for no reason at all, she felt the world was in tears and she wanted to bawl her eyes out.

Back at the house, fortunately, the men were still on the porch while Grandma Kezia was in the kitchen; nobody noticed her return. Rebekah felt cramps in her stomach, so she slipped upstairs, and after leaving her pastels in her bedroom, went into the bathroom to check what was wrong. Her panties were stained with blood and Wanda's voice half proud and half plaintive came back to her in a year-old memory. "I've got my first period, Bekah. Mama says I'm a woman now. The pain!"

Her tears flowed again. *Wanda was right,* she thought. *The pain.*

Chapter 6

After she showered and got dressed in a nightgown, Rebekah went to her bedroom. She looked at the drawings she had done that day – the one of the mangroves with the frangipani that had faded out – she could just see the faint outline of flowers – and the one the child had asked her to draw.

Then she thought of Grandma Kezia's mention of Rembrandt and her idea of doing a self-portrait. Rebekah wasn't quite sure who Rembrandt was, but he sounded important, and if he painted himself all the time, he had to be an artist. It occurred to her that she had never thought of drawing herself. She went to the small dressing table. On it was the cedar framed mirror her grandfather had made – it was a cheval mirror, Papa Malachi had told her. He said you could tell because it swung within a wooden frame. She leaned towards the mirror so that she could see herself more clearly. She used the tip of her pointing finger to feel her way around the contours of her face. Her face was longer than she had realised but her cheeks had curves. The shape of her eyes would be difficult to draw because they weren't as slanting as her grandmother's, but they weren't as round as her father's either. Somewhere in between, she thought. And they were the same colour as her father's, dark and shining – luminous. As for her nose – if she drew herself in profile it would have to be slightly upturned. And her hair, her mother's pride and joy, that was different from her parents' because it was silky with a hint of a wave to it. When she was little, everyone had complimented her on her hair. But these days it was unfashionable. Wanda said she'd have to perm it if she wanted an Afro.

Immersed in her own reflection, she jumped when Grandma Kezia came into the room, "What do you see, Rebekah?" she asked smiling.

"I dunno … Who was Rembrandt, Grandma?"

"A famous Dutch artist who was very good at portraits. Like you, Rebekah."

"Did you draw pictures when you were a girl, Grandma?"

"Sometimes. But we didn't have time for making pictures, for art. You had to do something practical. But I love colour, too, you know. That's why I make quilts and bedspreads. I couldn't afford paints but there were always scraps of material to make things out of."

Rebekah thought of her own bedspread at home which Grandma had carefully stitched in bright hexagon shapes and looked at the one on her bed in this room, done in a star pattern. She had never thought of it before, but Grandma was like her – she made things, pictures, only they were in quilts. She wanted to tell Grandma Kezia so, but she was looking intently at the drawing Rebekah had left on the bed. She picked it up. "Is this you?"

"No way. Does she look like me?"

"I'm not sure. Her eyes aren't like yours."

"No," agreed Rebekah. "My eyes don't slant as much. And they're a different colour."

"Who is she then?"

"Just somebody."

"Somebody in your imagination?"

"Maybe."

Rebekah couldn't explain because she wasn't sure herself.

If she put what she had seen into words, they would make no sense. *I don't need Grandma Kezia to think I'm crazy.* She changed the subject, looking again at herself in the mirror. "How come my hair's like this, Grandma?" It was something that sometimes bothered her.

"Don't question what God gave to you. Besides, it's good hair. You're fortunate." And then she said, "Have you seen your Grandma Violet lately?"

"No, Grandma. Why?"

"She has pretty hair as well. You get it from her, you know."

"I do?" She'd never thought about Grandma Violet's hair – usually it was hidden by a kerchief. She hesitated a minute and then came out with it. "Do you like Daddy's hair, Grandma?"

Grandma Kezia smiled.

"He's a free spirit, your daddy, and you can't argue with free spirits. You can try but there's no point to it."

"Do you think he should be a farmer, Grandma?"

"Child, it's up to him. He was always clever. He has the brains to be anything he wants. He's like Papa Malachi, you know, and he's like my daddy as well."

"What was your daddy like, Grandma? Was he a farmer, too?"

"No. He didn't like farming. It was the sea he always loved. You couldn't keep him away from it. He was always fishing, always on the water. I wanted to go with him. I was close to him, the way you are with your daddy."

"Why didn't you go to sea with your daddy?"

"Once he took me. But most times I had to look after my brothers and sisters. When I was older, I was a teacher, you know, like your mama."

"I didn't know that, Grandma."

"See, in our day, most girls stayed at school and taught the younger ones. The boys stayed on the land or they went to sea. I was going to train as a teacher – least I thought I was. But then

I met Papa Malachi. He wasn't a farmer, then, you know. He was supposed to follow his father and be a craftsman, but he never had the mind for it. He needed to be outside. He was like my father in that way. But he loved farming. After we married, we had children of our own. I looked after them and I helped on the farm. I have no regrets, mind. That was the way life was. It was hard work, but I enjoyed it. And now it looks like Jonah is going to farm, too."

"I wish Daddy'd come home, Grandma."

Grandma Kezia hugged her. "I know you do, child. But some things just can't be helped." She picked up Rebekah's drawing from the bed and traced her finger around the frill of the child's cap. "This is real nice, Rebekah. But keep the picture out of the sun. Her face is fading."

"It can't be, Grandma. I've only just drawn it." Rebekah held the drawing up and examined it anxiously. Grandma was right. The shading on the face was shrinking. It left only the outline of the head, sockets for eyes, and the brilliant white of the cap which was really only the white of paper. *If I can't keep the drawing, I must try to remember the face*, Rebekah thought. *But why can't I keep it? And why is this child so special to me when I'm not even sure I haven't made her up?*

"Rebekah?" Grandma hesitated for a moment as if what she was about to say was difficult to put into words.

"Yes?"

"Papa Malachi and I will always love you, you know, no matter what. So you don't need to worry about that."

Rebekah forgot about the drawing. Her face relaxed into a smile. They hugged again and Rebekah could smell the fragrant lavender perfume she always associated with her grandmother. It made her feel safe.

Chapter 7

The following Monday, Rebekah and Wanda made their way over the road and across the playing fields to the art room. It was in a cottage and in a way like its own kingdom.

"I hate art," Wanda muttered as they climbed the steps to the cottage. "It's all right for you. You're good at it."

"Mr. Fenwick doesn't think so," Rebekah pointed out. "He doesn't like what I do."

"He's crazy, girl! He's jealous cos he can't draw as good as you. 'Sides he doesn't like nothing anyway. Roger says he hates Bermuda."

Even if that was true, Rebekah thought, it didn't explain why he was always making nasty comments about her art and not about anyone else's.

"You're late," Mr. Fenwick snapped when they finally got to class. "Hurry up and sit down."

Rebekah inwardly sighed. Only half the class was there so they weren't the only late ones. *Why does he always have to pick on us?*

"Today," Mr. Fenwick shouted, interrupting her thoughts, "we shall look at the rules of perspective."

Rebekah's heart lifted a little. *Maybe I'll learn something today.*

"I'm going to hand out some pictures of houses and I want you to try to copy them."

Rebekah looked at the picture of a small house she was given. *It's not like any house I've ever seen,* she thought. It was made of red brick, for one thing, and it had strange grassy stuff on its roof. Obediently she drew it, the pencil in her hand steady and sure. Perspective was no problem – it seemed to come naturally to her. She finished the drawing in no time and seeing Wanda and other the students around were nowhere close to completing their drawings, she sneaked out her sketch pad and proceeded to draw a house of her own. She thought maybe it was one she had seen when going through Somerset, in Sandys Parish on the way to Royal Naval Dockyard. Sometimes she wasn't sure whether she had really seen it or had imagined it. The house was stone and it had a stepped-stone Bermuda roof and a large, large stone chimney. Its stepped shoulder rose against the gable end of the house. Drawing the shoulders and sides of the chimney gave her a surge of satisfaction – the symmetry was so appealing. She drew in small, rectangular windows with dark, wooden frames and shutters, as well as a closed door with a slatted vent above it. And she sketched in the shadows beneath the eaves and the shutters. Then she thought she'd try again but with the door open. So, she took another piece of paper and drew the house again. This time she thought she could see, through the door, one room with an open brick fireplace and iron pots and pans. There was a young woman bending over one of the pots. *Maybe it's the child,* Rebekah thought, *only more grown up. I'm sure she lives in this house – that's why I can see it. She wants me to see it.* But when the young woman turned around, Rebekah realised she wasn't the child at all. She was wearing a long, white, wide-skirted dress, the bodice low cut and showing her nut brown cleavage. Her eyes were very dark and round and her mouth wide and full-lipped. And then Rebekah could swear she heard a man's voice shouting, "Nancy, Nancy!" and afterwards a dog barking. And the woman's lips stretched even wider into a smile that Rebekah didn't think she could capture because it was happy and sad, humorous and bitter all at the same time. But she tried anyway, sketching in the figure with her hands on her hips and the face with that wide smile. But as Rebekah finished working in the smile, the woman's expression changed, frozen by the presence of another woman coming into the kitchen. As she pencilled in the door frame, Rebekah saw, the woman standing in the doorway was white and older, with washed out pale hair. She glowered at the girl in front of the fireplace with such hatred in her eyes, Rebekah felt a cold burning in her eyes and throat as her fingers sped along the paper bringing their expressions to life.

Who are these people; where have they come from, she asked herself, all the pleasure she had taken in the cottage's pleasing proportions evaporating.

"Have you finished, Rebekah?" Mr. Fenwick's nasal voice over her shoulder broke her concentration and shocked her into the present. Quickly, she slid out the cottage drawing he'd assigned towards him.

"Yes, Mr. Fenwick." He stood at her desk looking at her attempt.

"Very good. I see you understand what I've taught you." When he picked it up, though, he saw the additional drawings underneath. "Did I ask you to do these, Rebekah? Did I?"

"No, Mr. Fenwick."

"Did I ask you to draw a person?"

"No, Mr. Fenwick.

"So why did you draw these women? Why are you always drawing *people*?"

Wanda could not resist interfering. "Mr. Fenwick," she asked, "how come you don't like people? People live in houses, innit. So how come . . ."

"Hold your tongue, Wanda. Answer me, Rebekah."

"I dunno."

"Of course you know. You've copied these people, haven't you? Where did you copy them from?"

Rebekah shook her head. "I didn't copy them," she said quietly. *I wish I had,* she thought miserably. *I wouldn't feel so strange if I had copied them. I wouldn't feel as if I'm going crazy.*

"Does my class bore you, Rebekah Eve? You think your art is too good for my class? Is that the problem we have here?" He wagged his finger at her. "Well, let me tell you, young lady, I have taught at the Slade, the most prestigious art school in London where the best students of the land count it a privilege to be taught by me. Do you understand?"

Rebekah felt wretched – raw with shame. She wanted to tell him how important it was to her to learn from him because there was no one else who could tell her how to improve. Not her daddy, even though he appreciated what she could do, and certainly not her mama who wouldn't help her even if she could. But she couldn't find the words; besides, she knew he just wouldn't listen. "The rules of perspective have no interest for you?" he was saying. "Well, I suggest you leave the class and take your drawings with you."

"Yes, Mr. Fenwick." Rebekah's whole body felt heavy as she got to her feet and began to pack her school bag.

"Mr. Fenwick, you got to give Rebekah a pass," said Wanda. "Otherwise she'll get a detention for being out of class without permission and that's not fair."

"Wanda Lambert, do *you* want a detention?"

"I don't mind. I ain't got nothin' else to do."

Roger Peterson gave out a huge guffaw, making the whole class laugh with him.

Rebekah left before Mr. Fenwick exploded and made her

way across the playing fields, over the road to the main building, and up the stairs to the library. Mrs. Chatterjee was behind her desk, filling out book cards and talking to Rebekah's form teacher, Miss Spruce.

"Good morning, Rebekah. And why aren't you in class?"

"Good morning, Mrs. Chatterjee, good morning Miss Spruce."

"Have you a pass?"

"No, Mrs. Chatterjee. Mr. Fenwick didn't give me a pass. But he asked me to leave the room. Because I was drawing in class."

Miss Spruce raised an eyebrow. "In an art lesson? How unreasonable of you, Rebekah."

Rebekah looked at her doubtfully. *Is she being sarcastic?* It was hard to tell with British teachers. Sometimes, you didn't know how to take them.

"What were you drawing? Can we see?"

She took out the drawing Mr Fenwick had assigned first. "It's English – Miss Spruce, how come there's grass on the roof?"

"It's thatch, Rebekah – dried straw used to cover the roof. It's pretty."

"I wouldn't want it on my roof," said Rebekah.

"Then it's a good thing you weren't here in Bermuda in the 17th century because then people thatched their cabins with dried palmetto." Always the teacher, Miss Spruce couldn't resist dropping in a bit of history. "Actually," she continued, "when I was your age, I lived in a thatched cottage."

"Oh." And then, thinking that must have been a very long time ago, Rebekah asked very politely "How old are you, Miss Spruce?"

The teacher looked taken aback. "How old do you think I am?"

"Forty something?"

For a moment Miss Spruce looked so horrified, Rebekah was worried she was in trouble again. Mrs. Chattergee was smiling, though. And then Miss Spruce asked in a friendly way, "Now let's see what other drawings you did."

Embarrassed, Rebekah handed her the pictures of the Bermuda cottage, of the smiling girl, and of the white woman looking at her with hate-filled eyes.

The two women gazed at them in silence until Miss Spruce shivered a little. "They are excellent, Rebekah, but the drawings of the women rather give me the creeps. It's as if you have drawn a story from the past. And this from the girl who doesn't like history."

"I like history better now, Miss Spruce," Rebekah said earnestly, "specially when it's about people. Mr. Fenwick doesn't like the drawing because it's got people in it. But I can't help drawing people. That's what I like the best."

"Then you must carry on drawing people," said Mrs. Chatterjee. "You should always pursue what you're good at whatever anyone tells you. Which reminds me – I have a letter for your father."

"Who's it from?" she asked, anxiety tensing her stomach. "Am I in trouble?"

"Why should you be, child? It's not from Mrs. Drinkwater, if that's what is worrying you. I'm not sure who it's from. It arrived on my desk this morning. Be sure you give it to your father."

"Yes, Mrs. Chatterjee."

"Go and have your lunch now. And remember keep drawing from your imagination but not in Mr. Fenwick's class."

As Rebekah closed the library door, she heard Miss Spruce laughing, "Forty, for heavens' sake! I haven't reached 30 yet. Still, that child certainly has a gift. That Fenwick idiot. Can't he see how *brilliant* she is at art?"

I didn't think Miss Spruce liked my art, Rebekah thought, a warm feeling spreading through her. *I didn't think she liked me at all. Maybe she's not so bad after all.* Rebekah lingered a little to see if she could hear any more, then wished she hadn't.

"Mind you, Mrs. Chatterjee, I worry about Rebekah sometimes. You don't think she's a tad *disturbed*, do you? Imagining such things?"

Rebekah strained to hear Mrs Chatterjee's reply, but it was so soft she could hardly make it out. She thought she heard the word Trinidad and then, ". . . in our country we call it the sight."

On her way to her locker, Rebekah bumped into Wanda who was looking extremely pleased with herself. "Did Mr. Fenwick give you a detention, Wanda?"

"Yep."

"Girl, I'm sorry."

"No, girl. Roger got one too! Don't you think he's cute?"

Rebekah did not but she thought it better not to say so.

Chapter 8

Walking home from school, Rebekah thought about telling her mama about Mr. Fenwick and how nasty he was. But Mama didn't like her doing too much art anyway, so there wouldn't be much point. Besides, for the last couple of weeks her mama had been acting strange. She didn't seem to care as much about Rebekah's grades or about her painting instead of doing homework. She hadn't even commented on the pastels her daddy had given her – Rebekah had been sure she'd be angry about them. *But no, not a word. Mama's just too busy*, thought Rebekah, scuffing her feet. *She's always out at school meetings so that's probably why.* . . . It was better to think about the fun she would have on the weekend ahead. On Saturday, her daddy was going to pick her up and take her to Somerset for lunch.

The roar of a moped whizzing past jolted her out of her thoughts and she found herself nearly home. A shiny, red Toyota convertible with its hood down was by the side of the road. *Whose car is that*, she wondered. Then she remembered how Mama had always wanted a Toyota like Uncle Gabriel's. Had she bought one? But their battered, second hand Morris Minor was parked outside their house.

"I'm home, Mama," she called as she opened the front door.

"I'm in the kitchen," her mama called back. "I'm making dinner."

Rebekah walked in and was utterly shocked to find a white man, there at their kitchen counter, cutting onions and looking perfectly at home. Her mother was next to him slicing tomatoes. She looked up, smiling. "Rebekah, I want you to meet my – my new friend, Thomas, Thomas Forrest. Thomas, this is my daughter, Rebekah."

Rebekah stared at him, her eyes taking in the slate grey of his eyes, the thinning, wispy yellow hair – *how would you draw the texture of such hair?* His rather floppy, long mouth stretched even further into a smile.

"Hi, kiddo," he said. "Can't shake hands. Because of the onion. How about homemade hamburgers for supper? I know how you kids like hamburgers."

Rebekah looked at her mother as if to say, "What is this man doing here?"

"Say 'Good afternoon', Rebekah," her mama said.

"Good afternoon, Mr. Forrest."

"I'm Thomas to my friends," he said, his smile showing a muddle of muddy teeth. "And I know we're going to be real good friends."

"I don't think so," said Rebekah. "I'm going to my room, Mama." And she turned on her heel and walked up the stairs.

"Rebekah!"

"Don't you worry, Patricia. I know how to get on with kids. After all, I've got two teenagers of my own in Canada. We're going to get on like a house on fire, just you wait and see."

Rebekah sat on her bed. Rage rushed to her head. It clenched her hands, gripped her stomach so fiercely she had to lie down. So that's why her mama was out so much. So that's why she wasn't so uptight about grades and stuff. *How could she?* How could she be with a man who wasn't Rebekah's daddy and let him in their house? *And a white man, of all people? Let him cook as if he lives here!* Rebekah couldn't remember a time ever when a white person had come to visit their house, let alone cook there. The only time she ever met white people to talk to was at school or in shops or at the Aquarium. She couldn't begin to imagine what a white person's house would be like inside. She'd never been to one, not once. And as far as she could remember, a white person had never been to her house.

What would her daddy say if he knew this white man was cooking food in their house? She shut her eyes, feeling the heat of her tears against her eyelids. She would stay on this bed forever because there was no way she would go downstairs and see that man with his eyes like – like the sea on a very grey day. She would rather starve – she would starve.

The doorbell rang and hearing it gave a pause to her anger. She wondered if it could be her daddy; these days he did ring the bell before he came in. If it was him, what would happen? What would he do? Before her worry got the better of her, she heard her mother open the door and Wanda's voice saying, "Good afternoon" and her mother saying "Rebekah's busy right now."

But Wanda being Wanda took no notice. Rebekah heard the sound of her feet, flying up the stairs. And now Wanda herself, her perky face peering round the bedroom door. "You sick, girl? How come you're laying down on your bed?"

Rebekah sat up, her tears burning her cheeks. Wanda perched next to her. "Is it on account of that white man? Roger says he's your mama's boyfriend."

Roger Peterson? That nasty brat? Of all the people to know my business.

"What does he know," she muttered. "It's nothing to do with him. He better shut his mouth." She got off the bed, found her box of tissues and used one to scrub at her eyes. "How come you didn't tell me what Roger said?" Her rage surged back at the thought of everyone knowing about this man before she did. Because if Roger knew, everyone else knew.

Wanda shrugged. "I dunno. How come you didn't tell me your daddy moved out?"

Rebekah shrugged back. "I dunno."

"You wanna come with me to Green Shutters for a hot dog? I'm real hungry."

She shook her head. Just the thought of food made her feel ill.

"Wanda, you have to go home now." Mama walked into the bedroom, a plate in her hand. "You hear me?"

"Yes, Mrs. Eve."

"Well off you go then."

"Bye, Bekah."

"Bye." She lay down again on the bed, her back turned to her mother.

"Rebekah, here's your dinner. You can have it up here if you want."

"Don't want dinner."

Her mother put the plate on her desk and sat on the end of the bed. "I know you're upset, Rebekah, but when you get to know him, you'll see that Thomas is a very nice person."

"I don't want to get to know him. I want my daddy."

Her mama sighed. "I know you do but that's not my fault, you know. I didn't leave your daddy. Your daddy left me."

Rebekah had to admit the truth of this. But that was no reason for this man to march into her mama's life, was it? A thought occurred to her. She sat up. "Where did you meet him, Mama?" Where could they have possibly met?

Her mama started smiling. *If I drew a picture of her right now*, Rebekah thought with disgust, *she'd look really beautiful.*

"He's just joined the school's board of governors. After one of our meetings, he asked me out to dinner and . . ."

"How come he can be a governor? He's not Bermudian."

"He is, Rebekah. But he's lived his whole life in Canada because his father left Bermuda as a young man, just after Thomas was born. So naturally he has a Canadian accent."

Rebekah burrowed her face in her pillows again. "Why didn't he stay there?" she muttered.

"Well," Mama said carefully, "he was married but his wife left him. And then his aunt in Bermuda died last year. She didn't have any children, so she left all her property to Thomas. So, he came to Bermuda to see it and to work for a while. If he likes it here, he may stay. He's a lawyer, you know."

He would be, Rebekah thought. *He just would be.* The fact her mother had wanted her daddy and now her to study law was enough to put her off all lawyers.

"How come he's left his children?"

"What do you mean, Rebekah?"

"I overheard him say he had two teenagers."

"He hasn't *left* them. They're in college. Are you sure you don't want your dinner?

"Not hungry."

Her mama got off the bed and went to the desk to retrieve the plate when she noticed the envelope, addressed to Mr. Jonah George Jeffers Eve, which Mrs. Chatterjee had asked Rebekah to deliver. "What's this, Rebekah?" As she started to open it, Rebekah shot up from the bed and grabbed it.

"That's for Daddy, not for you. It's none of your business!"

"Rebekah, that's rude, you hear me? That's rude. Is this from your school? Are you in trouble again?"

"It's addressed to my daddy – see?" She pointed to her daddy's name on the envelope. It was written in small looped handwriting. It occurred to Rebekah that she hadn't known her father had more than one Christian name. Perhaps the same thought occurred to her mama because she looked at the lettering totally shocked.

"Where did this come from, Rebekah?"

"Mrs. Chatterjee gave it to me."

"Who wrote it?"

"I dunno."

"What do you mean, you don't know? Did Mrs. Chatterjee write it?"

"No."

Her mama pursed her lips. "This is very strange, very strange. I need to call Mrs. Chatterjee to find out who it's from. Give me the letter, Rebekah."

"No! Mrs. Chatterjee doesn't know who wrote it, but she asked me to give it to Daddy and that's what I'm going to do."

They glared at each other in silence. *I won't give in*, Rebekah thought. *I won't*.

Saturday morning, Rebekah crept out of bed at six, showered, and dressed. She made her way down the stairs, starving for breakfast. Peering out of the kitchen window overlooking the road, she could see that the man's car was gone. She ignored the pile of last night's dirty dishes, went to the cupboard and helped herself to cornflakes. As she sat down at the table to eat her cereal, Mama appeared in her jammies and dressing gown, her hair tightly rolled into curlers.

"Good morning, Rebekah."

Rebekah concentrated on eating her cornflakes. That way she needn't talk. She managed a tiny nod.

"I'm not surprised you're hungry. What do you expect if you didn't eat your supper? Well, you can help me with the dishes."

Rebekah felt a stab of outrage. If the man wanted to cook, why didn't he wash his dishes?

"No," she said.

"Rebekah! It's not like you to be so unhelpful."

"I didn't eat. No way I'm doing his dishes. No way."

"It wasn't his fault you wouldn't eat. Rebekah, you're going to have to get used to him."

Rebekah picked up her empty bowl and spoon, took them to the sink and washed them ignoring the other dirty plates and frying pan.

"I'm going to my room," she said. "Until Daddy comes."

When she got upstairs, she thought she would give in a little by cleaning the bathroom. But when she found yellow hairs in the basin, she felt like picking them up and smearing them all over her mother's pillow. Instead, she put the plug in, filled the basin with water and let the hair float to the top. *No way I'm cleaning that. No way. Mama can do it.*

Chapter 9

Rebekah's daddy arrived at 11:30 and called for her from the bottom of the stairs. She grabbed her sketchbook and portable box for pastels and charcoals, put them in her tote bag and then remembered the letter she was supposed to give him. That too went into the bag.

Once Rebekah reached the bottom of the stairs, her daddy gave her a huge hug. He pulled back, gazed at his daughter's face. "You all right, Bek? You look like you haven't slept."

She hesitated, eyes flicking to her mother standing by the kitchen entrance with her arms folded and her expression tight.

"How are you, Bek?" her daddy pressed.

"Fine."

Her daddy studied her a beat longer, then said, "I've a surprise for you. Uncle Gabriel and Aunty Gwen are driving us in their car – they want to come to lunch with us because they haven't seen you in a while."

It was true – they hadn't seen her since before her daddy had left. Sometimes she thought they didn't care about her now the family situation had changed. She'd known for a long time her mama and Aunty Gwen didn't get on although no one ever said anything to her. But she'd overheard Grandma Kezia talking to Papa Malachi when they thought she was too busy drawing to hear them. "It's sisters-in-law," she'd said, "jealousy."

"What's Patricia jealous of?"

"Are you crazy or what, Malachi? Gabriel's house. Everything they've got."

"And Gwen?"

"She wants a baby, of course. What do you think?"

"They're waiting in the car, Bek," her daddy said now.

She watched her mother's face tighten even more. If it were up to Mama, Rebekah could tell, there'd be no more family visits with Uncle Gabriel and Aunty Gwen.

"Well, I hope you will have time with Rebekah alone," her mother sniped after a stiff little silence. "A letter from the school has come for her."

"Not for me, Daddy, for you. It's addressed to you."

"With *all* your names," said Mama.

"All of them? That's interesting."

"Isn't that the truth?"

Rebekah accompanied her daddy to Uncle Gabriel's Toyota. Uncle Gabriel was sitting in the driver's seat, Aunty Gwen in the back. She tried to push away the knobbly feeling at having to share her daddy with them. It would be so much better if she could have him to herself, at least for the drive down. Besides, Papa Malachi's truck was more fun, even if it did smell of feed. You got a much better view of the scenery because the seats were high up.

"You want to sit in the back next to Gwen, Bek?"

"Yes."

What else could she say? But it would mean Gabriel would chat away to her daddy and there would be no time for her.

However, Aunty Gwen seemed happy to see her. When she proffered her cheek, Rebekah could smell her perfume; it filled the car. "That's a nice fragrance, Aunty Gwen," she said. "What is it?"

"Je Reviens," she said. "Worth."

"Mama likes that perfume, too." Rebekah wondered why she'd said that because it just wasn't true. Besides, Auntie Gwen knew her mama always wore the same perfume – L' Air Du Temps – she'd once commented on it, to her mama's annoyance.

Aunty Gwen didn't contradict Rebekah, though. "That's nice," she said smiling, looking, as always, happy and stylish. This morning she seemed happier still. Her dark eyes were brimming with light. "How's my favourite niece?"

"I'm fine. How are you?"

"Well, your uncle and I have a lovely surprise for everyone."

"What?"

"We'll tell you at lunch."

Once out of town, Uncle Gabriel took the Harbour Road as Rebekah knew he would. He liked to watch the ships glide into their berths and see them towering above the shore line. Sure enough, as he turned the corner, they could see the cruise ship the *Sea Venture* anchored against the backdrop of Front Street and the line of shops with their verandas facing the Harbour.

April to October of each year, the *Sea Venture* travelled regularly between Bermuda and New York. "When she leaves tomorrow, that will be her last crossing this year. It's been a good tourist season," said Uncle Gabriel.

"It has," agreed Aunty Gwen. She was in charge of a small, busy hotel on Pitt's Bay Road – where the guests so appreciated her positive personality, many came back year after year. "We're still booked out even though it's after Labour Day."

Slowly, the Harbour and the Great Sound with all its islets floating on the water faded out of sight as Uncle Gabriel drove down Burnt House Hill and on to Middle Road, heading west. Eventually, they reached Somerset Bridge. *If Uncle Gabriel tells me one more time it's the smallest drawbridge over the Atlantic…*

"Rebekah," Uncle Gabriel said, "did you know that Somerset Bridge is the smallest drawbridge over the Atlantic?"

"I thought we would eat outside," Daddy said as, eventually, they drove along Mangrove Bay Road past the house, which was once a prison, and into the car park of the Somerset Inn. "The sun's so bright; it's a shame to stay inside. Besides, I'm not even sure, they're serving in today. What do you think, Bek?"

"That's fine." Which it was. She loved the winter sun. There was never snow in winter though sometimes the north wind could chill you to the bone. But when the sun came out and the humidity was lower, its clear golden warmth felt so good on her face and arms and back.

They sat at a table on the terrace overlooking Mangrove Bay. Rebekah looked out to sea, her eyes taking in the chain of islets, stubbed with casuarina saplings, that stretched away from King's Point and the rocks ahead of her – home to small white birds swooping in and out of the water.

"Look at the longtails, Rebekah," said Uncle Gabriel. Rebekah didn't say anything, but she knew they weren't longtails – these birds were smaller and so were their beaks.

She felt a wave of love when Daddy said, "You crazy, bro? They're terns – but they're real late leaving this year."

He may not have as much money as Uncle Gabriel and he may not look as smart but he knows stuff.

A waitress came up to their table, her stern face contrasting with her courteous, "Good afternoon. And what would you like today?" From the way she winced as she turned to each of them, Rebekah thought maybe her back was bad.

"Do you want a hamburger, Bekah?"

Her stomach lurched. She never wanted hamburgers again. They made her think of Mr. Forrest. "No thank you, Daddy. I'll have fried chicken and French fries."

Sipping her fruit punch, waiting for the food to arrive,

Rebekah thought she would try to sketch the anchored boats bobbing on the water. Out came her sketchbook and vine charcoal. She had the idea of smudging the paper with the charcoal so that instead of drawing, she would use an eraser to rub out the shapes of the boats and the sun's lights flickering on the sea. She set to work. The conversation around her dimmed into the distance.

"Well now," Daddy said. "What's the surprise?"

"Expect an addition to the Eve family," said Uncle Gabriel, grinning.

"Yes," said Aunty Gwen, her smile stretching the width of her face. "I'm pregnant."

Rebekah almost dropped her eraser.

"Wonderful," said Daddy. "Congratulations, bro. When's it due?"

"June," Aunty Gwen said. "Aren't you pleased, Rebekah? You'll be like an aunty to the baby, being that you're so much older. We're going to need your help, you know."

Rebekah muttered and kept on erasing. Wanda had told her that once there was a new baby in the house two things happened. First you had to do more stuff in the house because you were always older and supposed to help. And second people paid you no mind because they were too busy checking out the baby. And Wanda should know because she had had to put up with *two* new babies, Troy and Trey.

So much change, Rebekah thought. *Daddy leaving and Mama with that man. And now Aunty Gwen's expecting.*

"How are you feeling, Gwen?" her daddy asked. "Morning sickness?"

Rebekah tried to tune out the conversation

At least I have my art. That's what she told herself, feeling annoyed at the unborn baby that was already grabbing the spotlight. *At least I'm good at that.* But then Mr. Fenwick's shrill voice nagged – *Why are you always drawing people?* She couldn't escape it, even in her own head. *Maybe I'm not good at art*, she worried. *He certainly doesn't think so. And even if I am . . . Mama doesn't see the point.*

Even as she doubted her drawing skills, a ship emerged through the charcoal. It had three masts, paler than the background charcoal but darker than the white of its full triangular sails billowing in the wind. But who was sailing the ship? Squinting, she began to sketch in a man at the bow of the vessel. She gave him a tricorn hat, a long blouse, breeches, and a neck cloth. His facial features began to appear – the beginning of pale eyes, thin strands of hair. *I don't like this man*, she thought, feeling faintly queasy. *I really don't.* She was frightened his face would come to life the way those women's had during Mr. Fenwick's art lesson. So, she rubbed his features out. But the man's figure remained: his head was bent, and he was steering the ship.

She smudged in the islets in the background but somehow the trees weren't right so she left them out, then wondered, as she'd wondered so many times before, how she would get the blues of the water the way she wanted them and the shadowy shapes beneath the surface. The thought of her pastels comforted her – at least she had them and a better chance of getting the colour of the clouds right as they ballooned over the sails. Her mind tussled with the problem of using her pastels to create white, or rather all the pinks and blues and violets you could see in white.

"Not anymore, thank goodness," Aunty Gwen was saying in the background. "It was real bad at the start. I couldn't look at food without being nauseated, could I, Gabriel?"

Who cares, Rebekah thought, putting down her eraser.

"Let's see your drawing, Bek," her daddy said. Rebekah tore out the page and handed it to him. Uncle Gabriel looked over his shoulder. "Girl, that's a Bermuda sloop. Man, you have some imagination. That's beautiful." Her daddy's face beamed with pride.

"Let's see," Aunty Gwen demanded. She took it from her daddy. "Who's the man, Rebekah?"

"I dunno. Just someone steering the ship." Just then the waitress brought their food and they were soon busy eating. As her Daddy finished the last of his pie, Rebekah could see a thought occur to him.

"What about that letter?" he asked. "Have you got it, Bek?"

"Mmm." She fished it out of her tote bag and handed it to him. He looked at the envelope and whistled.

"Check out the names, Gabriel."

Gabriel, seeing them, started to laugh. "Jonah George Jeffers Eve? There's only one person that can be from."

"Who?" asked Rebekah. "Mrs. Chatterjee gave it to me in the library, but she didn't know who wrote it."

"The library? Well, that settles it. It has to be from the Lady of the Library. She's the only one who knows your daddy has two extra names, other than the family, of course."

"Why?"

"I never use them," her daddy explained. "Jonah on its own is good enough for me. That's why we didn't give you middle names, Bek. Rebekah Eve seemed sufficient to me. But the Lady of the Library always uses all the students' names when she writes to them. She's known for it. And check out her handwriting – it hasn't changed all these years even though now she must be real old. She wrote to me once before – long before you were born."

"So, there is a Lady of the Library? How come she wrote to you?"

Her daddy looked a tad uncomfortable. "She had her point to make. Anyway, let's see what she has to say this time. She never writes without a reason." He tore open the envelope, unfolded a single piece of paper and silently began to read.

Glancing over his shoulder, Rebekah tried to make out the tiny looped handwriting. She could just see her mama's maiden name, *Miss Patricia Emilia Bascome* and after that the word *'mistake'.* But her daddy turned away slightly so she couldn't read any more. She began to feel annoyed.

"Well," said her father as he finished reading, "*well.*" And he handed the letter to Gabriel who read it and then handed it to Gwen.

"Oh Jonah, did she really write to you all those years ago?" asked Gwen after she had finished reading.

"Yes," he replied. "Patricia was real mad."

"Can't blame her. I'd be mad."

"Exactly."

Rebekah felt even more annoyed. "What is the letter about, Daddy? I can read it?"

"It's addressed to me, you know."

"Everybody else has read it. Is it about me?"

"Yes and no."

"How come I can't read it?"

He took the letter from Gwen and turned it over. "The second side is about you. Here you are."

She held it in her hand and quickly began reading:

He in his wisdom blessed you both with your daughter, Miss Rebekah Eve, who is fast becoming a most interesting young lady. Her gift for art has not gone unnoticed by me. Her extraordinary talent must be nurtured as a seed must be watered if it is to grow.

You will also recall that the Meridian School was once honoured to name our most eminent artist Mr. Everard Leopold Stowe as a member of its excellent teaching staff. I believe there was a time he tried unsuccessfully to teach you the principles of perspective and of colour. Unhappily, he left school after my retirement, mistakenly believing that his presence was no longer of value to our institution.

Mr. Eve, I have taken the liberty of explaining to Mr. Stowe, the importance of fostering your daughter's undoubted gift so that she can make her proper contribution to the rich culture of our people, which as you well know, has been for so long concealed.

He has kindly invited Rebekah to his residence for tea at 3.30 on Sunday, 3rd November so they might discuss how he may best assist her in her artistic endeavours. His address is as follows: Stowe Studio, Number 7 Fractious Street, Hamilton Parish. Mr. Stowe also requests that Rebekah bring with her as many of the drawings and paintings in her portfolio as possible.

I trust you will enable your daughter to keep this truly important appointment with Mr. Stowe so that one day she will achieve the destiny I am convinced awaits her.

Wishing you the greatest success with your farming pursuits, I am your former mentor and teacher,

Dr. Ella Bien-Aimée Delacroix

Rebekah's mind came alive with questions. Hadn't she wanted Mr. Stowe to teach her and hadn't she heard the sound of a cough behind the red door in the library with the silver knocker? Was it the Lady of the Library who had lent her the books on black artists? And how come she couldn't read the first part of the letter when everyone else at the table had read it? *What is it with grownups? They tell you stuff you don't want to know and keep from you the stuff you do want to know.* And the thought of that man and Gwen's baby and people writing about her behind her back and Wanda knowing her business made her so upset, she turned the letter over and read the first half:

Dear Mr. Eve,

You will recall I had reason to write to you on the occasion of your engagement to Miss Patricia Emilia Bascome. Unfortunately, it was my belief a mistake was about to be made, one that would have serious consequences for the rest of your life. It was my opinion that between you and Miss Bascome there was no marriage of true minds and that lack, in my view, was a grave impediment to a happy and blessed matrimony.

It seems that your recent separation has sadly proved me correct. And yet, Mr. Eve, I must confess that I am now most thankful the Almighty Creator saw fit to ignore my fervent prayer that the marriage between you and Miss Bascome would not take place.

"How dare she! How dare she say things about my mama and you, like that. I don't like this woman – I don't like her at all."

"Bek!" Her father looked horrified.

She got up from the table, stumbled across the terrace and into the inn's ladies' room. Fortunately, it was empty, and she was able to sit on the toilet in one of the cubicles and cry.

She didn't know how long her tears had lasted, but once they eased up she wiped her eyes and went out to wash her hands. There was Aunty Gwen patiently waiting for her. "I'm sorry, sweetie. I'm sorry."

"The Lady of the Library didn't have any right to talk about my mama like that. What does she know?"

Aunty Gwen didn't answer.

So Mama and Daddy are apart and Mama is seeing that man.

That still didn't give her the right.

"Aunty Gwen, that woman, she's poky."

"You're right, she always has been interfering."

Then Aunty Gwen changed the subject, to Rebekah's relief. "Do you want to walk on the beach, Bekah?"

She nodded. They walked back onto the terrace, down the steps and onto the narrow strand of creamy sand edging the gentle curve of the sea. The view soothed and distracted her into asking herself her usual questions. How would the colour of the sand be different in a painting from the sails of the ship? Or was it the texture that was different? And how could she create the palm trees framing the bay, their fringed fronds like green starbursts? But she couldn't concentrate; she couldn't get the letter out of her mind.

"Have you met the Lady of the Library, Aunty Gwen?"

"No. Nobody I know has, except your daddy, Papa Malachi, and Mr. Stowe. And Grandma Kezia, I think."

And my mama, Rebekah thought. *But you wouldn't mention her.*

"Well, how come she writes to my daddy?"

"Some students she takes a special interest in. Your daddy was one and now you're another."

"But *why?*"

"You read the letter, sweetie. She thinks you're special."

"But how come she hides away? How come she won't come out? It's creepy!"

"You'll have to ask Mr. Stowe that. They were teachers together once. She was his mentor. You ask Mr. Stowe when you go tomorrow."

"I don't wanna go," she said, resenting the idea of putting more effort into trying to understand the foolishness of adults. She just wanted to relax with her daddy.

"Oh, sweetie, you must go. He's a real nice man. And

everyone knows he's a brilliant artist. He'll help you, you know."

Rebekah thought about Mr. Fenwick and how he couldn't help her if he tried. "He can't be worse than Mr. Fenwick," she conceded.

Aunty Gwen looked startled. "You mean Stanley Fenwick, the English artist? He's having an exhibition in our hotel, you know. He's your art teacher?"

Rebekah sighed. "Yes. He doesn't like my art. Maybe he's right, maybe I'm not very good."

"Sweetie, I'm not even listening to you, you hear me? Stanley Fenwick's art sells, that's for sure. But I don't like it very much – it's got no soul, you know what I mean? I'm telling you, girl, he's probably jealous of what you can do."

"That's what Wanda says."

"Well, for once Wanda Lambert has some sense. Artists are only human, you know. They're just as competitive as anyone else." Auntie Gwen's eyes gleamed with humour. "Try buttering up his ego. Tell him you like his form and you'll have him eating out of your hand."

Rebekah was only half listening. "Maybe Mr. Stowe won't like my art either. What if he's competitive?"

"Everard Leopold Stowe is different – he's very, very special. Promise me you'll go?"

She nodded slowly. "I suppose."

Gwen looked at Rebekah then leaned in and gave her a hug. "We all love you, you know. You all right, sweetie?"

Not even close, she thought. What's all right about anything?

"I'm fine."

Chapter 10

When Rebekah's daddy dropped her off, her mama was out, which was a blessing because Rebekah really didn't feel like talking to her. *No way she'll be pleased about the baby. But I don't want to hear it right now. Auntie Gwen's not so bad.*

Slowly, Rebekah climbed the stairs to her room. Once there, she started sorting out her portfolio ahead of her meeting with Mr. Stowe. She took out the smaller drawings and paintings she kept in two drawers and checked her closet for the larger ones that she had clipped onto clothes hangers. There were so many, she didn't know which to choose. But the Lady of the Library had said to bring as many as possible. There wasn't enough room to spread them on her floor or the bed so she decided to take the pile down into the kitchen where she could spread them out on the table and the counters. Even though her mother wasn't there, she didn't dare take them into the living room. She was forbidden from drawing in there in case charcoal dirtied the furniture. The two armchairs and long sofa were covered in protective plastic so she couldn't see how the dust could hurt. But rules were rules. You couldn't leave anything in the living room, at least not overnight, not even a book. Not her school bag, on any account. And certainly not her drawings except the one of her parents she had drawn when she was seven. Her daddy, delighted and proud, had framed it and hung it on the wall over the mantelpiece.

Carefully she placed some of her pieces on the Formica counter and the table. Just as she was poring over the one she had drawn of Mr. Stowe, wondering whether it really did look like him, the doorbell rang. She thought about ignoring the bell, but curiosity got the better of her – besides, it might be Wanda. Although what she would tell her, she wasn't sure. Somehow, she didn't think Wanda would be interested in Mr. Stowe. Lately, Wanda didn't seem to be interested in anyone who wasn't Roger Peterson.

Rebekah opened the door and then promptly wished she hadn't. There was that man leaning against the wall, his fleshy red mouth stretched into a foolish grin revealing his grubby, crossed front teeth. And what was even worse, a nasty-looking, big, yellow dog lay panting at his feet.

"Hi kiddo." At the sound of his voice and maybe at the sight of Rebekah, the dog leaped up, barking and jumping on her. She was about to slam the door in its face when she saw her mother park her car – in front of his on the side of their lane – and emerge from the vehicle her arms full of packages.

"I don't like dogs," Rebekah said, trying to push the animal away.

"Oh, Jasper won't hurt you, he's just trying to be friendly." The creature jumped up again in an effort to lick at her face. "See? He likes you."

"Well, I don't like him." And she turned and stalked back into the kitchen.

Her mother followed her, her eyes taking in all the drawing papers on the counter. "You'll take these up to your room, Bekah?"

Rebekah didn't respond.

"So how was your lunch? And what was in the letter to your father? *Was* it from the Lady of the Library?"

"Did the Lady of the Library teach you, Mama?

"No," said Mama shortly. "She was teaching when I was at the Meridian, though. She had her favourites, that's for sure. I wasn't one of them. So what was the letter about? Thomas, you coming in?"

The dog, now off its leash, dashed in before Thomas, went for the kitchen table, took one of Rebekah's drawings into its mouth, and dashed out again.

"Mama!"

"All right, Rebekah, all right. Thomas, go get that dog and keep him in your car. We're not used to animals in this house."

"That's for sure," Rebekah muttered and then more loudly, "I want my drawing back."

She started to put her pastel paintings back into a pile as her mother began to unpack her shopping bags. "So, Rebekah, did the Lady of the Library write to your daddy?"

"Yes. She wants me to bring my paintings to Mr. Stowe. She wants him to help, maybe teach me."

"Mr. Everard Leopold Stowe?" Mama's mouth dropped open. "When?"

"Tomorrow. Mama, I want my drawing back."

"Here it is." Thomas sauntered back into the kitchen and handed it to her. "It's very good, Rebekah. You really are an artist. Who is it?"

She looked sullenly at the tooth marks in the corner and at her daddy stooped over the tractor that seemed to drive out of the drawing. She said nothing. But she bitterly resented the way the man had looked at her drawing without asking. It was so, so *rude*. He had no right. Mama did not appear to notice.

"Tomorrow?" she asked. "What about church, Rebekah? You know I don't like for you to miss church."

"Daddy's taking me to the studio in the afternoon."

"It's true Everard Leopold Stowe used to be a very good

artist, but he must be really old right now. In any case, you have your art lessons at school."

"Mr. Fenwick ain't no good."

"Isn't any good. Stop speaking like Wanda. It doesn't suit you."

"He don't teach me nothing."

"Anything. And that's rude, Rebekah."

"You're a really good artist," Thomas said again. "My mother wants a portrait done of me. Suppose I commission you?"

She would not dignify this suggestion with a reply.

"Rebekah! Say thank you to Mr. Forrest."

"Thank you, Mr. Forster . . ."

"Forrest," said her mama.

For a second Rebekah felt genuinely confused. "Forrest," she said at last. "But I don't draw white people."

"That's rude, Rebekah!" Mama's face was becoming tauter by the minute.

"Well, I can't draw them."

Which was totally untrue. Somewhere in the pile were superb likenesses of Miss Spruce and Mr. Enfield. Not to mention the strange woman in the house and the man steering the sloop. Quickly she scooped up the paintings, then turned to her mama and noticed a new piece of jewellery around her throat. It was a gold chain with a turquoise stone hanging from it. Mama's eyes shifted a little so that Rebekah immediately knew she had not bought it herself. The Forrest man had. And then she looked at her mother's hand and saw that her wedding ring was gone.

Chapter
11

Rebekah had never heard of Fractious Street, let alone been there. She said as much as they drove eastwards down the North Shore Road in Papa Malachi's truck. "It sounds weird, Daddy. Where's it to?"

"It's in Hamilton Parish. It connects North Shore Road to Harrington Sound."

"The same way Trinity Road does?"

"Exactly. It runs off Wilkinson's Avenue. I've heard it told the guy who built it named it after his horse."

"You mean the horse was named Fractious?"

"Maybe. I dunno. Maybe he was fractious – you know bad tempered and misbehaving."

"Oh."

"Papa Malachi had a horse like that – by the name of Patsy. Sometimes he couldn't get her to go up a hill for the longest while. Her ears would come up and she'd stop. Whatever you did, you couldn't hit her. She'd kick. She was a character, that horse. Brown with a touch of white between her eyes."

"Oh." Her mind drifted, thinking of her mama's hand without her daddy's wedding band. She looked at her father's bare hands on the steering wheel. He'd never worn a band, so it wasn't significant. But she noticed with dismay his finger nails were dirty. It wasn't his fault because he'd been working in the fields but what would Mr. Stowe think? And even though it was Sunday, he wasn't wearing a jacket. She sighed heavily.

"What's the matter, Bek?"

"Nothing. Did you always like working in the fields – even when you were small?"

"Yes. It was a beautiful life – it was like a picnic, Bek, provided you didn't mind working hard. See, I was an energetic little guy. I was always up at five. I used to feed the goats and the pigs. And Papa had horses then – I loved to ride. It was normal for boys to ride in those days. Better than a moped or a scooter, I can tell you."

Rebekah thought horses were frightening, worse than dogs because they were bigger and could trample you.

Her daddy fell silent, but he was smiling, probably enjoying more childhood memories of the farm and the animals. Rebekah looked out of the window to the ocean stretching out from the rocky coastline. Aunty Gwen said the visitors liked the South Shore best because it had a chain of beaches with pink, creamy sand and there was more surf. Plus, there weren't so many houses. But for Rebekah the North Shore was more home – she liked the patchwork of pastel coloured houses with their stepped, white roofs and their shadows. And she liked the way on windy days, like today, the waves rushed in short and snappy with foaming white crests. And the palm trees' trunks and leaves all bent the same way.

Her daddy slammed on his brakes, causing her to fall forward against the dashboard. "Oops, I nearly missed the turning. Here we go, Fractious Street, and there's the studio on the left. See the sign?"

There it was, a cedar sign printed in flowing, black letters and attached to one of the two pillars that announced the entrance. Her daddy swung the truck into the driveway dividing a large expanse of neatly mown lawn. Ahead was the house, single storey and washed white with wooden shutters and window frames – painted a vibrant sun yellow.

"That's a nice house." Daddy remarked as he cut the engine. "Bermuda stone – real nice. It's old, Bek. See the stepped roof? Just like Papa Malachi's but older, I think. See how it sags a bit in the middle? And the chimney?"

Rebekah nodded – the chimney was to the right of the house and was so much taller than the walls, it should have been out of proportion but somehow it wasn't. She liked the way the house seemed to lean into it and the smoke curling out of it. As they jumped out of the truck, the front door, panelled in Bermuda cedar, opened and there was Mr. Stowe smiling at them. Rebekah was startled to see that he was wearing exactly the red and yellow plaid jacket she had wanted for her drawing of him, as well as the navy Bermuda shorts with bright yellow knee socks. He must like yellow, she thought.

"Good afternoon, Jonah. It's been a long time since I've seen you, but you haven't changed. Just grown taller." The two men shook hands and Rebekah noticed with relief that Mr. Stowe had paint on his hands. Perhaps he wouldn't mind her daddy's dirty fingernails. She also noticed he had a voice like honey and an accent that was not familiar to her. It was English but not the same accent that Mr. Fenwick or Miss Spruce had. He sounded more proper somehow.

"Good to see you, Mr. Stowe. This is my daughter, Rebekah. It's very kind of you to see her."

Mr. Stowe shook her hand and gazed straight into her eyes in a way that might normally embarrass her, but strangely did not.

"I've heard a lot about you, Miss Rebekah Eve," he said. "I'm indeed happy to meet you."

She could tell he really was happy to see her. He wasn't just being polite. *Aunty Gwen is right*, she thought. *Mr. Stowe is different.*

"I think, Jonah, perhaps it would be best if you were to return at five. I can see that your daughter and I have a lot to discuss. And," Mr. Stowe added, smiling at the thick folder she held under her arm, "a lot to look at."

"I must go anyhow. Farming never lets you rest, let alone go on holiday."

"I heard you decided to take up farming. I applaud your decision."

"You do, sir? Not many folks do."

"Those of us who were here in the War remember how we needed our farmers. We all grew our own vegetables – it was very important. It still should be very important for us to grow our own food."

"Exactly," Her daddy looked at the borders at each side of the door. "Pretty roses. And I like the bitter aloe. My mama always grows it." He nodded. "Thank you again, Mr. Stowe. Rebekah, I will pick you up you at five."

"Thank you, Daddy."

Mr. Stowe ushered her through the door which led directly into the sitting room and gestured that she should sit down on one of the two settees, placed together in an L shape, while he would sit in the other. Rebekah stared around open-mouthed at the number of pictures on the oatmeal pale walls. Never had she seen so many paintings in a house before. There were many pictures of people, including one over the fireplace of a slim lady with bright hazel eyes, wearing a hat. "My wife," explained Mr. Stowe as he saw her eyes resting on it. She nodded, then looked at the others – pictures of houses in foreign cities, of seascapes and landscapes, and of flowers, lots of flowers. There were abstracts. *It will take me weeks to look at them all properly*, she thought. *Weeks and weeks and weeks.*

The room was interesting for other reasons as well. There was the fire in front of them, cedar logs burning brightly in the brick fireplace, just like at Grandma Kezia's. Rebekah's house had a proper fireplace, too, but Mama never liked real fires. She said the smoke spoiled the paintwork and anyway they were plain messy. She didn't like Grandma Violet's kerosene heater either – it smelled funny and gave off a thin blue haze. So in their fireplace they had an electric heater with pretend flames. In spite of the cold, damp wind that morning, Mr. Stowe's fire wasn't smoking. It radiated a cheerful heat and a cedar fragrance. In one corner of the room was a small upright piano with music on the stand. She recognised the name Johann Sebastian Bach because sometimes they sang his hymn "Sheep May Safely Graze" in the morning school assemblies all the students had to attend. Mr. Stowe would be good at playing the piano, she thought, on account of the size of his hands. She turned to look at them to see if they were as large as the ones she'd imagined. But sitting on his sofa he was steadily gazing at her again and the expression on his face was so familiar to her she almost laughed. He was doing what she so often did when she met someone – he was figuring out how to draw her. His eyes were taking in the angles and lines of her face, the proportion of her head to her body, the way her hair swept back in waves, the folds of her blouse and the lines of her skirt. He saw her smiling.

"What are you thinking about, Rebekah?"

"Nothing." It felt rude to tell him. But she smiled some more and handed over her portfolio. "I brought you some paintings and drawings because that's what the Lady of the Library said you wanted."

"The Lady of the Library?" he said smiling back. "A woman of strong opinions and convictions."

Remembering the Lady's opinion of her mama, Rebekah felt her mouth tighten. She didn't comment but waited for him to open the folder, her heart beating a little harder. What if he didn't like her work? What if he got mad like Mr. Fenwick? What if he agreed with Miss Spruce that she was disturbed?

He placed the folder on the coffee table in front of them.

Papa Malachi would like the table, Rebekah thought vaguely. It was made out of cedar – she could see the joins that Papa had told her were the mark of a real cabinet maker. It smelled nice too. When Mr. Stowe opened the folder and looked at the first drawing, he started to laugh, but Rebekah could tell he wasn't laughing at her. He was laughing because the drawing was the one she had sketched of him even though she hadn't known who he was at the time. "Well, Miss Rebekah Eve, well, well, well. I am truly honoured. An interesting portrait, indeed, if I might say so."

"I got your eyes wrong." She frowned as she looked at it. "Your right eyelid is not quite right. And your nose is not right either – it's too straight."

But he wasn't listening. He picked up picture after picture – the ones of Grandpa Malachi and Daddy on the tractor, of Grandma Kezia in the kitchen and bending over her herbs in the garden, of Grandma Violet sitting on an old metal chair in her kitchen – staring pensively out of a window. And of the cottage she had drawn for Mr. Fenwick. That one he paused over. "You have been to England?"

She shook her head. "No, Mr. Stowe. Mr. Fenwick brought a picture for us to copy."

"I see. Well, that is a typical English cottage. I saw many cottages like that when I was in England. But what is this?"

He lifted the next drawings – the ones of the Bermuda stone house with the large chimney and the vent with the slats. Then he pointed to the girl she had painted in the second drawing, the girl with the funny dress and the low cleavage. "And who is she?"

Rebekah shrugged. "I dunno. Just someone I saw."

"Does she have a name?"

Rebekah remembered the man's voice shouting. "Nancy. I think."

Next, he looked at the picture of the woman with the terrible eyes and the scraped back hair. "And this woman? Do you know her?"

"No," she said in a small voice.

"It's a very good portrait," he said calmly, putting it down and looking next at the picture of the ship with billowing sails tilting into the waves she had made yesterday over lunch at Mangrove Bay. And at the man with the tricorn hat.

"The captain?" But he didn't wait for an answer. He moved onto the picture of the child she had seen at Buildings Bay only the drawing was scarcely there. All the charcoal had faded leaving just the edge of the child's cap, a couple of smudges for eyes, a mere hint of a nose and no mouth. "What happened here?"

"She faded," Rebekah said. "I don't know why. I used lots of charcoal, but it got rubbed off."

"Could you draw her again?"

She shut her eyes, but somehow, she couldn't see her. "I don't think so. It would be very difficult. Besides, she changes."

"So you have drawn her before?"

She explained how when she had seen the child in Somerset, she did not have her sketch book with her. "When I saw her in St. George's, she was older. I just hope I see her again. But perhaps she'll look different."

Mr. Stowe was silent for a moment. "I have a difficult question for you, Rebekah. Do you want to paint what you see or what you imagine?"

"Is there a difference?"

"Now there," he said with an expression of sheer delight, "is the voice of a true artist. But in any case, you are clearly interested in history."

"I don't think so. I think history is boring."

"Your pictures say otherwise."

She nodded acknowledging that her painting drew her into the past – there could be no other explanation for the people she saw.

"You draw mostly in charcoal?"

"Yes. But my daddy bought me lots of pastels – 500

different colours. And yet I can never get the sea right. The blues aren't right – they don't – they don't sing the way they should. Mr. Fenwick doesn't teach us about colour – he goes on all about drawing and perspective."

"Some teachers like to start with the drawing basics. There's no harm in that, Rebekah. But perhaps I can help you with colour. You like pastels best of all, do you?"

She nodded eagerly. "I want to learn how to paint layers, do the underpainting, because I know everything behind the surface of a painting is important."

"Interesting. But you know underpainting can be important with other media. Oils, for example. And even watercolour though it's more subtle."

"I read something about pastels in a book in the library. It says with pastels there are no mistakes."

"Now that, my dear, is just not true. There are always mistakes. But the mistakes you can turn into truths."

She thought about this. "My ship drawing . . ."

"Yes, Rebekah?"

"I didn't draw it exactly. I rubbed out the charcoal and the ship came out and I don't think it is a mistake. But it's true I haven't put on colour yet. And if I do, I'll probably spoil it."

"Can you show me what colour you have tried?"

She showed him the scene she had attempted at Buildings Bay before the child had interrupted.

"See. The water is wrong and the leaves."

"Mangroves at sunset," Mr. Stowe murmured. "But what have we here?" He pointed to the thin suggestion of tree on the left of the bay. "Why didn't you finish this? It has a promising shape."

"Oh, it faded out of sight and so did the trees on the hill side. It was a nice tree with creamy flowers – it smelled nice."

"A frangipani?"

She nodded. "Yes. But it faded before I could paint it."

He paused for a moment. "Rebekah, let me get this right. Do you mean the frangipani in your picture faded? Or the real one by the bay?"

"I was drawing the real frangipani. When the child appeared at the bay, I couldn't see it any more. Or the trees on the hillside either." She tensed, her face hot with embarrassment. "I know it's strange, Mr. Stowe, but ..."

"Strange, perhaps, Rebekah, but not impossible."

She relaxed, her breathing easier now she could trust him not to dismiss her as strange or crazy.

"I am sure one day we will find an explanation. Until then, keep drawing."

She nodded as his eyes turned back to the faded frangipani. "But you like painting flowers?" he asked.

"Yes. Though not as much as people. The colours of flowers are too difficult, 'specially white ones."

"We'll see about that. Certainly, I will help you with colour. But I warn you, Rebekah, it will be a lifetime study. Now, would you like to see my garden? And my studio?"

Of course, she would. She always liked to see new places and she liked to see the tools other people used. "Yes, yes please."

They got up and he led her through a door to the kitchen. Before she could take in the details of the kitchen, he slid out the lower bolt of the cedar stable door and turned the knob of the top half. Rebekah gasped with pleasure because there before her was a wonderland of trees, supports for all sorts of vines scrambling across them. And from their branches hung hundreds of plants with unusual flowers in pots and miniature homemade wooden baskets. She pointed to them. "They are so pretty – I've never seen them before. What are they?"

"Orchids and bromeliads. I grow them. I collected them on my travels throughout South America. Many of them are epiphytes. That means they grow on other plants. See?" He pointed to an exquisite orchid hanging from a tiny piece of driftwood attached to a twig. The flower was orange-yellow and speckled and to Rebekah it looked more like a butterfly than a flower. "That is Mrs. Stowe's favourite." Mr. Stowe led the way through the trees along a narrow pathway edged on one side with the aloes, cochineals, and agaves that she recognised from her grandparents' garden. But on the other side was a mass of red and orange flowers. Mr. Stowe stopped for a moment. "Do you know what this is, Rebekah?"

"I don't think so."

"It's called milkweed and is vitally important for our Monarch butterflies. They lay eggs on it and when the eggs hatch, the caterpillars feed on the plant until they are ready to turn into chrysalises." He pointed to a caterpillar with greenish yellow and black and white stripes undulating along one of the stems.

"It looks creepy," Rebekah said.

"Does it? Think of the beautiful butterfly it becomes."

They reached the end of the path and there was Mr. Stowe's studio which looked like a smaller version of the main cottage. It, too, was white with the same yellow trim and it, too, had a cedar stable door. He took out a large key to open the top half, unbolted the second and stepped in, beckoning her to follow him. Apart from a bathroom, there was just one room though it was long and spacious. There was a sink and plenty of room for the three wooden tables and the shelves containing his supplies. And what art supplies! She had never seen so many. Box after of box filled with tubes of oil and water colour paints, and one large drawer filled with pastels. Stacks and stacks of paper just waiting to be used. Dozens of brushes, all different sizes, stored in trays and jars. She saw bottles of ink as well and different nibs. Palettes and palette knives, pots of glue, and scissors. Everything in its proper place. She remembered Wanda saying it was OK for creative people to be untidy – it was proof they were artistic. But Rebekah never agreed with that theory. Papa Malachi had taught her that you must respect your tools or they won't work for you. His office with all the bits of paper in it might be untidy but his work shed was just so. *Mr. Stowe's studio is just the same*, she thought.

Her eyes took in his three easels holding unfinished paintings – one a Bermuda scene all in shades of blue. She opened her mouth to ask him about it – why not any other colour? But he was still talking about the butterflies.

"Do you know what a symbol is, Rebekah?"

"Something that stands for something else, like scales for justice."

"Exactly. I think the caterpillar, particularly the monarch, has important symbolism for the artist. The stuff that dreams are made on. Your dreams are important, you know."

Rebekah sighed. "That's what my mama says. She wants me to be a lawyer or a doctor – something like that."

"And what do you want to be, Rebekah?"

She sighed again. "I dunno. I don't feel right unless I'm drawing but mama says…" She broke off, distracted by one of the titles of the books in the shelves lining the walls. "I've read that book – *The Paintings of Henry Ossawa Tanner*. I *love* his paintings."

"You do, do you?"

"I like *The Banjo Lesson* best."

Mr. Stowe took out the book and turned the pages until he found the painting. They sat down together at one of the tables. "I do too," he said. "It speaks to me. What does it speak to you about?"

"Papa Malachi," she said promptly. "When he's telling me stuff. I think this man is a grandfather too."

"And what do you like about it?"

"I like their expressions. I like the way he's teaching the boy and the boy listening and I like the light in the background because it makes them seem rich."

He smiled at her. "Where did you come across the book, Rebekah?"

"Mrs. Chatterjee found it on her desk one morning, along

with some others. She didn't know where they came from because they're not proper library books. But I think, I think . . ."

"What do you think?"

"I think the Lady of the Library put them there."

"Really?"

"Does she really live behind the door in the library?"

Mr. Stowe's eyes slid away from her. "The Lady of the Library is an extremely private person."

"How come? How come us children never see her?"

"That is her choice. But one thing is for certain, she certainly sees you."

Rebekah shivered a little but decided it could be rude to say the Lady of the Library was creepy.

"She never goes out of her room?"

"She will when she needs to. Tell me, Rebekah, the child you drew, the one that faded. Does she have a name?"

"She didn't tell me it. But she called me Bek."

"She spoke to you? Did she say anything else?"

For a second, Rebekah couldn't quite remember. Then a phrase came back to her. "Maybe I imagined it, but I thought she said, 'No finery'. And she told me to draw her."

Mr. Stowe seemed to think about it. Then he said, "Rebekah if you draw her again, I want you to telephone me immediately. And I will come and see your drawing. Do you promise me?"

"But why?"

"Just humour me, child. And now let's plan the work we will do together. I would like for you to come here every Sunday afternoon."

Her heart filled with pleasure at the thought of his attention and she smiled at him.

Chapter
12

During the next few weeks Rebekah didn't know what she would have done without her Sunday lessons with Mr. Stowe – they were the only bright spot of her week. Her daddy, so busy with the growing season and the crops that should be ready for Christmas, only just managed to take time off to take her to the studio. She was worried that he'd ask her mama to take her instead and then when would she see him? So far, though, he was honouring the wishes of the mysterious Lady of the Library.

Mr. Stowe's exercises didn't bore her like Mr. Fenwick's. He would ask her to colour in squares so that she could practise creating graduating shades for each family of colours. And he would talk to her about colours, about how some are warm while others are cool, and about how you can create different effects using colours that are opposite to each other. Some subjects, he said, require you to make the colours luminous so the light appears to shine through them. After an hour or so, he would let her draw a subject he chose or one of her own while he continued with his own work.

Unlike Mr. Fenwick, he never minded if something unexpected appeared on her paper. In fact, something unexpected often appeared on his paper. There was the time he painted a woman dancing and gave her bright red hair that to Rebekah's eyes looked odd against the woman's dark complexion.

"Why not?" he said when Rebekah expressed surprise. "Art is all about the unexpected. Many black women want to change their hair." Rebekah would never dream of dying her hair red. Given her mama's preoccupation with straight hair, she could just imagine her reaction.

"Sometimes art is about how we see ourselves and sometimes how we would be if only life would let us. Your child, for instance. Sitting on the rocks. Have you painted her again?"

"No."

Whenever Rebekah tried to conjure her, the details of the child's face and eyes would not come to life and she was left with the desolate feeling that she had lost something precious. The house in Sandys Parish – the one she had drawn in class, unsure if it was real or not – stayed with her. She drew it from all angles – the huge chimney, the windows. But it was the front door that fascinated her and the thought of the people inside. She would sketch the young lady with the long, low cut dress, standing at a kitchen table. Rebekah thought she could see the other scary woman, her skirts trailing on the floor, hovering by another door inside the kitchen. It was too tricky to draw a door within a door, Rebekah thought. Besides, she wasn't sure she should draw that woman again. The thought of it made her sick. She saw again the front door of the house and then the back view of a man on his way through the door frame. She couldn't see his features at all, but she could see his dress. That's when she thought he might be the same man from her charcoal picture of the ship. Only she wasn't quite sure, though he did have the same breeches and shirt.

Sometimes Mr. Stowe would take her out into the garden, which was much bigger than she had first noticed. To the left of the studio was his vegetable and herb garden with rows so neatly planted Grandma Kezia and her daddy would certainly approve. Mr. Stowe would tell her the names of the flowers and plants and she would choose the ones she wanted to paint for the still life exercises he told her were important to master. She was willing to try any subject he suggested, even a bowl of oranges that Mr. Fenwick also had once ordered the class to paint. But Mr. Fenwick never explained the different ways you could suggest colour. He just criticised when she got them wrong. Mr. Stowe, on the other hand, would talk and demonstrate, encouraging her all the while. "Dark to light," he would constantly remind her. "And not too much light orange. There's not nearly as much orange in an orange as you think there is."

Still, as she told him, it was people she loved best to draw, and houses because they told you about the people who lived in them.

"Well now. You'll have no problem with Christmas presents, Rebekah. Folks love to have portraits done – of their children or of themselves."

An expression of distaste crossed her face.

"What's the matter? You don't like to give your drawings away? I agree it can be painful. To this day I regret selling a painting I did of a friend of mine. I needed the money, you see . . ."

"I don't mind giving my pictures away but . . ."

"But?"

She hadn't told anyone about her mama's boyfriend – she worried that if she did, they would think badly of her mama. Yet Mr. Stowe was so accepting, so lacking in judgement, she thought she could risk a confidence.

"My mama. My mama, she has a boyfriend. Mr. Forrest. He wants me to call him Thomas. But I don't want to. And . . . and he wants me to do portraits of him so he can give them as Christmas presents to his mama and aunties. I don't want to do that either. Even though he says he'll pay me."

"I see. I believe that is your prerogative, Rebekah."

"How do you mean?"

"Your right as an artist to choose."

Rebekah didn't feel like she had much choice in anything – in her daddy leaving, in her mama bringing Mr. Forrest into her life. In anything. For one thing, she had so little time with her mama alone. Many evenings, Mama was out, and the house was lonely without her. Occasionally, Wanda would stop by but as the weeks wore on, she was less and less interested in staying in and more and more interested in hanging out at discos, preferably with Roger Peterson. She started wearing really short skirts, huge platform shoes and glittery nail varnish.

"Why don't you come, Bekah? It's fun and the music's real good."

"My mama won't let me."

"Your mama won't know! She's always out. So why don't you hang out with us, Bekah?"

Somehow the prospect of going out and her mama not knowing was worse than getting caught. What if she got caught and her mama didn't care?

"You're real boring, Bekah! All the kids are hanging out. It's cool."

"How come your mama lets you go out?"

Wanda looked shifty. "She don't know either."

"How come she don't know?"

"She thinks I'm with you!"

Rebekah didn't like that either.

When Mama was at home, the house didn't echo but it was still lonely because the man was always there and always talking. Rebekah couldn't stand his voice going on and on about law cases he had done in court in Canada or her mother looking so proud while he spoke. Rebekah just knew she was imagining her daughter with a barrister's wig and gown, looking important. If Mr. Forrest wasn't talking about law, he was going on and on about dogs. How everyone should have a dog because a dog is man's best friend. Sometimes he would bring Jasper into the house and the dog always went straight for Rebekah, tail wagging and saliva dripping. *Yuck.*

"I think Rebekah should have a puppy," he said once, that stupid grin on his face. "Don't you, Patricia? Dogs teach kids a bit of responsibility. How would you like a puppy for Christmas, Rebekah?"

Before Rebekah could voice a strong objection, her mama fortunately disagreed with him. "Rebekah doesn't like dogs, and I have to say, I don't either. So that's enough on that subject, Thomas."

Other times he'd bore her with stories about his family, which he said he was only just getting to know about. "I was born in Bermuda. But my family left when I was very small. We moved to Canada but . . ."

Pity you didn't stay there, Rebekah couldn't help thinking.

"Somehow, I feel as if I really belong in Bermuda, which isn't surprising when you think about it. As I was telling your mother, Rebekah, I've been doing some research in the archives about my family on my father's side. Do you know his family came over to Bermuda in the 1600s and years back they often sailed to Turks and Caicos to rake for salt . . ."

Why people have to go on and on about the past, I don't know. Even Mama gets bored when he rambles on about salt raking in Turks and Caicos. Her face takes on a funny expression he's too foolish to notice.

So, when he was over, Rebekah spent most of her time in her room.

One Thursday evening, when he was there for supper, her mother came up to her room to find her drawing. "I hope you've finished your homework?"

"Mmmm."

"Well, I wish you'd come downstairs. I need you."

Rebekah didn't say anything. She just kept on drawing.

"I need you, Rebekah," her mama repeated.

"Why? You've got company."

"It's Grandma Violet. She has just arrived, and I know she wants to see you."

"Grandma *Violet*?"

"Yes," Mama said, her face all embarrassed. "She's just arrived."

This was very strange because the only time Grandma Violet ever came to their house was when Rebekah's mama or daddy drove her. Although her house wasn't very far away, Grandma Violet never walked very far if she could help it. Rebekah figured that was because she had spent so much energy cleaning for other people, she just wanted to sit down all the time. "How did she get here?"

"Her friend brought her."

"But … why?"

Her mama shrugged, her eyes still embarrassed.

Then the penny dropped. *Of course*, Rebekah realised, *she wants to see the man; she wants to check him out.* And for the first time in weeks, apart from when she was at Mr. Stowe's, she felt like smiling. There was something endearing about her grandma being poky about her mama. *Well*, she thought, *poky's better than sad and it's better she's being poky about Mama than about me.*

"Will you come downstairs and see Grandma Violet?" her mama asked. "You can bring your pastels. We'll sit in the kitchen."

Rebekah brought down some of her pastel boxes as well as paper and charcoal.

"Hi kiddo," said the man, sitting at the kitchen table, the usual smile on his face. "And how was school?"

"Fine."

"Just fine, huh?"

If only he weren't so friendly, she thought, *so remorselessly cheerful all of the time.* She half nodded to him and went up to Grandma Violet who was sitting at the other end of the table, her hair neatly covered as usual with a kerchief. "Good evening, Grandma Violet. It's good to see you." She kissed her grandmother on the cheek.

"It's good to see you, child. I've come to meet Mr. Forrest."

"Thomas," he said quickly.

Grandma Violet did not appear to hear him. "You still drawing?" she asked Rebekah.

"She's always drawing." Her mama sighed.

"She's real good at it," Mr. Forrest said.

Rebekah could have sworn Grandma Violet winked at her, but she knew she must have imagined it. Grandma Violet was not the winking kind.

True to form, she did not crack a smile. *I must have imagined it*, Rebekah thought.

She took her paper and pastels to the counter and sat down on one of the kitchen stools. Eventually, Mr. Forrest and her mama started to talk while Grandma Violet sat silently – her face sad, as usual, but determined. That was new. Rebekah tugged the corner of her mouth with her finger, holding in a smile. It was obvious her grandmother wasn't going anywhere. Rebekah decided to tune the adults out and, picking up her charcoal, soon let her mind lose itself in her drawing. Her imagination was once again pulled towards the Sandys house she couldn't seem to stop drawing. Quickly, she sketched it in and then she saw the white man again with the shirt and breeches, and she was sure that he was the same man as the one she had seen on the ship and by the door frame of the cottage. But this time he was facing her so she could see his face – his mouth, a straight line, and his eyes, the colour of a stormy sea, gazing into the distance. Her hand flew over the paper and there he was, lazily leaning against the cedar front door of his house, holding a long whip loosely in his hand. She picked up one of her pastels to add a touch of colour to the eyes. But instead gave in to an overwhelming compulsion to tear off another page and start his portrait again.

On the new page, though, she found herself drawing the girl with the long dress she had seen in the house instead. The one she thought was called Nancy. Once Rebekah had outlined the head and shoulders, she realised the girl was struggling to escape. She sketched in Nancy's eyes; then used a hint of pastel to show the contrast between her irises and whites. The effect was one of sheer terror, emphasised by the screaming shape of her mouth. Only then did the man enter the picture.

This time she drew him grabbing the girl. She shaded in the straining muscles on his neck and across his shoulders as he raised his other arm to lash the girl with his whip. His face was in half profile – mouth snarling, teeth bared, eyes crazed.

She put down the pastel and stared in horror at the picture. *What's wrong with me that I see these terrible people? Are they real?* She remembered how she had asked Mr. Stowe whether there was any difference between what you see and what you imagine and how pleased he had been that she had asked that. What would he think now? What kind of person was she to imagine people as cruel as this and people like this young woman suffering for it? Just as she was thinking it would be better to destroy the drawing, Mr. Forrest walked over to her and peered over her shoulder. "Hey, girl, what are you drawing?" Seeing the two drawings, he exploded. "You say you can't draw me and then you draw me like that? I'm not a racist – how dare you draw me like that! How dare you? Patricia, look at these drawings! Look at them! Look how she's drawn me."

Rebekah looked at him and then at the drawing. "But this isn't you!"

"Of course it's me." He looked again, his eyes furious. "Why lie about it?"

All of a sudden, he flung the drawings onto the counter and, picking up the tray, hurled the pastels on to the kitchen floor where many broke into pieces.

Rebekah felt as if he had struck her. "My daddy gave me

those pastels. My daddy gave me those. And you've broken them! You've got no right to touch my property."

Tears of anger pouring down her face, Rebekah dropped to her hands and knees to pick up the pieces before he ground them into dust.

Mama shot up from her chair, shaken. "Thomas, you shouldn't have done that. You shouldn't."

"Well, she shouldn't have painted me like that. It's racist."

Mama picked up the drawings. "What's the matter with them?"

"Look at that picture, Patricia! She's drawn me as a slave master."

Mama looked at the first drawing and then more carefully at the second, sharply drawing her breath.

"That's not racist, Thomas. These days, she often draws from her imagination, don't you, Rebekah?"

Rebekah didn't answer. She was too busy looking for a dust pan and brush to sweep up the tiniest fragments. She would put them in a bag. Mr. Stowe kept all his pastels, however small. He'd said that you never knew when they'd come in useful.

"You didn't mean to draw Thomas in that picture, did you Rebekah?" And when Rebekah still didn't answer, "Well, did you?"

Rebekah's head throbbed so violently, she couldn't stand any more questions. "I don't know why I drew it. I just drew it!" she shouted at Mr. Forrest. "It's none of your business who I draw."

"It is when you draw me as a slave master – it's libel."

"Patricia." Grandma Violet's calm voice shocked them into silence. They had forgotten she was there. "I would like to see Rebekah's picture, please."

Mama put it on the table in front of her.

"Well, I have to say it does look like you, Mr. Forrest," Grandma Violet said after taking her time to absorb the drawing. "So how come you're acting so upset? Slave masters existed. You've gotta know that."

"Not in my family!"

Rebekah watched her grandmother, interested in spite of her headache. It was so unusual for Grandma Violet to express an opinion on anything, let alone smile – the way she was smiling now.

"Honey," she said to Mr. Forrest, "go back far enough in a white person's family and you'll find a slave master some place; same as when you go back in a black person's family, you'll find white blood somewhere. No need to get upset, that's just a fact."

Rebekah, calmer now, said, even as she continued checking the floor for pastel fragments, "You said your mother's family came over in the 1600s. Back in those days most white folks had slaves. That's what my teachers say."

"That may be true," Mr. Forrest said at last. "But slavery in Bermuda was not like slavery anywhere else. I've been reading about it. We didn't have plantations. Slaves were like members of the family."

"Still slaves," Grandma Violet said.

Mama was silent. And Rebekah saw she had exactly the same funny expression on her face that had appeared when he talked about salt raking in Turks and Caicos the other week. *She doesn't like hearing about his past any more than I do.*

"Maybe now's not the time for this conversation," Mama said.

"Are you saying I'm in the wrong?" Mr. Forrest demanded. "Is that what you're saying? I'm not the one who painted a lie. That child of yours has got problems. She needs professional help. Are you going to draw me like that again, Rebekah? Are you?"

Somehow, in spite of all the emotional turmoil pounding behind her eyes, Mr. Stowe's words came back to her. "That is my prerogative," she said.

"Your what?"

"My right as an artist to choose."

Chapter 13

The next Sunday at the studio Mr. Stowe lent Rebekah an easel and she enjoyed the new angle from which she worked so much she felt a sense of release and freedom. The picture of a woman came into her head – not Nancy, someone much happier and more independent although about the same age. Eventually, the vision appeared on the sheet of paper: a short, dark skinned, young woman dressed in a white blouse with long puffed out sleeves and a necktie paired with a flared, navy blue skirt belted in to a narrow waist. She wore shoes with silver buckles and her dark hair was piled up. Rebekah used the flat edge of the brown pastel to create eyes brimming with vitality and promise, and red pastels for the books the woman carried under one arm.

Mr. Stowe stood next to her, gazing steadily at the depiction. "Do you know this lady, Rebekah?"

"No, of course not. I made her up." Then she remembered she thought she had made up Mr. Stowe as well when she drew him. It was Mrs. Drinkwater and her daddy who had put her right on that one. *Could this drawing be of a real person as well?*

"Do you know her?"

Instead of answering, he asked a question of his own. "Do you like her?"

She gave him an "Are you crazy or what?" look.

"I'm serious. Do you like the person you have drawn?"

She thought about it. "Yes. I do."

"Good."

"Why?"

Mr. Stowe smiled. "Because I like her too."

Rebekah's eyes drifted back to the image. "She looks like somebody even though her clothes have come out funny." She fell silent for a moment, her eyes thoughtful but sad.

"What's the matter, Rebekah?"

"Remember I told you my mama's boyfriend wants me to draw him but I don't want to?"

"Yes, certainly I remember."

"Well, he thinks I drew him anyway and he was upset."

"Have you brought the drawing with you?"

Rebekah went to the folder of work she had brought with her to show him and picked out the picture of the man leaning against the door. Then, nervously she pulled out the one of the same man beating the older girl. Would Mr. Stowe think badly of her? Miss Spruce's voice came back to her: "You don't think she's a tad *disturbed*, do you?"

When Mr. Stowe looked at both drawings, he let out a small whistle of air. "I expect he was upset, Rebekah. You did not think you were drawing him dressed in historical costume?"

"No."

"Now that you've had time to think about it, does it look like him?"

"I didn't mean it to be him." Rebekah's face creased at the awful memory. "He was so mad. He broke some of my pastels on purpose." Once again she saw her beautiful colours in fragments on the floor.

"I hope you kept them. It is indeed distressing when our pastels break for the first time. But they can still–"

"Come in useful," she said smiling. "I knew you'd say that."

"Rebekah. Do you think he would have hit you?"

"I don't know. Maybe. Maybe not."

"Are you frightened of him, Rebekah?"

She struggled with a huge temptation to lie. Because if she said she was frightened, maybe Mr. Stowe could find a way to tell her mother and then maybe her mother wouldn't see Mr. Forrest anymore. It would serve him right because he had thrown her pastels on the floor and he was trying to push in where he wasn't wanted. But still – it wasn't right to lie, especially to a person as special as Mr. Stowe. She shrugged her shoulders. "He's – he's foolish."

Mr. Stowe handed her a fresh sheet of paper and another piece of charcoal. "I want to see what you think he looks like. Draw him for me, if you please."

After shutting her eyes to recall his face, she let the charcoal speed over half of the paper. There the man emerged, one hand holding the frying pan, the other flipping the hamburgers, his face creasing into an amiable grin. Then she drew him again, the way she remembered him looking after throwing the pastels. Mr. Stowe peered at the drawings.

"What did you say his name was, Rebekah? Mr.?"

"Forrest, Thomas Forrest."

"I know this man's father, Rebekah."

"Yeah?"

"He's a lawyer you said?"

"Yeah."

"His father was a banker. He helped my mother secure her mortgage way back in the 1930s."

Her eyes widened even as she wondered, *What does that matter to me?*

"In those days, that was a big thing to do for a widow, especially for a woman of colour. Mr. Forrest senior wasn't a bad man."

"What happened to him?"

"He left the country with his wife and child because, like everyone else, he lost his investments in the Depression. Thomas would have been a baby then. As I said, his father wasn't a bad man though some said he lost them their savings. His son doesn't look like a bad man either. Weak, perhaps, but not fundamentally … evil. He looks like his father."

"He looks like the man with the whip as well," Rebekah pointed out. "Though I don't know why."

"Perhaps we will never know why. And yet, and yet I think a story may be unfolding."

"It's not a nice story," Rebekah said in a small voice.

She saw a flash of understanding cross Mr. Stowe's features. "Sometimes we have to paint the truth – however unpleasant, however cruel. Picasso understood that in his Guernica painting of war. We will look at it one day."

He smiled at her. "Painting the ugliness does not mean there's something wrong with the artist, you know."

Rebekah gave a hint of a smile back. He understood her so well.

"You still have not seen the girl with the cap you saw in St. George's?"

"No, Mr. Stowe."

"Remember what I told you. Phone me immediately if you do see her. In the meantime," he said, pointing to her picture of the lady in the navy blue skirt, "I would be most grateful if I may keep this. I like it very much. Would you mind?"

Mind? A great artist wanting one of her pictures? How could she mind? How could she thank him for the compliment? Her heart felt alight. All she could do was smile sweetly and say, "No, I don't mind."

"Then please sign it. Thanks much."

Chapter
16

Usually, Rebekah loved the lead up to Christmas, but this year all the signals of the season left her feeling flat and uncertain. At the beginning of December, the Corporation Christmas trees arrived on the dock and were soon all over the City of Hamilton shimmering with lights. The island's Christmas lights competition was in full swing and, though in previous years she loved to drive round the island with her parents to check out the illuminated reindeer and nativity scenes that transformed folks' gardens, this year she could hardly bear to go with her mother. At least that man was not invited but it felt so wrong to be in the front seat of the car instead of the back, and somehow the lights dotted around hedges and along rooftops, instead of being magical, appeared plastic, cheap, and tawdry.

And then there was the uncertainty. Where would she spend Christmas Day? Her mama wasn't saying, and her daddy was so busy making sure the vegetables would be ready in time for the season, he wasn't thinking. Most years they spent the morning together, her daddy, her mama, and Grandma Violet, who would always be so quiet, you hardly noticed she was present. They'd go to church, go back to their house for lunch, and eat turkey and cassava pie with all of the trimmings. And then, after taking

Grandma Violet back to hers in back of town, they'd drive down to St. George's to spend Christmas night and Boxing Day with Grandma Kezia and Papa Malachi and Uncle Gabriel and Aunty Gwen. And a fire would be crackling in the living room and however full they felt, they'd have turkey and cassava pie and the trimmings all over again. And nobody minded except perhaps her mama because she and Grandma Kezia were never comfortable with each other, not even at Christmas. But somehow Rebekah could put that unsettling thought to the back of her mind, taking pleasure in the Christmas tree Grandma Kezia always dressed with ornaments she had made herself, as well as the hum of conversation among adults.

But this year?

At school, she was constantly reminded of the problem because of all the Christmas activities. There were Christmas carols in the morning assemblies and the school choir, of which Wanda was a member, was constantly practising. You could hear the music wafting out of the assembly hall. Paper and tinsel decorations went up in the form rooms. Even the library, Rebekah's one refuge at school, had fairy lights strung across the tops of the shelves. Mrs. Chatterjee sported a Santa hat and earrings that flashed first red, then green, and lastly gold. Above the silver knocker on the red door, Rebekah noticed, was a small wreath made of cedar and Mexican pepper with red berries.

Wanda didn't seem pleased by Christmas either. She didn't like being in the school choir because Roger wasn't in it – his voice was only half broken. When Rebekah pointed out that singing would help her be a good actress, Wanda said, a bit sulkily, that she wasn't sure she wanted to be an actress after all. "It's boring," she said. But everything was boring for Wanda these days, everything and everyone but Roger Peterson. Wanda particularly resented the times her mother asked her to take care of her little twin brothers because that meant she spent less time with Roger. However, even she couldn't refuse to take the twins to see Santa arrive for his parade on Front Street. Her mother was out on her second job cleaning offices and her father, a bartender, was always out at night anyway.

"You gonna come with me?" she asked Rebekah.

"Why don't you ask Roger?" Rebekah couldn't resist; she was so tired of hearing about him.

"Are you foolish? I couldn't ask Roger. He'd think I was acting childish."

So, on the evening of Santa's arrival, they stood with crowds of parents and children on Front Street, holding the boys' hands and trying to control them as they jumped up and down in a frenzy of excitement. Santa was to arrive by ferry, and they could just see the light on the funnel before the boat made the turn into the ferry terminal. Minutes later they could hear the clanging of the fire engine, which would carry Santa into Front Street. "We'd better lift them up so they can see," Wanda said with resignation. "I'll take Troy. Troy wriggles more than Trey but I'm used to it."

"Do you want to sit on my shoulders, Trey?" Rebekah asked. He nodded and climbed onto Rebekah's back, his arms around her neck. The bells of the fire engine came nearer, and soon the swarms of people cheered and waved as a fully robed Santa came into view on top of the gleaming, red fire truck, grinning and waving back. *I've never painted crowds before*, Rebekah thought vaguely, *maybe I should. Being in a crowd makes you feel different somehow, not quite yourself because you're so caught up with everyone else.* Then she glanced at Wanda and saw it wasn't true of her at all. Her petite frame struggling with Troy's writhing weight, she looked on the scene with such a lack of enthusiasm, Rebekah had to smile. But unexpectedly her own view of Santa on top of the truck slid into darkness. All she could hear was the siren. Her vision cleared in time to see the fire engine just as it slowly drove past them, and she could swear the scarlet figure she had seen previously was different. *It isn't Santa at all, it's an old woman.* An ugly, bent old woman cackling and shouting at the mob. *Why is she shaking her fists at us? Why is she laughing at us?* She glanced around. Nobody else could see the woman, she was sure. Wanda didn't seem to notice and neither did the twins. They were cheering with everyone else the whole while. "Santa, Santa, Santa!" Meanwhile, the cackling woman on the truck raised and shook her fists again, and Rebekah saw that her hands were bound at her wrists. She shivered.-

Around her, the crowd continued cheering. "Santa, Santa, Santa!" And then, through the swell of the crowd's shouting, Rebekah thought she heard the old woman yell, "No use you hurrying, folks. There'll be no fun till I get there."

Get where, Rebekah wondered, *get where?*

But by then the truck had driven past and was now well to her left, and the old woman was vanishing. And just as the shouting around her started to die down, Rebekah saw that she was gone altogether. She could just see the back of Santa's scarlet hood and robe.

I imagined it. I must have done. What is the matter with me?

"Bye bye, Santa," Trey said.

"What's the matter, Bekah?" Wanda asked. "You're real quiet." The event over, Wanda had insisted on going to the Kentucky Fried Chicken restaurant on Queen Street as a treat for the twins. Rebekah looked listlessly at her wings and fries. *If I told you*, she thought, *you'd say I was crazy.*

"Nothin'. I'm just tired."

"Now you know what I go through when I look after the twins, which is most of the time. Hey girl, guess what Roger told me about Juan?"

Rebekah gave an inward sigh. *Here we go again*, she thought. "What?"

A memory of Juan in their last year at Primary School shot into her mind. One day, they had stayed in their classroom at lunch break because the rain was so heavy the yard was like a lake. The boys were talking excitedly about the football game they were to play the next afternoon against another school. Roger Peterson had caught sight of Juan who was sitting at his desk, his quiet, gentle face intent on reading a book while the rain hammered on the roof. Roger, never one to waste an opportunity, winked at Rebekah and said, "My daddy's gonna watch me play in the game tomorrow. Your daddy gonna watch you?"

Juan said nothing, his eyes on his book. Roger snatched his book away. "Your daddy gonna come to the game? I don't think so. You ain't got no daddy. Everybody knows that, don't they, Rebekah?"

Juan stood up. "What you mea, mea, mean, I ain't got no daddy?"

"I mea, mea, mean, you ain't got no daddy."

"You mea, mean my daddy's dead, is that what you're, you're saying?"

Rebekah remembered Juan's eyes boring into Roger's, remembered wanting to save him from Roger's mockery but not being able to figure out how to do it. Suddenly, words miraculously fell freely from Juan's mouth.

"My daddy's in New York. You think my daddy's in the ground where people stamp on him? You think he's a clock that goes tick tock, tick tock? You think my daddy's in space, up in space? You think my daddy's in the lighthouse for tourists to go up and look at? You think my daddy's dead? My daddy's in New York."

"Bekah?" Wanda's voice jerked her back into the café. "Roger thinks Juan is soft on you."

"Roger's foolish."

"No, girl. He says Juan is always in the library trying to find you."

"*Please.*"

"He says he saw Juan there twice today."

"Girl, shut your mouth!"

"I'm serious."

"Right." Just as she was thinking about how to change the

subject, Roger walked in, an older boy, a young man, really, beside him. They walked up to the service counter to order their food. Rebekah heard Roger's voice giving his order. *Typical*, Rebekah thought, *the one person you don't want to see is right in your face. Please, Lord, don't let Roger notice . . .*

"Hey Wanda," he shouted, turning towards them.

Wanda's eyes lit up. "Roger!" She beckoned him to the empty table next to them. Then she pulled it closer to theirs. Once the boys were given their plates of food, they made their way to it.

"John, this is my friend, Wanda, and these are her little brothers, Troy and Trey," Roger said. "Wanda, this is my elder brother."

John put down his plate – salad, Rebekah noticed. No fries. "Good evening, everyone." He gazed down at the twins. "How you doing, boys? Having a good time?" They stared at him, speechless with admiration.

Rebekah looked at John curiously, taking in his large Afro, glasses that gave him a studious look, and tall, lean frame. *Not pudgy like his horrible little brother*, she thought, smarting from not being included in his introduction. *Not stupid looking either.*

"Evening, John," Wanda said, her eyes shining in the excitement of meeting someone new. "How come I've never seen you at your house?"

"Oh, that's because he lives in our apartment." Roger started to tuck into his hamburger. "He only comes upstairs when–"

"Good evening, John." Rebekah interrupted, deciding not to let Roger get away with it.

John smiled at her. "And you are?"

She was about to answer but Wanda wouldn't let her. "This is my friend Rebekah Eve."

"Good evening, Rebekah. Good to meet you."

"Good to meet you."

"You come here a lot?" Wanda asked. "I've never seen you."

"I'm treating Roger, being that it's Christmas. For some

crazy reason he likes it here."

Roger washed down his fries with some soda. "John likes healthy stuff. He's a freedom fighter, you know," he added proudly, as if there was a sequitur here somewhere. "He likes politics, don't you, John?"

"I do. Life's not fair when some people suffer and others don't, you know what I mean? Are you interested in politics, girls?"

"I've been interested in politics for a while," Wanda said quickly, "but . . ."

Rebekah practically choked. Whenever a politician came on the television, they both turned off the set or switched channels. "Boring, boring," Wanda would say.

John turned to look at Rebekah. She could see behind his glasses that unlike Roger's, his eyes were more green than brown. They had a seriousness to them that Roger's lacked but a gleam of humour, too.

"You like politics, Rebekah?" He looked as if he genuinely was interested in her answer.

Before she could answer, Wanda cut in. "Bekah's an artist, you know, so she doesn't have time for politics."

"That's nice, Rebekah," he said.

He was pleasant enough, far more so than his brother, but she had to put him right about art.

"Being an artist isn't nice. It's just the way you are."

He nodded slightly, as if her correction intrigued him.

Wanda laughed loudly. "Bekah, it's late, you know. You should be going." Her eyes danced with amusement, but Rebekah knew it wasn't amusement; it was spite. *She wants all the attention. She always wants all the attention.*

Wanda turned her eyes to John. "Bekah's such a mama's girl. She's not allowed out late."

Rebekah got up, hoping John couldn't see her face burn with embarrassment. *How dare Wanda humiliate me like that? How dare she!* She decided to go on the attack. "The twins need to be in bed, Wanda. It's not fair to keep them up."

"That's very mature of you, Rebekah," John said. Then he quickly winked at her as if to say, "Is Wanda a pain in the neck or what?"

"The young are our future so we must take care of them properly. That's why I do a lot of work with a youth group."

Rebekah took pleasure in the annoyance flashing across Wanda's face that John was not talking directly to her, but she was also curious. "You do?"

"Sure. We have a club on the Admiralty House property. You must come and check it out. We need our artists to show us who we are. It would be great, Rebekah, if you could help out with the art side of things."

Rebekah got to her feet. "I might just do that. Bye, everyone." Wanda glared at her and Rebekah left with the satisfaction of knowing she was absolutely furious.

When Rebekah reached the house, she was appalled to see Mr. Forrest's car on the street outside. She had not seen him since the evening he had broken her pastels, and, as far as she knew, neither had her mother. They had spent several evenings together without him being around. Her mama had not even mentioned him much. Rebekah had hoped that meant the relationship was over but had not been able to bring herself to ask.

One of the few times her mother had mentioned him – out of the blue as Rebekah pored over her papers preparing to draw pictures of Grandma Kezia and Papa Malachi for Christmas presents – was to apologise on his behalf. "I'm sorry about your pastels, Rebekah. That was wrong of Thomas."

"That's all right, Mama."

"He's nice to me you know, but he's foolish sometimes, like a lot of white folks."

"Mmm," Rebekah really didn't want to discuss it. *Why couldn't her mama just get rid of the man and have her daddy back?*

"They just can't confront the issue, you know."

"What do you mean, Mama?"

"Slavery. They won't talk about it – they won't face it."

"Oh."

"You made him see it and he didn't like it."

Rebekah shrugged her shoulders. *What's it to me?*

"But maybe you should stop drawing and painting for a while because it can't be healthy drawing these painful things, Rebekah. It can't be good for you. And you know your other school work is far more important."

Rebekah had felt her face tighten in resentment and knew her mother had noticed it when she sighed and put on the TV. Thankfully the subject was over. Still, Rebekah hadn't been able to stop thinking about it. She found herself wondering whether she really wanted to be an artist after all. *Maybe I should be a lawyer; that way Mama will be happy, and I won't paint these pictures, and nobody will be upset.* But deep down she knew she really had no choice at all, whatever her mama wanted, whatever Mr. Forrest wanted, or anyone else. As long as the pictures came to her, she would bring them to life as sure as she'd keep breathing.

Tonight, her mind reeling under the sight of that crone on the truck, the last thing Rebekah felt like doing was facing, let alone talking to Mr. Forrest. She hoped she could creep up the stairs to her bedroom but when she unlocked the front door, as quietly as she could, the click of the key was enough to alert her mother.

"Rebekah. You're home."

Course I'm home, she thought, *what do you think?*

"Thomas has something for you, Rebekah."

There was no chance of escaping up the stairway, she realised, so she reluctantly entered the living room. The portrait of her parents was still above the mantel piece. She wondered for how long. And there was Mr. Forrest. He got to his feet, put his hand through his yellow hair and then held it out to Rebekah. Not knowing how to respond, she found herself shaking his hand. "I have an apology to make to you, Bek."

"Rebekah." *What right had he to shorten my name the way my daddy did?*

"Rebekah. I'm sorry." Then he picked up a parcel from the coffee table and handed it to her. "I've been on business, in Boston. I went to an art shop on Massachusetts Avenue. I felt that was the least I could do … Well, open it. It's not a Christmas present, well, it's … Here you are."

She didn't want to open it, but somehow his anxious expression, while making her irritated, made her feel almost sympathetic. She took the oblong parcel and opened it to find a box containing the colours he had hurled onto the floor plus some extras. They were the same make, exactly the same colours. It couldn't have been easy for him to find them and she knew her mother must have helped.

"I'm sorry I broke them, Rebekah, really sorry."

She nodded. "Thank you."

"They're the right colours?"

She nodded again.

"Well," he said, looking so amiable, so harmless, "how are you drawing me now? Who else am I whipping? You know, Be – Rebekah, I have never laid a hand to anyone in my life."

"It wasn't meant to be you."

"But it looked like me. Why?"

"I dunno." She shrugged her shoulders. "The picture just came out that way. That's all. Mama, can I go to my bed now? I'm tired."

Chapter
15

The last day of term, most of the teachers ran out of steam and out of things for the students to do. "Today, you may draw or paint anything you like," Mr. Fenwick announced during their art lesson. "That will probably please one young lady in this class who always does what she wants anyway."

All eyes looked to Rebekah who dropped her eyes to the floor. *How come he's always so much nastier to me than anyone else?*

"You may paint or draw a person, a landscape, a still life, anything you like, even an abstract. All I ask of you is to put your name on your paper and today's date. Is that too much for any of you?"

Wondering yet again why teachers from England had to be so sarcastic, she picked up her charcoal. Out of nowhere, the vision of a basket came into her mind, an old-fashioned basket woven with dried palmetto leaves. In it, she saw tiny, yellow green apples; a woody stem of green leaves; and, out of the stem, a droplet of white sap. Obediently, she printed her name and the date: the 18th of December 1972. Using a charcoal, she sketched in the basket; she then chose her pastels to create the fruits. "Don't forget the light," Mr. Stowe's voice echoed in her head. "Remember you must always think about where the light falls and where it's in shade even when you're painting the smallest of objects."

She built up the colour in layers, as he had taught her. First the darks – reds and blues and violets; next the greens and the yellows – especially where she imagined the light falling. And there were the fruit, all but popping out of the basket, and the oval leaves, almost menacingly shiny, with thick pale ridges down their centres. She stared at her picture, appraising it. Deciding it needed something more, she sketched in a toad – with white, greenish skin and bulging, pond water eyes – perched on top of the fruit. Then she added two bundles of knotted rags next to the fruit.

"What are those, Bekah?" Wanda asked, staring over her shoulder at the apples. "Loquats?"

It was true they were the same size, but Rebekah was sure they weren't loquats. Like most of her friends, she loved the sweet, tart taste of those ripe, yellow-orange fruits which come out all over Bermuda in February. Looking at these fruits she had conjured, she started to feel nauseated.

Carrying spare sheets of paper, Mr. Fenwick walked up to her desk and regarded the drawing. "Apples, Rebekah?" he asked. "Rather small for apples. Crab apples, perhaps?"

To her astonishment, he was affable. "I like the toad," he continued. "The eyes are most effective. The colour's unusual." Just as she was wondering why he was being so uncharacteristically friendly towards her, he said, "So you are Gwen Eve's niece?"

Her mouth dropped open, but then she remembered how Aunty Gwen had told her Mr. Fenwick's pictures were being exhibited in her hotel.

"Yes," she said.

"What a delightful lady she is." He handed Rebekah another sheet of paper saying, "Why don't you try something else now, a little more Christmassy, as Wanda is doing? Hmm?"

Wanda in fact was painting a lopsided version of Santa

coming to town on the fire truck, a subject which, after that strenuous evening with the twins, had no appeal for Rebekah. But it did remind her of the woman she thought she had seen on the truck. Shutting her eyes, she tried to summon the old woman's features. However, it was the house in Sandys that came into her mind. Once again, she could see the open door of the kitchen and the pots and pans and the hooks. A woman, that pale faced woman who had stared at Nancy with such hatred, was seated at a rough wooden table chopping vegetables. But this time the woman was smiling, smiling at someone who sat opposite her. That other person's face was hidden because it was bent over a pot. When she did raise her head, Rebekah let out a gasp – it was the child she had seen in Sandys and St. George's, she was sure of it. As fast as she could, Rebekah used charcoal and then pastels to draw her, her eyes taking in the white shift, the tousled curls under the cap, and the smile lighting the green of the child's eyes. *Why, the child likes that woman!* Rebekah realised in astonishment. *How can she like such a horrible woman?*

The scene went dark; then lightened so that the fireplace came back into view. From behind, she saw a young woman in long, full skirts bending towards the fire. Nancy, Rebekah assumed, but, as the young woman turned, Rebekah saw it wasn't Nancy at all. It was the child again but somehow older with a fuller figure. *It's the dress*, Rebekah thought, as she ripped another piece of paper from her book in her haste to get the drawing down. *The bodice is so low cut, her breasts half show. It's like Nancy's. I don't like it and neither does she. I can see she doesn't like it at all. Her eyes are so huge and so frightened.* But, of course she was frightened. There was the man who had beaten Nancy leaning against the door, watching her with those dreadful eyes.

Rebekah raced her pastel against the paper, against time. All the while, she thought she could hear the sound of male laughter in the distance.

The bell rang, pulling her out of the scene and causing an instant cacophony of scraping chairs and shouting children. "Be quiet!" Mr. Fenwick shouted. "Hand your work in."

No way, thought Rebekah, remembering Mr. Stowe's directive to call him. She had to keep both the figure drawings to show him, and somehow, she thought it important to show him the basket as well – he might know about the fruit.

Gathering up her work and equipment, she raced to the door, taking advantage of the fact that Mr. Fenwick was surrounded by her classmates. Wanda followed close on her heels. "What's your hurry, girl? It's only maths. Boring."

"I'm not going to maths."

"How come?"

"I'm just not. If the teacher asks, say I'm not well."

Mr. Fenwick emerged from the throng behind her. "You seem in a hurry, Rebekah Eve. Have you handed in your work?"

Turning, she nodded weakly at him, her hand tightly clutching her folder. Just in time, Aunty Gwen's words came back to her: "Tell him you like his form and you'll have him eating out of your hand."

"I've seen your pictures in the hotel where my Aunty works," Rebekah said, "I really like your form, you know."

The expression on his face was so beatific she thought it was pathetic.

"What was that about?" Wanda asked as they fled the classroom.

"You don't want to know. I'll see you, Wanda."

Rebekah rushed up the steep stairs to the library. To her relief, no one was there but Mrs. Chatterjee who was busy stamping some books.

"Good morning, Rebekah. How are you?"

"Good morning, Mrs. Chatterjee. I am fine, thank you."

"What can I do for you this morning? Do you want to take

books out for your vacation? I have a new book on the French Impressionists that might interest you."

"Yes please. But Mrs. Chatterjee, may I make a phone call?"

"To one of your parents?"

"No, Mrs. Chatterjee. To–"

"Then I can't allow it, I'm afraid. No personal calls except in an emergency. I see you have some paintings with you. May I see? I always enjoy looking at your work, you know."

Silently, she handed them over, wondering what to do next. Mrs. Chatterjee was the least strict person in the school. The staff in the office were much stricter, especially the head school secretary, Mrs. Goodchild, and asking the headmistress, Mrs. Drinkwater, would be impossible. There was no way she would say yes. *But I have to speak to Mr. Stowe*, she thought. *I have to.*

Mrs. Chatterjee gazed intently at the fruit and the leaves. "We have this in my country, Rebekah, in Trinidad. We call it the manchineel tree. Do you know what else we call it?"

Rebekah shook her head, a burning nausea beginning to rise in her throat.

"Sometimes we call it 'the little apple of death' because it is so poisonous, you see. The manchineel is one of the most dangerous trees in the world. I'm surprised you've heard of it, child. And the white toad, that's poisonous, too. Your picture is certainly accurate. Who is the young lady? She looks terrified."

Rebekah had no answer to that and was too anxious to call Mr. Stowe to even pretend to think of one.

No need, as Mrs. Chatterjee continued, "You have such an active imagination, Rebekah. I think you should be an illustrator, you know."

She gave Rebekah back the paintings. "Wait a minute, I'll get the book on the Impressionists I thought you'd like. I put it aside for you." She got up, went to the stock cupboard and, returning, handed it to Rebekah.

"Here it is."

Rebekah flipped through the pages. "Mr. Stowe will be pleased. He often talks to me about the Impressionists."

Mrs. Chatterjee's eyes widened. "Mr Stowe? You can't mean Mr. Everard Leopold Stowe?"

"Yes. He's my art teacher. He teaches me every Sunday."

"He does? You fortunate child. Why he's very famous!"

"I know. Mrs. Chatterjee?"

"Yes?"

"It's Mr. Stowe I need to telephone. You see, I promised him I would and–"

"That's a different matter, my dear Rebekah." Mrs. Chatterjee's face creased into a broad smile. "If Mr. Everard Leopold Stowe has asked you to telephone him, then you must do so at once."

Mrs. Chatterjee led Rebekah to the telephone that she kept on a small table in the stockroom so as not to interrupt readers in the library. When she dialled the number Rebekah had given her, the whirring sound of the dial seemed to echo in the library. Mrs. Chatterjee handed the receiver to Rebekah. "I'm going out for a while so I'm going to lock the library door. If you go before I come back, be sure to lock it again behind you."

The phone rang and rang and rang but Rebekah held on remembering that it was in the main house so it might take a while for Mr. Stowe to pick it up.

Finally, his voice came on the phone. "Everard Leopold Stowe speaking. What can I do for you?"

"It's me," she said. "It's Rebekah. You told me to tell you if I saw the child."

"And you have?"

"Yes. This morning in art class."

"Have you drawn her?"

"Yes. Twice. I saw her twice. The second time she was older.

She looked scared. The first time she was with ..."

Mr. Stowe interrupted her. "What did you use to draw her?"

"My charcoal and some pastels – burnt sienna and ochres, a touch of green."

"Where are you now? In the office?"

"No. In the library. Mrs. Chatterjee let me use the telephone."

"Good. Have you kept the pictures?"

"They're with me now."

"Stay where you are, Rebekah, until I come to you. Do you think you can do that?"

"Yes."

"Good. I'm leaving now. Just wait for me."

Hearing the click as he put his phone down, Rebekah placed her receiver down and taking her paintings and school bag, went to sit on one of the library chairs. She put her head down on the reading table, too tired and drained to read or even look at a book. The sensation of nausea still clung to her throat and she wondered about the tree Mrs. Chatterjee had mentioned. Had she really drawn poisonous fruit? Her head felt so heavy she didn't want to think about it anymore. All she wanted to do was sleep. She drifted off.

"Are you all right, Bekah?"

A boy's voice jerked her awake. Confused for a moment about the time and where she was, she raised her head and was astonished to see Juan gazing down at her with an expression of concern.

"I must have fallen asleep. How come you're in here?"

He gave a shy smile and, remembering Wanda's tease in the restaurant, Rebekah began to wonder whether there might be some truth in it. Juan's face had changed, she realised with a shock. It was still a gentle face but there was more confidence in it. His nose was longer, his mouth firmer and behind his glasses, his eyes were still soft but more determined. Why, she'd like to try drawing him.

"The library's for all of us, isn't it?"

"Yes but . . ." Her brain kicked into gear. "The library's locked – Mrs. Chatterjee locked it. So how could you get in?"

He shrugged and laughed. "How come you're not in maths?"

She'd forgotten all about maths. "I have an appointment. How about you?"

"Me too."

"Who with?"

He hesitated. "I had to see a teacher."

"I didn't see you."

He smiled with a hint of mischief. "Course not. You were fast asleep. Who are you meeting?"

"Mr. Everard Leopold Stowe," she answered promptly. "He should be here by now."

A broader smile lit up Juan's face. "Mr. Stowe's teaching you art."

"What makes you think that?" Rebekah asked, annoyed. "Are people talking about me?"

"Not in a bad way. To be taught by Everard Leopold Stowe? Girl, you're something else. But I'm not surprised – you were always a genius at art."

"Thank you, Juan. That's nice." Something was nagging at the back of her mind, something was not quite right but she couldn't think of what it was. Just as she was wondering what to say next, the library's door handle turned 180 degrees but the door itself did not open. There was a knock and then Mr. Stowe's voice, "Rebekah, are you there?"

She looked accusingly at Juan. "Mrs. Chatterjee did lock the door."

His eyes turned, seemingly of their own volition, to the maroon door. It wasn't ajar, Rebekah noticed. But Juan was not exactly looking at the door; he was looking at a tiny circular object on the wall to the left of the door. A door bell? It appeared to be one.

"Rebekah?" Mr. Stowe knocked again.

"You can't keep Mr. Stowe waiting. You'd better let him in." As he spoke, Juan turned his back to the door of the Lady of the Library.

Quickly, Rebekah walked across the library to lift the catch and open it. "Good afternoon, Mr. Stowe."

There he was, so familiar somehow with his lopsided smile, his plaid jacket and his Bermuda shorts and long, yellow socks. Round his neck was a camera Rebekah had never seen. It was a big and serious looking piece of equipment with a lens attached to it.

"Good afternoon, Rebekah. I am sorry I have been so long coming." Catching sight of Juan, he nodded. "How are you, young man?"

"I'm fine, Mr. Stowe. Just fine."

"And your mother is well?"

"She's fine too."

"That's good. That's good. Shouldn't you be in class, Juan?"

"Yes sir. I'm on my way. Bye, Rebekah."

"You know Juan, Mr. Stowe?" she asked as Juan left the library.

"I've known him since he was born. His mother is my wife's niece. Juan's in your class?"

"Yes. He has been ever since we were in Primary."

"I see."

Looking at the gleam in his eyes, Rebekah had the uncomfortable feeling Mr. Stowe was thinking they were boyfriend and girlfriend. *He couldn't be more wrong about that,* she thought. Her mind jumped and she understood what had been tugging at her. In that whole conversation Juan had not stammered. Not once.

Mr. Stowe turned away from the door to Rebekah. "Where are your drawings? Let me see. Let me see."

Rebekah led the way to the table where she had left her stuff. They both sat down. First, she took out the painting of the child sitting opposite the pale woman and handed it to him.

"See, it's the same woman I drew the other day – the woman with the horrible eyes but here she doesn't seem so horrible. And the child, well, she looks as if she . . ."

"Trusts her," said Mr. Stowe. "Well, well, well. This is very interesting Rebekah, very interesting. And the second time you drew her today?"

Rebekah pushed the painting of her in the tawdry dress towards him. "She's scared and she's more grown up. And there's the man who looks like ... the man who beat Nancy."

"The girl's very different from the first time you saw her?"

"Oh yes. The first time I saw her she was so young, much younger than I was. A tiny child."

"You told me once you don't remember her. How do you know that if you couldn't remember her?"

"It's difficult to explain."

"Just try. Take your time."

"I never forget her exactly. It's just I can't remember how to draw her – I can't, I can't see her properly. But this time she was, she was . . ."

"Yes?"

"Well, at least my age. Thirteen. Maybe older. Although the dress makes her older."

"I agree. But she certainly isn't a very young child." Mr. Stowe noticed the other painting of the basket she had laid on the table, "What is this, Rebekah? When did you draw this?"

"It was in art class this morning. We could do anything we liked. I don't know why – I drew this . . ."

"Yes?"

"Well, it frightens me. It makes me feel ill. And Mrs. Chatterjee says the fruits are poisonous. She recognises them. I've never seen them before, but I think she's right. I think they are poisonous."

"You are right, Rebekah, they most certainly are poisonous. Why did you put in the rags? What made you think of those?"

"I dunno. I just did."

He picked up the painting of the girl again. "You heard her call out Beck once?"

"Yes. She definitely knew my name."

"It all fits," he said.

"What do you mean?"

He was silent for some time, his eyes seemingly a million miles away. Rebekah felt so tired she was tempted to rest her head on the table again.

"She's a beautiful young lady," he said finally.

Rebekah looked again at the painting of her in the full-skirted dress, at the green eyes. "She was a beautiful child. But now her eyes look different."

"They are very frightened eyes."

"Yes," she said. "I told you she's scared. It's that man. But do you think she's frightened of the basket? Because it frightens me. And yet she's not in the painting of the basket. I saw her after I saw the fruit."

"Look!" Mr. Stowe's voice became urgent. He pointed to the painting of the girl with the pale woman and the one next to it of her with the man watching. "Look, she's beginning to fade."

It was true. Her curls, the colour of her face were draining from both the papers. Mr. Stowe quickly lifted his camera and adjusted the lens. "You don't mind, Rebekah?"

"No, I don't mind."

He stood up and directed the camera over the paintings which he'd laid flat on the table. As he pressed the shutter release, the camera flashed. At that very moment both the paintings of the girl burst into flames on the table. In a matter of seconds all that remained was a pile of ash.

They both stared in astonished silence.

"Lord have mercy!" gasped Mr. Stowe. "I've never seen a camera do that before."

"Mrs. Chatterjee will be vexed if the table has burn marks," Rebekah said in a shaky whisper.

Mr. Stowe gently pushed the ash with his finger. The table was unscathed. "I don't think you need worry yourself with that. I hope my camera is all right. Maybe I got the photo before . . ." He twisted the knob to wind the film forward until it was finished. But when he opened the back of the camera, though the metal reel was intact, the film had shrivelled. There was no hope the photograph had survived. They both looked down at the pile of ash.

"I've lost her again," said Rebekah sighing. "She *always* disappears, I don't know why. Do you know why, Mr. Stowe?"

He shook his head, picked up his camera from the desk, examined it, and shook his head again.

"Extraordinary," he said. "Quite extraordinary. But the fruits aren't disappearing, Rebekah."

He was right – they were becoming brighter by the minute, so bright she thought they could burn the paper as well. She could almost feel their heat. And the white toad positively glistened. "I wonder whether I'll see her again. Perhaps I won't."

"Oh, I think you will, Rebekah. I'm certain you will because clearly you are important to her. Although it seems some remarkable force is trying to prevent you from recording her. That in itself is very interesting. You dated the pictures?"

"Yes. Mr. Fenwick asked us to."

"The 18th of December?"

"Well, that's the date today, isn't it?"

"To tell you the exact truth, Rebekah, I'm never sure of the date. Let's look at Mrs. Chatterjee's calendar. He got up and went to her desk to look at the calendar on the wall. Sure enough the 18th was circled in red, a smiley face next to it and "LAST DAY OF TERM printed in capitals. "Mrs. Chatterjee obviously needs her vacation," he remarked. "I remember the feeling. Now Rebekah, I need to make a telephone call."

"The phone is in the stockroom," she told him.

"So it is. I want you to leave your paintings with me. Take your school bag and wait for me in the office. I won't be long."

"Shouldn't I be in class?"

"As Mrs. Chatterjee's calendar reminds us, it's the last day of term so I don't think you will be missing anything important. Just tell the secretary I've told you to wait for me."

Reluctantly, she did as he wished. Because she was absolutely certain he was not going to use the telephone at all. He was going to visit the Lady of the Library. *Why can't I go with him, I want to know.* The question irked her. But she was glad he was keeping the painting of the basket – she didn't want it anywhere near her with the fruit getting brighter and brighter and creepier and creepier.

As she made her way down the library steps to the office, she saw Juan rushing his way up them, his head down. *How come he's going back to the library? Anyway, there's no way he'll get in. I heard Mr. Stowe lock the door behind me.*

But a locked door hadn't stopped him this morning. Thinking back to when she had been waiting in the library for Mr. Stowe, she realised the only way Juan could have got in was if he had already been there before Mrs. Chatterjee had left. If that were true, there was only one place he could have been. She knew for a fact he hadn't been in the library itself. All the tables had been empty. And given all the bookshelves were flat against the walls, there was nowhere he could hide. So that meant he'd been visiting the Lady of the Library. *Is that where he's going now? How come he gets to see her and I don't? I wonder if she only likes men,* she thought. *First there was my daddy. And now Juan. How come she doesn't like girls? She didn't like Mama, that's for sure. But if she doesn't like me, why did she fix me up with lessons?*

Rebekah finally reached the school office and was relieved to see that Mrs. Goodchild, the scary secretary, was out for lunch and not there to interrogate her as to why she wasn't in class. She sank into a chair and waited for Mr. Stowe, her head still buzzing with questions.

Chapter 16

After driving excruciatingly slowly and waving to everybody they saw on their way to Fractious Street, Mr. Stowe finally turned his ramshackle station wagon between the pillars into the driveway. There was Mrs. Stowe waiting for them. It was the first time Rebekah had met her because on Sundays his wife was involved with church all day. But she instantly recognised her as the slim lady with a hat in Mr. Stowe's portrait of her hanging above his mantel piece. Today, she was not wearing a hat. Rebekah noted her mahogany complexion and black hair pinned into a smooth French twist and her eyes that were a dark hazel, soft and warm, yet inquisitive though not in an irritating way.

"So, you are Miss Rebekah Eve, child. I've heard a lot about you. Come in, come in, you must be hungry and thirsty. And so must you, Everard, with all this commotion. You're not going to the studio before you've eaten, you hear me, Everard?"

"I hear you, Ianthe."

After lunch Mr. Stowe suggested that since it was still light and sunny, they should sit in the garden and sketch or paint as they wished. "There's little point you going back to school on the last day. I'll see you get home safely. Just wait until I get the key for my studio so I can get paper and paint."

"May I do the dishes?" Rebekah asked Mrs. Stowe, who shook her head but with an approving expression that plainly said, "Well, I can see you have been raised right."

As she followed Mr. Stowe into the garden, Rebekah reflected how she always seemed to see something new each time. Today, it was two citrus trees, one orange, the other lemon, their fruit almost ripe in time for Christmas. And then there was another previously overlooked narrow pathway with a rustic cedar trellised archway. She couldn't miss it today because of the red, red roses that covered the lattice work.

"You like that, Rebekah?" Mr. Stowe asked, noticing her rapt expression. "Agrippina climbing roses – they do so well in Bermuda. Mrs. Stowe loves them. Would you like to draw them? We can have a good view from this bench."

In companionable silence they took out their pads. While Mr. Stowe seemed to focus on the roses, Rebekah was fascinated by the cedar tracery half hidden by the crimson of the blossom.

"Your sketch doesn't have to be exact, remember, Rebekah. Try to draw what the flowers say to you. And try to relax."

She only half heard him. In her mind's eye the interweaving cedar branches of the trellis formed a huge, looming pattern so that she could no longer see the archway or the roses. Just the pattern. Then she saw the pattern transferred to the naked back of a young woman wearing only a ragged long skirt and a turban. And though Rebekah could not bear to look, she knew she had to so that she could draw this figure and the cruel tracery of those livid welts. Her charcoal flew across the paper, shading in the lights and darks to create the merciless embossment branded on the woman's back. Then she added touches of red pastel to make the welts more livid. After she'd finished, she closed her eyes, willing the woman to turn around so that she could see who she was, but the vision in her mind faded until another took its place. Tearing her picture from her sketchpad, Rebekah took up her charcoal again, now drawing a bent old woman with a ragged top and long tattered skirt trudging along a narrow, beaten path that twisted through a thin, sunlit woodland of cedar and palmetto. The woman held in her brown hands the palmetto woven basket Rebekah had drawn in her art class. But on this occasion, it contained just the two filthy rags – the fruit and the toad had disappeared. As Rebekah watched, the path curled left, the house in Sandys abruptly coming into sight. The old woman approached the door and Rebekah could see her face. *It's the old woman I saw laughing on the fire truck the night of the Santa parade*, she realised, *I'm sure it is.*

Rebekah drew the old woman knocking at the door and then the door opening. There at the entrance was the white woman, with the young girl in that horrible dress, next to her. She pushed the girl forward and the old woman bent towards the girl pulling her outdoors. There was something about the way the old woman and the girl looked at each other that made Rebekah realise they were related. *It's her grandmother*, she thought, *it has to be her grandmother.* The old woman was saying something, and her granddaughter was nodding. Then the girl ran to the side of the pathway, sat down on the slope and looked fixedly at the bend ahead, as if she was keeping watch for anyone coming to the house. Rebekah sketched her in the picture as a distant figure. She focussed on the white woman who gazed steadily at the old woman, a curious expression on her face – part fear, part dislike, part reluctant respect – then she stared down at the rags in the basket as if mesmerised. The old woman whispered to her, pointing to first one rag, then the other. Then she pointed one finger to her granddaughter watching so patiently by the pathway. The white woman's eyes followed her finger before turning back to the old woman and it seemed to Rebekah, as she watched their eyes engage, they had reached an agreement. The old woman handed over the basket, turned and headed back along the pathway paying the child no mind whatsoever. The white woman watched her for a few seconds, then closed the door leaving Rebekah on her seat, the trellised arch with the tumbling red roses in front of her and the pile of sketches on her lap.

"May I see, Rebekah?" Mr. Stowe asked her. That was another aspect to Mr. Stowe, Rebekah really appreciated. He always asked; he never demanded. Handing the sketches to him, she felt anxious. "Mr. Forrest said I needed help," she said. "If he saw these, he might take me to have my head seen to at St. Brendan's!"

Mr. Stowe didn't respond. His eyes rested on the picture of the young woman's back. After a time, he asked, "Did you see her being whipped? And yet … there's no blood."

"I saw the pattern on the trellis and then I saw it on her back."

"I see. And the roses reminded you of blood, perhaps?"

"I didn't think about the roses – it was just the pattern on her back. There wasn't any blood. But there would have been, wouldn't there? Lots of blood."

"Have you ever seen her before?"

"No."

"And this elderly lady with the basket? Have you seen her before?"

"I think so." And she explained about the parade and the woman she'd seen laughing on the fire truck.

"Did you see anything else this afternoon, Rebekah? Anything at all? That you haven't put into this drawing?"

"I think the old lady's the girl's grandmother, you know."

"You do? Why is that?"

"I dunno. I just think she is. It was the way they looked at each other."

"I see." His eyes were thoughtful yet accepting of what she was saying. "What else did you see?"

"Nothing really. The old lady talked to the white woman for a while . . ."

"You are sure, Rebekah? You are absolutely sure the white woman and the old black woman talked to each other?"

"Oh yes." She saw him looking intently at her, his face uncharacteristically urgent. "That's important, isn't it?"

"Yes, it is Rebekah. You are sure?"

"I'm absolutely sure."

"And then the old woman gave the white woman the basket?"

"Yes."

"She didn't give it to the girl?"

"No. She gave it to the white woman and the white woman took it and shut the door behind her."

"Did the old woman enter the house?"

"No. She walked back the way she came."

"Extraordinary. Quite extraordinary."

"Why? Do you understand what is happening with the old lady and the basket, Mr. Stowe?"

It seemed to Rebekah that his face was falling. If she were to draw him now, the humour would be gone from his eyes. "I thought I knew, Rebekah. But your pictures have changed things somewhat."

"How?"

"I can't tell you now."

"Why not?"

"It's important I don't influence you, Rebekah. It's your vision that counts, not my opinion of what might be happening. I don't want to spoil the integrity of what you see. Do you understand me?"

She wasn't sure but she nodded because he so obviously wanted her to grasp what he was trying to tell her. "It's about the past, isn't it? Because it's history? I'd rather see the future if I have to see anything. It would be more useful."

"No, Rebekah. What you are doing is so important."

"Why?"

"Because you may be revealing what was unknown to us, although some force seems to be at work to try to prevent you."

"What do you mean?"

"Your picture exploded when I tried to photograph it, remember? There has to be a reason for that. Some force at work that doesn't want the world to see your revelation."

"But I don't understand what I'm seeing."

"Perhaps you don't. Not now. But we will help you."

"We? Who's 'we'?"

"Dr. Delacroix and I."

"The Lady of the Library? She doesn't want to help me! At least, she doesn't want to see me. She doesn't care about girls."

"Rebekah, why do you think that?"

"She sees Juan, I'm sure she does. But she won't see me."

"She has her reasons, Rebekah. She will be there for you when the time comes, I promise you. And because she is a brilliant historian, she will help us understand your visions when it is necessary for her to do so."

Rebekah wanted to ask him what he meant by "when the time comes", but he was packing up and gesturing that she should do so as well; it didn't seem right to press him. Besides, the sun was sinking fast and as she watched the Spanish bayonet and palmetto shrink into spiky silhouette, she felt the chill of the damp winter evening air. Once inside the main house, she was surprised to see her daddy sitting in the kitchen talking to Mrs. Stowe. He got up as soon as he saw her and gave her a quick hug.

"Bek."

"What are you doing here, Daddy? I thought you'd be working."

"I was home early today, fortunately. That's why I could take Mr. Stowe's call."

Rebekah gave Mr. Stowe a querying look.

"I called your father when I went to get the key, Rebekah. It has been a difficult day for you, and I think you need him."

"Does Mama know you've come to get me?" Rebekah asked as her daddy drove her towards Pembroke.

"Not yet."

"Well, I don't think . . ." Her voice broke off because she couldn't figure out how to tell him.

"Don't think what, Bekah?"

"I don't think we should surprise her."

"Bek," his voice even softer than usual, "I know all about Thomas Forrest."

"You do?"

"Yup."

Did Mama tell him, she wondered. *Doesn't he mind?*

She sighed. "I wish you'd come back to live with us, Daddy. Then that man would have to leave us alone."

"It's not possible, Bek. I'm sorry but it's not going to happen."

She was so tired she couldn't cry. Instead, a dull ache seemed to spread from the pit of her stomach through to her back.

"We can't stick together because we just don't have anything in common anymore, except you."

She thought of that marriage of true minds stuff the Lady of the Library had written in her letter and felt annoyed. *Why isn't a child enough to keep parents together?*

"Do you have a girlfriend, Daddy?"

"Nope. I don't have time for a girlfriend so don't you worry about that. Just remember you're my number one, you hear me?"

Huh, she thought. *If that's true, why aren't I important enough for you to come home? And would I be your number one if you knew just how crazy I'm getting?*

Chapter
17

Rebekah woke to a blue, bright Christmas morning. Her daddy had promised to come at midday to take her to Grandma Kezia and Papa Malachi's for Christmas dinner. But the memory of Christmas Eve without him was so dreary she didn't know how she would survive the morning. Mr. Forrest had come later in the evening, and he and her mama had talked the whole time, her mama paying her no mind at all. Rebekah couldn't help remembering the Christmas carols her daddy used to play on his eight-track tape recorder for them to listen to while they all prepared the cassava pie and the stuffing for the turkey. This Christmas Eve, though, she sat on the sofa grimly staring at the tree and then at the television. She hated the tree – usually she and her daddy went to a supermarket to choose one of the real pines specially imported every year from Canada; this year Mama had her own way, insisting on an artificial silver one. She had bought baubles for it, all the same shade of electric blue, and Rebekah hated those as well. They might as well have taken an already decorated tree out of a hardware store. All the ornaments she had made as a child were nowhere to be seen and neither was the nativity set Papa Malachi's father had carved many years ago. It was as if her mama had taken a knife and cut away everything to do with the Eve family. It was as if nothing mattered but *that* man. No special Christmas cooking. Not even any presents under the tree. It seemed that all her mama wanted to do, apart from go to church, was to spend the day with Mr. Forrest.

So, when she reached the kitchen and her mama wished her a cheerful happy Christmas, Rebekah felt her face stiffen into a glare – *What could possibly be happy about this Christmas?*

"Don't have an attitude, girl. It's Christmas. Come and have breakfast and then we'll get ready for church."

"What about Grandma Violet? Isn't she coming to breakfast? Are we going to pick her up?"

There was a little pause and, behind her mother's smile, Rebekah thought she saw embarrassment.

"Grandma Violet's not coming this year."

"Not coming? Why not? Where's she spending Christmas to?"

"She didn't want to come this year. We must respect her wishes, you know. She never really enjoys Christmas with us anyway."

It was true that Grandma Violet never looked happy. Most of the time Rebekah drew her, she was staring sadly through a window at a world where Rebekah sensed she could never reach her. And often that would irritate Rebekah because it was no fun to be with someone who was sad all the time. But still, alone for Christmas? It wasn't right. If her daddy were here, he just wouldn't allow it. He was always the one to go get Grandma Violet and coax her along. And usually by the time lunch was over he'd got a smile from her.

"Now hurry up, Rebekah. Time's getting late for church."

"I'm not going."

"Are you foolish? Of course, you're going."

"I'm not going without Grandma Violet."

Her mama's face tightened, and Rebekah felt a surge of the

old apprehension. Before that man appeared on the scene, she had almost always given in to her mama because going against her was so stressful. This time the whole of her body stiffened in defiance.

"You'll get dressed at once, Rebekah, do you hear me?"

She let her eyelids half close and stared at her mother from under her lashes.

"Don't you be insolent with me, young lady!"

Rebekah knew her expression was upsetting her mama. It felt good. *At least Mama's really looking at me for once,* she thought, *instead of thinking about Mr. Forrest.* She lowered her eyelids a little further and put her hand on her hip.

And *wham.* She felt the smart slap of her mother's hand across her face.

Turning on her heel, Rebekah went back up the stairs to her room. The slap smarted in more ways than one. Her mama hadn't hit her since – she couldn't remember when. But she'd felt a bitter pleasure in provoking a real reaction out of her. The pleasure didn't last long, leaving just the painful heat of the slap and a lingering heartache. She stared sadly at the small pile of presents she had wrapped the previous night. Perfume for her mama and for Grandma Violet, and the pictures she had drawn for everyone else. Well, she'd get showered and dressed and wait on the bed for her daddy to get her. There was no way she'd go to church without Grandma Violet. "If Mama wants me to go to church and pretend to be happy, she'll have to lift me up and carry me." Saying the words out loud strengthened her resolve and made her feel better.

Half an hour later, her mother, dressed in a rich emerald suit and a dark red hat with a broad brim, walked in to find Rebekah sitting on her bed, sketchbook in hand. She was showered but with her bath robe on. Her bright red Christmas dress hung over the chair.

"Rebekah!"

Rebekah tried to concentrate on her drawing – yet another one of Grandma Violet staring out of the window.

Her mother sat on the bed next to her, her anger seemingly spent. "I'm sorry I slapped you, Rebekah, but ..." Then she set eyes on the drawing and was cross again. "You're irritating, Rebekah, you know that? Grandma Violet doesn't want to spend Christmas with us, I promise you."

"Did you ask her?"

"No. I didn't need to. She told me she didn't want to weeks ago."

"So how come you didn't tell me?"

"It's not your business, Rebekah."

Christmas is my business, Rebekah thought. *It's everyone's business. And Grandma Violet shouldn't be on her own.*

"So hurry up. Put on your nice dress and let's get started."

"No."

"Please, Rebekah." To Rebekah's surprise, her mama's voice took on a wheedling tone. "Don't let's ruin Christmas."

You ruined Christmas. Not me.

"No."

And that was that. Total victory. But after her mother had driven away, the victory did not taste so sweet. The walls of her room drew in on her, making her feel it was a little waiting room where she had to sit and sit and sit until somebody ushered her into the real room where life would begin again.

Eventually, she heard the sound of Papa Malachi's truck. After slipping on her Christmas outfit, she went down the stairs to open the door. There was her daddy looking so unusually smart in shirt, jacket, and tie, she could smile for the first time that morning. Grandma Kezia must have nagged him. They hugged.

"Happy Christmas."

"Happy Christmas, Daddy."

"You look beautiful, Bek."

"Thank you, Daddy."

"Where's your mama?" he asked, walking into the living room. His eyes took in the tinsel tree.

"At church."

"How come you're not at church with her?"

She shrugged her shoulders. "I didn't want to go."

"On Christmas morning? That's not like you, Bek."

She shrugged again.

"I guess we'll wait for your mama and Grandma Violet. I want to wish them a Happy Christmas before we leave."

"Grandma Violet's not coming to Mama's for Christmas this year."

Daddy's voice sharpened. "What do you mean, she's not coming?"

"Mama says she doesn't want to spend Christmas with us. She says we must respect her wishes. That's what she says."

"I see." And Rebekah looking at the unusually stern expression on his face saw that he saw everything.

"Well now, Bekah, go and get your suitcase while I wait for your mama."

"Suitcase? Am I staying the night?"

"Course, what did you think?"

She hadn't known what to think. Nobody told her anything. She sped up the stairs, her whole mood miraculously lightened. Maybe the day wouldn't be so bad after all.

As she packed all her presents, save the one for her mama, her sketch books, pastels portable box and clothes into a case, she heard her mother unlocking the front door and her father's, "Good morning, Patricia."

"Good morning, Jonah. Rebekah's upstairs."

"And Violet?"

"Now don't you start, Jonah. I won't have it, you hear me?

Mother doesn't want Christmas here this year and that's the end of the matter."

"What kind of person are you, Patricia, to let that poor old woman be on her own Christmas Day? It's disgusting."

"It's none of your business, Jonah. It never was as a matter of fact. And it certainly isn't now."

Rebekah waited. It was bad enough hearing them argue without having to watch. But their voices fell silent and she thought it safe to come down with her case.

"So, you've decided to get dressed at last?" her mama said tartly. "You missed a good service, Rebekah. The minister asked after you. And so did Wanda and her parents. You really were missed, you—" Noticing the present Rebekah held in her hand, she stopped. "Is that for Grandma Violet?"

"No, Mama, it's for you. I'll put it under the tree." When she bent to put it there, the small package made the tree seem so pathetic, Rebekah couldn't wait to get out of the house.

"Bye, Mama."

"Rebekah, I have something for you, you know. I was going to give it to you but . . ."

"It doesn't matter, Mama."

Her mother's face had such a forlorn expression, Rebekah felt racked with guilt. *It isn't my fault*, she told herself. *I would have stayed with her if Mr. Forrest wasn't going to be here. She'll have a good time when he gets here.*

Her daddy swung the truck out from the street and drove it in the direction of back of town, instead of taking his normal route along the North Shore Road.

"Where we going, Daddy?"

"Grandma Violet's, of course. She can't be alone for Christmas Day. She has to come with us to St. George's."

"Will Grandma Kezia mind?"

"She'll understand. There's always room for one more on Christmas Day."

As they negotiated the crisscross of roads behind Hamilton's main grid of streets, Rebekah thought of Grandma Violet with some trepidation. She was glad her daddy didn't want to leave her grandmother alone on Christmas Day, but she had to admit to herself she never really enjoyed going to her grandmother's apartment because it was often not too clean and had far too many ants and cockroaches. Frequently, it would smell so strongly of fried fish, Rebekah would feel sick. Mama didn't like it either, she knew, because it reminded her of being poor when she was a girl. But Rebekah didn't blame Grandma Violet for it because of what she had said once to Mama: "You know, Patricia, when you've cleaned as many houses as I have for other folks, you don't much feel like cleaning your own." But besides the smells and the dirt, visiting didn't make Rebekah feel comfortable because Grandma Violet so rarely said anything to her. She just looked sad.

Her daddy parked the truck easily – there were hardly any cars parked on Grandma's street.

"I feel bad, Bek. I don't have a gift for her. And your mother didn't give me one for her."

"I've got something for her – some perfume. It's in my suitcase."

Quickly she opened her case, delved into it and found the package.

"You're a good girl, Bek."

Grandma Violet's home consisted of three rooms at the top of a two-storey house which was divided into two different apartments. As they walked towards the building, Rebekah thought how even more run down the house looked than normal. The pink paint was peeling and smudged while the roof was so blackened with mould, it looked dangerous. Like everyone's in Bermuda, Grandma Violet's supply of running water largely depended on how much rain she could catch from her roof into her outdoor tank. *I'm not drinking Grandma Violet's water,* Rebekah thought, *even though she does keep guppies in the tank to eat the mosquitos.* The outdoor steps leading up to her apartment were littered with old leaves, scraps of old newspapers and plastic bags.

Two steps up, they both stopped in surprise as they heard the Jackson Five yelping out 'Santa Claus is Coming to Town'.

"That can't be Grandma Violet," Rebekah said. "She doesn't like music, does she?"

"Well, I never knew she liked the Jackson Five. Maybe it's coming from the downstairs apartment."

But when they reached the door, they realised the music was certainly coming from Grandma Violet's. Seconds after they rang the bell, an elderly gentleman came to the door, a glass filled with a yellow liquid in his hand. He was wearing a crisp white shirt and a black tie. His hair, parted and half straightened into waves, was still dark, although his neat moustache, if Rebekah were to draw it, would have some grey. *His eyes,* she thought, *might be tricky to draw since they don't fit with the maturity of his face.* They were the mischievous eyes of an eight-year-old.

"Good morning, and the Season's Greetings to you both. What can I do for you?"

"Grandma Violet," Rebekah stammered – she was so taken aback. "Is she here? We've come to see her. Is she–"

She stopped short as she saw her grandmother step forward, smiling. Grandma Violet who never smiled! She was wearing a long, silky, green evening dress, a sparkly necklace and lots of gold and silver bangles on her arms. Her hair, which Rebekah had only seen before covered with a kerchief, was hanging loose in soft waves.

"Grandma Violet! You look beautiful."

"Why thank you, honey. Are you two coming in, or you just going to stand there?"

They all walked into the kitchen and Rebekah could smell the turkey and the stuffing roasting away in the oven.

"I want you to meet my friend, Mr. Sidney Gomes. Sidney this is my granddaughter, Rebekah and her daddy Jonah Eve."

The two men shook hands. "Would you like a drink, Jonah?" Mr. Gomes asked him.

"Thank you kindly. But I'm driving."

"You both must have eggnog," Grandma Violet said. "Sydney, Jonah, go fix them." She beckoned Rebekah into the tiny living room that was as poorly furnished as Rebekah remembered – a shabby, stained sofa, a couple of metal chairs and a table – but infinitely more cheerful. Paper chains and tinsel lanterns festooned the ceiling and a small artificial Christmas tree flashed different coloured lights. Grandma Violet went to the record player perched on a small coffee table and turned down the music.

"I didn't know you had a record player, Grandma."

"Sydney brought it with him. Sydney's my honey, you know."

"I didn't know you have a special friend, Grandma."

"Why should you? I never told you, not your mama neither. Anyhow Sydney says you can't have Christmas without music. I sure do like the Jackson Five's Christmas Album. So is this a present for me, Rebekah?" her eyes falling on the parcel in Rebekah's hand.

"Yes, Grandma. I hope you like it."

Grandma swiftly unwrapped it. "Why thank you. That's real nice, my favourite perfume. But how come no picture this year?"

"I'm sorry, I . . ."

"That's all right, girl. To tell you the truth, I really like your pictures of everyone in the family but not the ones you do of me."

"Why not, Grandma Violet?"

"I always look so sad. It's depressing."

Rebekah wanted to say, "But you do look sad. That's the way you look." but said instead, "I'm sorry they come out that way."

"It's not your fault. You usually draw me in a situation when I'm with your mama and there's something about your mama that makes me feel sad. She always did, you know. Because all she wanted was to get ahead – I'd see her coming down the Meridian's school steps and there she'd be, pushing everyone out of the way."

Talking about her mama made Rebekah feel acutely uncomfortable – she wished people wouldn't do it. So, she said nothing.

"Your mama's still going with that Thomas Forrest?" Grandma Violet didn't stop for an answer. "His father was a banker, you know, and he lost folk's money."

"Did he lose yours, Grandma?"

Grandma Violet burst out laughing. "I never had no money to lose, Bekah. His son's a lawyer, right?"

Rebekah nodded.

"Well, I wish her more luck than my mama had."

"What do you mean, Grandma?"

"Your mama never told you?"

Rebekah shook her head.

"I should have figured that. My daddy was a white man, you know. He was a Scottish soldier up at the Garrison in Prospect. He left my mama when I was a few months old – went back to the white wife and children he had in England. The only thing he left me was my hair – he had really dark, wavy hair."

"Meaning you're half white, Grandma?"

"Most folks got some white if you go back far enough."

I've never heard Grandma talk like this, Rebekah thought.

Maybe I can ask her stuff I can't ask Mama.

"What was my grandpa like, Grandma Violet?"

"Your mama never told you that neither?"

Rebekah shook her head. "She always told me he was dead."

"He may as well be. She never knew her father cos he left the island before she was born. I never told him I was pregnant. He was a coloured man on the American Base in St. David's."

"That must have been terrible for you, Grandma."

"There are worse things to happen, you know. People said the usual things, wouldn't talk to me for a while but they got over it."

Her eyes looked into the distance, a touch of sadness back. "Trouble was your mama couldn't get over it. Truth to tell, she was born angry, as if she knew I wasn't the right mama for her. Life wasn't easy cos we were poor. But we got by. After the War, the hotels opened again. There was always work cleaning. And your mama done well. She got a scholarship to the Meridian and then she went away to college."

"Mama wants me to go to college," Rebekah said with a sigh.

"Course she does. A clever girl like you. But remember, girl, life's too short not to have fun while you can."

Just as Rebekah was thinking about her grandma's surprising piece of advice, the two men walked in with the eggnogs and a glass of red wine for Grandma Violet.

"I'm sorry for taking my time pouring your drinks, ladies," said Sydney. "Jonah and I got talking in the kitchen."

"Not to worry," Grandma smiled accepting her glass of wine. Yet another surprise because Rebekah never knew Grandma drank alcohol; her mama certainly never touched it.

Raising their glasses, they all chorused, "Happy Christmas!"

"Well now, Violet," her daddy said. "I can see we didn't

need to be worried about you on Christmas Day."

"You always was a kind man, Jonah Eve. But I'm fine, just fine."

"I'll make sure of that," Sydney put in, his eyes smiling, his whisky in hand. "We're gonna have ourselves a merry little Christmas."

"I believe you." Her daddy drank the eggnog in a single swallow. "Bekah, we must be going or we'll be late for dinner. Have a good one, Violet. Nice to meet you, Sydney."

After they got back into the truck, he said, "Your grandma is something else."

"I've never seen her like that, Daddy. I mean, she was acting happy."

They could hear the music blaring again. Both of them started to laugh. Michael Jackson was screaming out, "I saw Mommy kissing Santa Claus!"

Chapter 18

Grandma Kezia and Papa Malachi used their dining room so rarely, Rebekah often wondered why they bothered to have one. Her mama sniped that it was the only room in the house that could fit their old-fashioned furniture. But, today, the room came into its own. The gleaming table and sideboard filled the room with cedar fragrance. Grandma had placed a large bowl, filled with the dusky oranges she had picked, on the sideboard. Greenery surrounded it and brass candlesticks were placed on either side. The table was beautifully laid with Grandma's best china, cutlery, glasses, red linen napkins, and arrangements of scented jonquils and Brazilian red pepper berries. She and Papa Malachi sat at either end of the long cedar table and Rebekah just knew he would tell them again how his father had made it and the chairs. Sure enough, "Look at the feet," he said. "See the Queen Anne claws – my father carved them, you know. Out of a cedar tree from his garden."

Everyone started to laugh until Grandma Kezia worried they'd never start eating. "Stop your noise, you children. Malachi, carve the turkey before it gets cold."

The food was plentiful – turkey and ham and cassava pie and fresh carrots and broccoli from Daddy's fields and mashed potatoes and stuffing and macaroni cheese and gravy. Not to mention the three different stuffings Aunty Gwen had made.

Rebekah sat next to her father on one side of the table while Aunty Gwen and Uncle Gabriel sat across from them, in front of the sideboard. Above the sideboard was a large horizontal mirror in an old frame. Reflected in it were two portraits, fixed on the wall behind her. They were ones she'd drawn of her grandparents a previous Christmas.

"Where are you going to put this year's portrait, Grandma? I don't think these are that good anymore. Maybe the new one should go in their place?"

This year, Rebekah's presents to everyone, except her mama and Grandma Violet, had been her portraits – one of her aunt and uncle sitting together out on the balcony of their house; another of her daddy, his locks longer now and his face beaming as he carried a sack of potatoes on his back. Mama had seen that one and not liked it at all. Rebekah could tell from the way her mouth had tightened when she looked at it. The one of Grandma Kezia and Papa Malachi was the best. Rebekah had done it under Mr. Stowe's supervision – he was showing her how to create effects with a limited palette of colours – and the result was spectacular. The picture of her grandparents tending to the goats glowed with earth tones – ochres and reds and yellows and browns.

"We'll see," Grandma Kezia said in response to Rebekah's suggestion. "We love all your pictures. Now, what does everyone think of my cassava pie?"

Daddy patted Rebekah on her knee. She knew exactly what he was thinking. His tasted better – more crumbly; Grandma's – thicker and moister – cos she'd used too many eggs though neither Rebekah nor her father would dream of saying so. Her daddy's cassava pie was something she, her mama, and her daddy all enjoyed, something they used to enjoy together. It would never have occurred to her that her daddy wouldn't be with her and her mama on Christmas Eve stewing the chicken and pork, beating the eggs and the butter and the grated cassava for the batter. "Nutmeg," she remembered her daddy saying, "nutmeg is very important. And I like to add grated orange rind." She bent her head so the others wouldn't notice her tears welling.

"It's delicious, Kezia," said Aunty Gwen. "Real good."

Auntie Gwen touched her stomach to stress the point, her hand lingering to cradle her baby bump. "Isn't it funny to think there'll be an extra Eve in the family next Christmas?" she said smiling.

One Eve more and one Eve less, Rebekah thought. Although maybe her mama had never counted as a real Eve. But then again Aunty Gwen wasn't a blood Eve either. It all cancelled out. Maybe.

"Do you think it's a boy or a girl?" Papa Malachi asked Aunty Gwen.

"I don't know. I don't mind as long as it's one or the other."

Rebekah wished passionately that if there had to be a baby at all it would be a boy.

"We can't agree on a name for the baby," Aunty Gwen said. "I like N'Keisha for a girl but Gabriel says . . ."

Rebekah felt like raising her eyes to the heavens – all this stuff about names. She tried to concentrate on her food, which was truly delicious, and tune out the conversation about baby names. She looked across the table, and up at the mirror and her heart halted, then thumped double time in shock. The mirror had turned totally dark even though the dining room lamps were switched on. The pictures of her grandparents were gone. She looked at the others around the table but nobody else seemed to notice. She tried to concentrate on listening to Aunty Gwen instead of staring at the mirror, but the darkness of the mirror drew her in.

Half squinting, Rebekah saw two faint flickerings in the mirror. As they grew brighter, she realized it was candlelight. The candles were on a cedar table much like this one, only covered with different dishes filled with fish and roasted birds. Nobody was seated at the table. A girl came in. Rebekah could not see her face, but she was wearing a long blue dress and carrying two more dishes which she set on the table. And then, the girl turned and stared straight out of the mirror, straight at her. It was *her* girl, older now. She beckoned to Rebekah, then turned and walked out of the room. Rebekah stayed seated but her eyes somehow were able to follow the girl into the kitchen, to the kitchen door where she stood looking out. The white woman – the one Rebekah had seen before – was right there, furtively reaching up to place in the slats of the kitchen door some damp and dirty rags. The scene in the mirror blurred, the woman receding into darkness. Rebekah watched as the girl went down some steps to the basement, to a figure asleep in the corner, huddled under a rag. It was Nancy. She looked ill, dreadfully ill, her face covered with sweat and contorted in pain. Rebekah could see the back view of her girl just standing there, staring down at Nancy for a few seconds until they both faded.

Seconds later, Rebekah could see the child was back in the room with the table again. But this time, two figures were seated at each end of the table, the white woman and white man – the man she'd seen before, with the cruel face and the whip. They were dressed in odd-looking clothes – a long white dress with a low neck and a triangular scarf for the woman; a white shirt with flared frills on its sleeves for the man. They stared at each other in silence.

The woman – her yellow hair drawn tightly back from her face, her complexion yellowish – took meat from her plate, slowly lifting it to her mouth, then putting it down again. Once more she lifted it to her mouth and swallowed it. *She's forcing herself,* Rebekah was convinced, *she's forcing herself to eat even though she knows the food is poisoned because then she won't be found out. If she's ill, no one will think to blame her.* The woman's eyes, vacant of all expression, still rested on the man at the other end of the table.

If I were to paint her eyes, Rebekah thought, *there'd be no light in them, no light at all.* And the man – he was the one she'd drawn on the ship; and outside his cottage beating Nancy; and looking at the young girl in such an evil way. And, yes, he was the one who looked so like Mr. Forrest, so like. But he was now ashen-faced.

Around Rebekah, cutlery clattered against the plates, conversation sputtered but all she could see was those figures in the mirror – still and silent. And the girl, whose face Rebekah longed to keep in her painting, was there, too, leaning against a wall, her haunted eyes watching, watching.

"Bek, Bek! You're missin' girl?"

She could feel her daddy's hand shaking her arm.

"You still with us, child?" Grandma Kezia asked.

Clearly, nobody else could see the tableau in the mirror. Was there something wrong with her brain that made her see these people? *Mr. Stowe thinks what I see is important,* she told herself. *He told me so. He doesn't think I'm crazy.*

Slowly, the faces in the mirror receded, the candle light went out, and once again her pictures were reflected in the glass.

"You all right, Bek?"

"I'm fine."

"Do you want some more turkey, Rebekah?" Papa Malachi was asking. "There's plenty, you know."

But she shook her head. Remembering the food she had seen in the mirror and the white woman forcing meat into her mouth made her feel sick. A second helping was the last thing she needed.

The telephone rang. "Shoot," said Grandma. "Sometimes I wish there was no such thing as a telephone." All the same, she got up and went out to the kitchen to answer it.

"You all right, Bek?" her daddy asked. "You're not eating very much."

"I'm fine. I was just thinking."

Before he could ask her what she was thinking about and before she could think of a lie as there was no way she could tell them about the scenes in the mirror, Grandma Kezia came back in. "Wrong number, thank goodness."

And in a flash Rebekah remembered how annoyed Grandma Kezia had been the last time a telephone call had interrupted dinner, the time her mama had called, just after Papa Malachi had told her the story of Sally Bassett and Grandma had explained about the poisonings.

That old woman standing outside the house with the basket and the rags must be Sally Bassett. She was the one handing the poisons to the white woman. And the girl I've been seeing since that day we had lunch in Somerset, she's Sally's granddaughter. She must be.

And then the implications hit her. "The child didn't do it! She didn't. The white woman did it." Rebekah heard herself scream. But the sound must have been in her head because all the adults were still placidly eating as if they had heard nothing at all. *Thank goodness.* What would they think if she told them she had seen Sally Bassett? And her granddaughter, too? And that the story Grandma Kezia had told her about the granddaughter just wasn't true? *They'll think I'm crazy,* she thought miserably.

Papa Malachi brought in the steaming Christmas pudding and set it down on the table and Grandma Kezia served everyone a helping, as well as her warm vanilla cream sauce. Rebekah tried to calm herself so that she could eat. There sure would be a fuss if she did not eat Grandma Kezia's Christmas pudding.

"Rebekah," Grandma was saying something to her. She

forced herself to listen. "Did you bring your bathing suit? We're swimming tomorrow."

"I forgot, Grandma. But that's all right. I'll watch you both. It's too cold for me to swim."

"You're not made of sugar, child!"

Papa Malachi shook his head as if to say, "What's wrong with you children today?"

"Where are we swimming tomorrow?" her daddy asked. "Tuckers Town?"

They all laughed because they knew he couldn't be serious. All the beaches in Tuckers Town, in Hamilton Parish, were private. Rebekah had often driven past the adjoining two golf courses, but she had never been to any of those beaches. She couldn't think of one of her friends who had been to one of them either. You had to belong to the prestigious Mid-Ocean Golf Club to visit them or stay at the Castle Harbour Hotel. And that meant you had to have a lot of money. She didn't know anyone like that. Who did?

"Well now," said Papa Malachi, "I used to swim in Tuckers Town, you know."

Uncle Gabriel and her daddy smiled because they knew the story well, but Rebekah did not and she was interested, if only to take her mind off what she had seen in the mirror.

"You're serious, Papa Malachi?"

"I stayed there with my parents and my grandparents, child. You didn't know that? My grandfather farmed in Tuckers Town. Other coloured folks did, too. We could swim wherever we liked. And then, in the 1920s, the powers that be – the Forty Thieves on Front Street – they made us leave on account of attracting rich folk from the United States for the new Club and the golf courses. They paid us money for our land but still – I haven't swum in none of them beaches since I was six or seven years of age."

"That's not fair," Rebekah said.

"It's more than unfair," said Uncle Gabriel. "It's downright racist."

"Do we have to talk about this on Christmas Day," Grandma Kezia said. "Rebekah doesn't need to be hearing this."

"But I want to, Grandma."

"Quite right." Uncle Gabriel smiled at her. "You're a young lady now, old enough to know about the uglier side of our past. See, even if you had the money to join the Club or buy the new properties going up in Tuckers Town, you couldn't do either if you were black."

"Exactly," said Papa Malachi. "Exactly."

"Don't even get me started on voting rights," said Gabriel. "Do you realise that until ten years ago you couldn't vote in the elections unless you had property?"

Rebekah began to lose focus. Who cared about voting rights? She said as much.

Her daddy shook his head. "You should care, Bekah." Then he said, smiling, "One day you will, if the Lady of the Library has anything to do with it!"

Papa Malachi leaned forward. "Did you say the Lady of the Library, Jonah?"

"I did. She is taking a personal interest in Bek. She is the one who asked Everard Leopold Stowe to give Bek art lessons. She wrote to me."

"She did, did she? So Dr. Ella Bien-Aimée Delacroix is still taking an interest in our family. That's nice. That's real nice."

"I don't know about that," said Grandma Kezia. "Remember what the Lady of the Library said the last time she wrote? There was trouble in the family, I can tell you."

"She didn't like my mama," Rebekah said remembering how upset she had been when she'd read the letter in Somerset. "Why didn't she?"

Jonah shifted in his seat.

"Daddy?"

But she could see he didn't want to answer. Nor did anyone else. So, it being Christmas and all, it was better to change the subject.

"How did you get to know the Lady of the Library, Grandma? Cos you and Papa didn't go to the Meridian, did you?"

Papa answered instead. "Course not. I left school when I was 13. But Miss Delacroix came to meet my father in our house, not long after she started teaching at the Meridian. He was a cabinet maker – I told you that – and she wanted him to make her a cedar writing box. He was happy to."

"What's a writing box?"

"Well now, when you rested it on a table, opened the lid and laid it flat, you had a nice little sloping writing surface. You could lift the surface up both sides of the box and underneath was space for paper. She did a lot of writing on that box. She was always writing to the newspaper and to children she thought would do well."

Rebekah thought then of the letter – the two letters – the Lady of the Library had written to her father.

While she was imagining her using the box to write them on, she heard Papa explaining how the Lady of the Library had been a history and elocution teacher at the Meridian as long as he could remember. "She was famous."

"Was she French, Papa? Names like Bien-Aimée and Delacroix – they're not Bermudian, that's for sure. Where was she from?"

"No one knew. She just arrived here one day off the boat, a bit like a hurricane. Some people thought she was from Haiti, or from Martinique, one of them French colonies; but she never let on. She had a degree, which was unusual for a coloured woman back then – unusual for a white woman as well. And if she was French, she didn't have an accent. She spoke proper English like the King himself."

He went on to explain that although she eventually received her doctorate from Oxford University, she was never accepted as headmistress, even though she applied, because until Mrs. Drinkwater's appointment, every head at the Meridian had been a man. But most likely, he said, they didn't appoint her because she spoke out publicly against racial segregation in the schools and the hospital, in the hotels, restaurants and cinemas. She spoke out about everything that was unfair, especially the economic disparity between races.

"That disparity still goes on today," said Uncle Gabriel. "As the Black Beret members will tell you."

Rebekah's brow wrinkled. "Who are the Black Berets, Uncle Gabriel?"

"A group of black young men still fighting for equal rights in Bermuda. Our very own Black Panthers."

To her, he sounded impressed with them. "I don't always agree with their methods, mind," he was careful to say, "but they have a point, a strong point."

But Papa was still focussing on the Lady of the Library. "The white people on the boards of the banks didn't like what she said. Some folks say that's why she never had a mortgage. They say that when she retired, she refused point blank to leave the school. Not even the headmaster could make her. That's when people started to call her the Lady of the Library instead of Doctor Delacroix because they thought she stayed in secret rooms next to the library."

"Does she?" asked Rebekah.

"I think so. The school board members don't let on and the teachers aren't saying so nobody knows for sure."

I do, Rebekah thought. *I do.*

Chapter 19

Once Grandma Kezia's clock chimed midnight, Uncle Gabriel and Aunty Gwen said their goodbyes and Rebekah made her way to her room, her arms full of Christmas presents. She set them down on a side table and then walked over to the open window overlooking the cove where weeks ago the strange child had begged her to draw her. The half-moon shone on the water and she could just see the shadowy roots of the mangroves. The room was filled with the sound of tree frogs singing after a sudden rain shower. Rebekah's brain brimmed with the revelations of the day; so many revelations, she couldn't settle. She thought of Grandma Violet in her lovely green dress and what she had told Rebekah about her father. *How surprising was that?* But not as surprising as the people she had seen in the mirror, especially the white woman putting the rags into the kitchen door slats. *I must draw her*, she thought, so *Mr. Stowe can see what I saw. It wasn't Sally Bassett's granddaughter who poisoned the family, I know it wasn't.* She walked to the dressing table and sat in the chair with her sketch book and charcoal. Her charcoal pencil darted along the pages, bringing to life all the figures and scenes she had seen in the mirror. There was the white woman at the door; Nancy writhing on that dirty floor and finally the white man and his wife at the table. She examined the last sketch, unsure she'd got their features exactly right. But she knew the woman's dress, with the scarf around her low neckline, was accurate.

Beyond tired, Rebekah closed the book, put down her pencil and thought about going to bed. Looking up, she stared into the cheval mirror at the circles under her eyes. Grandma Kezia's suggestion that she do her own portrait came back to her. She took a strand of her hair in her hand. *Maybe I could draw me with an Afro*, she mused, *and then I'd know whether it would suit me*. The tree frogs fell silent and as she looked intently at the reflection of her eyes in the mirror, she saw them lengthen into almond shapes, the dark brown of their irises lightening to seaweed green. Her hair turned to a tumble of tight curls and her skin tightened, making her cheek bones more prominent. The reflected lips in the mirror became tauter, thinner than Rebekah knew hers to be. She saw these foreign lips on her face part to let out the whisper, "Draw me, draw me."

"I'm always drawing you!" Rebekah said out loud. "No matter what happens, I can't seem to keep my drawings of you."

Again the reflected lips parted. The murmur was so soft she could hardly hear it, "Draw me, draw me."

"Tell me your name, then I'll draw you. What's your name?"

"Bek."

"No, your name, not mine. What's your name?"

"Bek."

Rebekah felt a chill on the back of her neck. Bek was the girl's name. Just like hers.

Rebekah opened her sketch book and picked up her charcoal. She looked up again at the tilting mirror and straightened it. Then she focussed on the face before her, taking in the sad knowingness of the girl's eyes. So different from the lightness she'd seen in them at their first few meetings. She sketched the face, taking care to capture the haunted expression in the eyes, the dark circles below them and the shadows on one side of the face. It was tricky to look in a mirror and draw a reflection that wasn't her own. But eventually she finished, and when she did, the lips in the mirror parted again to murmur, "Show me, show me."

Tearing off the page, Rebekah held the drawing up to face its mirror image. She thought she heard a sigh. But when she took the sketch away from the mirror the only reflection there was her own.

Boxing Day morning, Rebekah woke late. After she dressed, she checked her drawing to find the girl's face unchanged – it had not faded in the slightest. I must call Mr. Stowe, she thought, excited, but when she asked her daddy for permission, he shook his head.

"Why not, Daddy?"

"He called this morning while you were asleep. He didn't want to wake you."

"Well, I'll call–" Her daddy's concerned expression stopped her. "What's the matter? Is he ill?"

"No, no. But he's going away for a time."

"Going away? Where's he going to?"

"He didn't have time to explain, Bek. But he asked me to tell you he has written you a letter – he gave it to Mrs. Chatterjee, apparently, so you'll get it when school opens. All right?"

It wasn't all right at all but there was nothing she could do about it. All she could do was wait. The holiday dragged until she found herself back at the Meridian in the assembly hall listening to Mrs. Drinkwater lecture the children about New Year resolutions and how they should commit to doing more than their best this term.

Wanda sighed heavily, "Boring!" And she pulled out her

pick to fluff out her Afro. Bored herself, Rebekah looked up at the ceiling and observed for the first time a small square glass window just above the stage where the Principal, her deputies, and Mr. Darrell, who played the hymns on the piano, sat. It was a funny place to have a window, she thought, and she saw that it was sparkling clean, unlike the grubby windows on the outside wall, but there was no sky behind it. Nothing at all that she could see.

As soon as the lunch bell rang, she sprinted up the steps to the library. Mrs. Chatterjee greeted her warmly. "Why good afternoon, Rebekah, I was just thinking about you. Did you have a good Christmas?"

"Good afternoon, Mrs. Chatterjee. Yes, thank you. I hope you did too. Mr. Stowe said he gave you a–"

"A letter for you? Yes, he did. Here it is." Mrs. Chatterjee picked up a sealed envelope from her desk and handed it to Rebekah. "Here you are."

Rebekah sat down at a table, slit open the letter with her thumb, and began to read.

"Stowe Studio"
7, Fractious Street,
Hamilton Parish.
24 December

My dear Rebekah,

Mrs. Stowe's sister, who lives in Atlanta, has been unwell and so my wife is staying with her to nurse her back to health. In the meantime, I have decided to take the opportunity to travel to parts of the world I have not seen before and to find further artistic inspiration. I will start by exploring different parts of Africa, but I also hope to visit Australia, New Zealand and also the island of Tahiti, once, as you know, the home of Paul Gauguin. Hopefully, I shall end my travels in the Caribbean before returning. I am not exactly sure when I will be back but I will most certainly return by June when once again we may renew our lessons together.

June, she thought with horror. *No lessons until June?*

I am sure I will have all sorts of new techniques to show you as I will be attending different workshops. One must never stop learning, you know.

I know you will continue to sketch and to paint – I do not need to tell you because, like me, you must always have art in your life. It is the way our Almighty Creator made us.

As for your visions of the young lady, I think you will find she will no longer fade.

How did he know that would happen?

If while I am away there are further developments in the story I believe is unfolding, I feel certain you will receive the help you may require. You may be assured of that. But I suspect there will be little activity until my return.

Why not? How could he know that?

Please convey my kindest regards to your father and, of course, to your mother.

My very best wishes,
Everard Leopold Stowe

The thought of six months without her Sunday lessons filled Rebekah with despair. She folded up the letter and put it back in the envelope, feeling her stomach clench. Then she took the letter out again and reread it.

"I feel certain you will receive the help you may require."

What does he mean by that?

Her eyes glanced instinctively at the red door with the silver knocker. Struck by an impulse, she got up from her chair, crept over to the red door and examined the round object she had seen Juan looking at. It wasn't a door bell at all, she realised. It was a peephole. She bent down to squint through the hole. At first, she saw nothing but an expanse of velvety red, the upholstery of a sofa perhaps, but then, to her embarrassment, the iris of an eye appeared right in front of her, dark brown and beady. For what seemed an eternity their eyes were locked. Then the bell rang. Not wanting to be late for class, she went back to the table, picked up her bag, and carefully put Mr. Stowe's letter into it, with more slowness than each of these actions required, lingering to see if the red door would open. But nothing happened. The door stayed closed and she left, locking the library door behind her.

Chapter 20

Soon the term slid into spring. Come February, Rebekah noticed the longtail birds were back, swooping in pairs along the coastlines of the island and in and out of the harbours. She never tried to draw them, however. Even she was not fast enough to catch them in their courtship flight. By March the wild freesias were out, too, dotting people's lawns with the palest white, gold, and purple blooms.

One Sunday morning her daddy asked her to come with him to Somerset. "I've got something real nice to show you," he said. "Bring your sketchbook and pastels – you'll regret it if you don't."

She was glad to go with him because Sundays were hard without him driving her to Fractious Street and without Mr. Stowe's lessons. Once they got to Hog Lane, her daddy parked the truck and took out some wooden crates, secateurs, plus his transistor radio which these days he always took to the fields to keep in touch with the news. They walked together until they reached the field that in September had been fallow. Now, the whole field was filled with the nodding trumpet heads of white Bermuda Easter lilies. Rebekah had never seen a field of flowers so beautiful. Their heady perfume filled the air.

"Oh, Daddy," she said, "I love them."

"I'm glad," he said. "Papa Malachi doesn't approve at all."

"Why ever not?"

"You know Papa Malachi. If you can't eat a crop, what's the point of growing it? But they're nice – real nice, fit for the Queen. Every Easter, we send a bunch of our lilies to the Queen. Did you know that?"

She shook her head, all the while wondering how she could possibly capture these amazing blossoms in pastel.

"You sit here, Bek, while I cut the flowers – folks buy these at this time of year, and I want to make sure I pick enough for my orders. I think I'll leave the radio with you."

As country and western music played in the background, Rebekah watched him for a while using his secateurs to cut the stems – all, she noticed, exactly the same length. She then turned her attention to the problem of painting the flowers. Mr. Stowe's voice came back to her. "Remember to look for all the colours you can see in white. White is not just white."

I need the palest blues, mauves, pinks, and creams, she thought. *So maybe I'll charcoal the flowers first – find their shapes and paint them at home.* She set to work. When she came back to herself, the music had stopped, giving way to the news. "His Excellency the Governor Sir Richard Sharples was fatally shot last evening, together with his Aide-de-Camp, Captain Hugh Sayers and his dog, Horsa."

That's terrible, she thought.

"You all right, Bek?" Her daddy came up just then, back for another crate.

"The Governor's been shot. And the ADC."

"What? When?"

"Yesterday evening. Must have been after the news."

Together, they sat on the grassy edge of the lily field listening to the details. The Governor and his wife had held a small dinner party at Government House. After it was over, the Governor decided to take his Great Dane for a stroll in the grounds. His ADC accompanied him and was the first to be ambushed and killed. "The killer has escaped," the announcer said: "The deaths of the two men come exactly six months after the killing of Police Commissioner George Duckett."

Rebekah listened as the announcer speculated that some black activists, who wanted independence and argued against racial and economic inequality, were responsible. Vaguely recalling what her Uncle Gabriel had said at Christmas about the Black Berets and their fight for racial equality, she found herself wondering ... *Is that cause, any cause, worth a life?*

"It's not right to kill people, is it, Daddy?"

"No, Bek, course not. But, if I'm being honest, I wish white people would listen more to what's important to other people ... not just themselves. Some people thriving while other people suffer, sometimes the sufferers run out of patience."

Something in the way her dad spoke just then reminded her of that time she'd met John – Roger's elder brother – in the Kentucky Fried Chicken Restaurant after the Christmas Parade. What had he said? "Life's not fair when some people suffer and others don't." Something like that.

Her daddy dropped her off late that afternoon, giving her a bunch of lilies for the house. Her mama was in the kitchen with Mr. Forrest. She took one look at the flowers and said, "You can take those right out of here, Rebekah."

"Why don't you like them?"

"They smell of death and there's far too much death around already."

"You mean because of the Governor and all? I heard it on the radio."

"Uh-huh. I just hope the wrong people don't get blamed. Everybody was talking about that at church."

"That won't happen, Patricia," Mr. Forrest said. "We have a British legal system."

"Thomas, you may have been born here, but you're foolish about Bermuda sometimes."

Isn't that the truth, Rebekah thought.

"Well," Mr. Forrest said, "I believe in the law. It's all we have. I must say it's a terrible shame about that Great Dane. Why did they have to kill the dog?"

Rebekah placed the lilies in a jug in her room and spent the afternoon trying to get their white right. In the end, she gave up in frustration. She looked sadly at the postcards Mr. Stowe had sent her over the last few months. They were pinned to her wall – pictures of zebra, giraffes, and elephants in Africa; Maori warriors in New Zealand; ochre quarries in Australia; and tree houses in Tahiti. Why that man had to go travelling for so long, she didn't know; he could be helping her instead.

The following day, she decided she would actually give Mr. Fenwick a chance to teach her. She needed the help and he had been nicer lately. Maybe because of Aunty Gwen. Whatever the reason, there was no one else to ask. "I don't see the problem, Rebekah," he said. "Your painting is good."

"The colours aren't right," she pointed out. "They're not – they're not luminous. They're not luminous enough."

"They look fine to me," he said, "but I'm not a pastels man. You could try watercolours and then just use the white on the page for the lilies, adding shadows."

She opened her mouth to say something, but his expression turned dismissive. "You're fussing too much, Rebekah. It's really not that important."

"Of course, it's important! Everything you do in a painting is important. Every artist knows that."

"You do take yourself seriously, don't you? Who do you think you are, Rebekah? Monet, perhaps?"

His question burned into her and, in the midst of her fury, she had to answer him.

"I would like to be someone like that one day," she said quietly. "I would like to be a great artist."

"My dear girl, how many famous female artists have you heard of?" he asked, his tone so gentle she felt worse than if he had shouted at her. He continued. "How many ones from islands as small as Bermuda?"

Rebekah felt something twist inside her, even as he smiled faintly and dismissed her.

"Off you go now, or you'll be late for your next class."

And with that, he turned his attention away from her, intent on clearing the clutter left by the class. She wanted to hit him, scream at him, "I am an artist, a better one now than you will ever be. How dare you mock who I am! How *dare* you?" But she felt impotent. His mind was made up. She wasn't an artist because she was just a girl from Bermuda. *A black girl,* she thought. *He didn't say so but that's what he meant.*

Outside, Rebekah looked at her lilies and felt like ripping them up. *If I can't be a good artist cos I'm female, what's the point? Nobody cares about my art – except Mr. Stowe and he's not here. And family doesn't count – besides Mama doesn't want me to be an artist either.* The sad thought came to her that there was absolutely no one she could tell about how she felt. Wanda was no good. They were still always side by side in assembly and they sat together in class. But at weekends, Rebekah hardly saw her. That meeting with Roger and John Peterson after the Christmas parade had created a chasm between them that only seemed to get wider by the day. *Wanda only cares about being cool,* Rebekah thought. *Nothing else is important, specially my art.*

"Bekah! Wait for me!" She turned and there was Juan

Symonds sprinting towards her.

Her heart lightened a little. Juan liked her and she liked him. They weren't boyfriend, girlfriend, though. Nothing foolish like that.

"Good morning, Juan," she greeted him.

"I was washing out some brushes in the bathroom and I overheard what Mr. Fenwick said to you, Bekah. It's not right!"

"Maybe he is right, you know. I never thought about it before, but I haven't heard of many female artists. Maybe I can't be a real artist."

"Are you crazy, girl?" Juan was shocked. "Course you can. Your art is brilliant. Mr. Stowe wouldn't be teaching you if you weren't. He doesn't normally take students."

"How do you know that?"

She thought he looked uncomfortable.

"My mama told me," he said after a pause. "One day, you'll be famous; I believe that."

She was warmed by his support though not surprised. These days he was interested in the pictures she drew of the people around her, asking her about them, and wanting to know why she chose certain colours and strokes. But he wasn't an artist himself. *So what does his opinion matter?* Besides, being famous wasn't the point. She remembered Mr. Stowe asking her, "And what do you want to be, Rebekah?" And how she had told him, "I dunno. I don't feel right unless I'm drawing", not realising how important her answer was. There was only one person she could be and here was this horrible teacher telling her it wasn't possible. If only Mr. Stowe were here now.

Chapter 21

The weeks seemed to creep by. Rebekah felt so depressed. School dragged and being at home wasn't much better because of that man. Nobody cared about her. Wanda still wasn't speaking to her and when the phone rang it was never for her. So, she was astonished when one Saturday in May her mama called up the stairs, "The phone, Rebekah – it's for you."

She dashed down the stairs with a feeling of anticipation only to feel crushed when she heard who it was.

"Rebekah, it's Roger."

"Oh," she said, thinking he'd never called her in his life.

"Do you want to come and check out the youth group at Admiralty House today?"

Why would I, she thought. "No thank you," she said, ready to slam down the phone. "Bye."

But Roger surprised her. His voice sounded serious, even urgent. "Don't go yet. I wish you would come. My brother wants to speak to you." Then she heard him shout, "John, Rebekah is on the line."

"Hey there, Rebekah." John's voice sounded so friendly, it helped lift her spirits. "If you haven't got anything to do today, you're very welcome to visit our youth club. There's a sort of open

house for new members. I thought we could show you around
and then we could talk about setting up an art club."

She remembered he'd mentioned the youth group at
Kentucky Fried. *Why not? There's nothing else to do. And I don't
have to pay Roger any mind.* "Okay," she said. "I can do some
sketching?"

"Course you can. Meet me at the gate at three."

Admiralty House was on Spanish Point Road, a half a mile
or so from Rebekah's house so it was easy to walk there. As she
walked towards the gates, carrying her sketch book inside her
tote bag, she could see John Peterson sitting on the veranda of the
old ball room and talking to a bunch of teenagers. The ballroom
was the only room left intact in this tumbledown house, which
once many British admirals had called home. He got to his feet to
greet her. "Afternoon, Rebekah. It's great you could come. In a bit
I want to introduce you to the girls who are interested in starting
an art club. But I thought I'd show you around the property first.
If we go down to the Cove, we can find somewhere to sit and you
can sketch."

"Okay. Roger's not coming?"

He rolled his eyes. "He said he was. But that's kid brothers
for you. He's got better things to do."

Rebekah laughed, relieved she wouldn't have to tolerate
Roger. "I expect he's with Wanda," she said.

"Yes. He led her along the thin pathway, edged with clumps
of purple Bermudiana irises. At one point it was so rocky, she half
stumbled all the way down to the bottom of the hillside.

"Careful now," he said.

At the bottom, the path followed the coast line and at one
stage of the walk they could look out to the open sea and to the
mostly derelict buildings of the Royal Naval Dockyard on the
peninsula curving to the west. Against the sky were the thick,
grey stone walls of Casemates Prison. Rebekah shivered a little,

thinking of the prisoners condemned to confinement there. Walking on, they reached two adjacent creamy, little beaches tucked around the cove and lined with asparagus fern. One of the strips of sand was below a grassy slope.

"Shall we sit on the grass?" Rebekah asked.

John pointed to a stone slab stuck in the middle of one of the beaches. "Let's sit on that."

It was, in fact, a grave stone. Before sitting down on it, she peered at the faint inscription: "Charles Francillon, midshipman on board HMS Spartan, son of Mr. Francis Francillon, purser in the Royal Navy, died April 12, 1813, in the sixteenth year of his age."

"He was so young," she said. "I wonder what he died of."

John smiled as he sat down and patted the stone for her to join him. "You like history, Rebekah? You do, don't you?"

"Sometimes I think history likes me," she said.

"That's a strange thing to say."

You'd think it even stranger if I told you about my visions, she thought. On a blank page, she tried a rough outline of the cove and the water, but she was too self-conscious drawing in front of someone she did not know, too anxious the drawing would not be good enough. She didn't need to lose even more self-confidence. "I'm not in the mood for drawing today," she said.

"That's okay," he said. "But can I see some of your drawings?" She handed him the sketchbook and he flipped through it, coming to a loose sheet she had forgotten sliding between the pages. He pulled it out. It was the drawing she had done of the man beating Nancy, the one that had so upset Mr. Forrest.

He examined it intently, then looked at her with what she could see was definite respect.

"You really get it, don't you? The evil of the colonial system? It's right there in every muscle of that man's face and body."

"Are *you* interested in history?" she asked him.

"History is about the past. It's true, history helps us understand the present, but some people use it to stay stuck. I refuse to stay stuck. That's why I'm Zende Azikiwe now, not John Peterson."

"You've changed your name?"

Can changing your name make so much difference, she wondered. *Can it change who you are? I don't think so.*

"No. It was the Petersons who changed my family name," he corrected her. "I refuse to bear the name of the white slave master. I am going back to an authentic name. That's what I want you to call me."

"Does Roger call you that?"

"No," he admitted. "He keeps forgetting."

For once Rebekah felt a smidgeon of sympathy for Roger. "What name did your mama give you?"

He looked surprised. "John, of course."

"Well," she found herself saying sternly, "I think you should go by the name your mama gave you. It's wrong if you don't."

He was silent for a moment. Then he said, "Look, Rebekah, I am dedicating my life to justice for our race and that means I fight for change."

"What kind of change?" She thought of Papa Malachi and Uncle Gabriel, and what they had told her at Christmas about injustice in Bermuda.

"As black people, we should be in charge of our own destiny instead of being under the yoke of a British Governor."

"But the Governor was shot ... wasn't he?" She wondered what John thought about that. It was confusing because killing had to be wrong so how could the Governor being shot be a good thing?

John's eyes narrowed and for a moment she was frightened – his expression was suddenly so fierce. He looked again at her paintings. "You and Wanda are tight, aren't you?"

The sudden change of subject surprised her. She didn't quite know what to say.

"You talk a lot to each other, right?"

"We used to. Not so much now."

"May I ask why not?"

"I dunno, she . . ." Rebekah's voice trailed off. She scuffed her shoes in the sand, looked at the cove ahead, the water like sunlit emeralds, and at the poinciana trees bursting into leaf on the hillside behind.

"She thinks I'm too young for her, I guess."

John placed her drawing back in the sketchbook and handed it to her. He watched her put it back in her tote bag. "She's the child, Rebekah, not you. You, you have – soul. Your pictures tell me that." His expression was softer now.

Rebekah felt a warm glow. *At least someone appreciates my art.*

"Come on, let's go back up the hill before it gets dark. The girls should be here by now."

They stood up from the gravestone and made their way back up to the ballroom where now some girls had indeed gathered. She didn't recognise any of them, though. They weren't from her school or her neighbourhood.

"Hi girls," John said. "This is Rebekah Eve. She's an excellent artist. She might be able to help us with the art club."

The girls greeted her in a friendly fashion. "That's cool," one said.

"Nice earrings," said another. "Unusual. Can I have a closer look?"

"Sure." But as the girl touched one of her earrings very lightly, Rebekah froze. *Something is wrong*, she thought, *something is terribly wrong.*

"Pretty," said the girl.

But Rebekah wasn't listening. Something down the hill

was forcing her to look down. She didn't want to look down but she *had* to. The hillside and beach had changed. The poincianas had vanished. Instead, there were many more cedars, a thick palmetto grove, and leafy trees and shrubs she'd never seen before. The gravestone was gone, and the place where it had been was scattered with driftwood and seaweed. The asparagus fern edging the beaches had disappeared too and so had the jetty. In the pink golden light she could just see the ghost girl, *her* girl, only so much taller, a woman now, standing by the water in Nancy's dress.

She's turning away Rebekah thought. She mustn't disappear. She mustn't!

"Rebekah? What's wrong?"

She turned towards John, noting the concern on his face but compelled to run to Beck before she disappeared. "I've forgotten something," she said. "I'll go get it." She was moving, running down the hill, her bag on her shoulder before he had a chance to respond. It was a struggle to keep her balance on the rocks, at that speed. But she reached the edge of the water, without tripping. Within seconds, she and the girl – who blessedly had not disappeared – were standing face to face. She was surprised to see the girl's hands resting on her stomach. *She's pregnant*, Rebekah realised. Impossible for it to be anything else, the girl's – no longer a girl's – stomach was so large. *She's scared, she's so scared.* Rebekah felt the usual urgency to draw her.

Rebekah whipped her sketchbook and charcoal out from her bag, opened a page and frantically began to sketch the girl. But, for the first time, it felt as if there was no need to be frantic. The young woman just stood there patiently.

After Rebekah had finished the sketch, the girl picked her way in bare feet along the path by the ocean. Glad she had shoes, because the way was rocky, Rebekah followed the girl until she too could look out to the open sea and to the Dockyard. But all she could see was a line of trees and the distant billowing sails of two tall sailing ships. No Casemates prison, not a building in sight; instead, just tree covered hills. They both watched as the bright burning sun began to dip. Once the ships disappeared over the horizon, Rebekah felt the girl's finger touch her shoulder. She turned and so must have the girl because there they were facing each other, the girl's expression so urgent. Rebekah saw the girl's lips part but the only sound she could hear was John's voice from the top of the hill. "Rebekah!"

As Rebekah watched, the girl faded from sight.

And once again, her own world re-settled around her. Looking across the ocean, she saw again Casemates Prison and the lonely buildings of the Dockyard.

"Rebekah!" John was still calling out to her. She wondered how much time had passed.

She turned and began her climb back up the hill.

Chapter 22

The lunchtime break bell rang, rudely interrupting Rebekah's memory of seeing the girl at Admiralty House. Wanda, as was normal lately, quickly packed her bag and was out of the classroom before Rebekah had time to close her books. Rebekah decided to go to her locker in the hallway to put away her backpack and retrieve her lunchbox. The backpack – bulging with her sketchbook, folder of drawings, and art books, as well as her normal texts – was too heavy to carry around. As she opened her locker, she heard a squeal and then a choking sound coming out of the assembly hall. No one was allowed in the assembly hall during break times. She slipped through the door, which was not quite closed, and was amazed to see Roger Peterson pinning Wanda against the wall, his hands around her neck.

"You get your hands off my friend," Rebekah screamed without a second thought. "You hear me?"

But Roger ignored her. His hands around Wanda's neck, he kept kicking her with his boots in a fury.

Rebekah lifted her school bag high and bonked him on the back of his head. He jerked around so that Wanda was now free. "Run, Wanda, run!" But Wanda either wouldn't or couldn't. She stood there coughing and spluttering, her eyes pouring tears.

Roger clenched his fists and made to attack Rebekah.

"You touch me and I'll scream," she hissed. "You leave Wanda alone."

"Well, she should leave my brother alone. And mind her own business." He moved towards her with his fists still tight.

Rebekah lifted her bag again, heavy though it was. "Come near me and I'll hit you again. So do yourself a favour and get out of here. Go on, get out!"

To her relief, he obeyed. The bag must have hit harder than she realized. He scowled at Rebekah as he slunk into the corridor.

Rebekah put her hand on Wanda's shoulder, "You OK, girl?"

Wanda nodded. "I think so. Just a bit shaken up." She picked up her lunchbox which had fallen to the floor.

"We'd better get out of here or we'll be in trouble," she said, leaving Rebekah no choice but to follow her out.

Rebekah quickly put her bag in the locker and followed Wanda out of the main building. Walking outside, they made their way to a clump of trees on one side of the school yard. They sat there, under one of the cedars.

"I forgot my lunch," Rebekah said sighing. "I'd better go take it out of my locker."

"The bell will go by the time you get it. You can have mine – I don't feel like it."

"You sure you're all right?"

Wanda nodded again.

"So what was that all about? I thought you liked Roger."

Hot tears started to trickle down Wanda's cheeks and she brushed them away angrily. "He's mad with me."

"Why's he mad with you, Wanda?"

The words tumbled out of her mouth. "We were at John's apartment – well it's not his really – it's his parents' – they have an apartment underneath their house and John lives in it. I made

Roger take me there, cos you know me, I always like to see where people live."

It was true. She did.

"Anyway, John went into his kitchen to get us something to drink and I was sitting on the couch. I could see a chest with drawers in it on the other side of the room. It was pretty and I don't know why – I wanted to see what the drawers were like inside. I didn't think he'd mind – so I got up and opened one and I saw a gun."

Rebekah gasped. "You can't have done, Wanda!" Immediately after the Governor and his ADC were killed, the government had made owning a gun illegal – people were given ten days to hand in their guns. Papa Malachi said it was an amnesty. He was annoyed he had to give up his shot gun – he used it to shoot pigeons and crows. "Poisoning the birds is far crueller than shooting them," he'd told her.

"It must be a toy gun," she said now. "Real ones are illegal now."

"Then why was he so angry? Besides, it looked real – like the kind of gun I've seen on *Hawaii Five-O*."

"But, Wanda, what would he want a gun for?"

"That's what I asked him. He got so mad. He said it wasn't my business and I had no right to search his things. I said I didn't mean to search his things, I just wanted to see what the inside of the drawer was like. He said I was stupid. He said if I told anyone he'd kill me and my family. He said I'd better believe it."

Rebekah's stomach lurched. She remembered how fierce his face had turned when she mentioned the Governor being shot.

"He said he was fighting for rights for the black man and I was too young and too stupid to understand that. And then he swore at me. I thought he was going to hit me. I was so scared – I ran out of his house."

"When did all this happen?"

"Last Thursday."

Thursday. It hit Rebekah then that maybe John had invited her to Admiralty House on Saturday because he wanted to know if Wanda had said anything to her. To see if she knew about the gun. Talk about the art club was just an excuse. She remembered their conversation when they had sat on the gravestone, and how surprised she had been at the sharp turn in conversation when he'd brought up Wanda. "You all right, Bekah?" Wanda's voice jolted her out of her thoughts.

"I'm just thinking. Was Roger still there when John attacked you?"

"Yes."

"So why did Roger attack you just now, Wanda? Did you say anything to anybody about John?"

"Nope. I'd just got my lunch from my locker when he jumped me and dragged me into the assembly hall. Jeest I was scared! And nobody noticed. Except you, Bekah. He said I ruined his brother's life. And then he tried to choke me. Maybe he's worried I'll go to the police."

"Do you think you will go to the police, Wanda?"

"Are you crazy, girl? If John found out I'd been to the police … what if he hurt my family, if he hurt Troy or Trey? You won't tell anyone about John, will you, Bekah? You promise?"

"I promise."

The school bell shrieked across the yard. Obediently, the girls got up. Wanda touched Rebekah on the shoulder. "Bekah?"

"Yes?"

"Thank you!"

"You're welcome."

"We're friends again, right? I didn't like not being friends."

"Me neither."

That was true, Rebekah thought, but she wasn't sure she'd be able to be friends with Wanda the way she used to be. They used to tell each other everything. But ever since they'd both been accepted into the Meridian there was so much she hadn't been able to tell Wanda. Not about her daddy leaving and certainly not about the visions. *If I told her about those*, she thought, *Wanda would say I was crazy, I know she would. Maybe I am crazy.* She decided she wouldn't tell Wanda about meeting John at Admiralty House either, not unless she absolutely had to.

Once the girls reached the school's veranda, the sky turned black and pelted torrents. All afternoon it rained and rained. Miss Spruce, who was teaching the class *Macbeth*, or trying to, was able to joke: "'Fair is foul and foul is fair', indeed."

Five minutes later, water gushed out of the ceiling followed by a shower of plaster. Part of the school's roof over their class room could not bear the weight of the downpour. It was the last class of the day so everyone was delighted, hoping it would bring school to an early close. But their hopes were dashed.

"No, you can't leave early! We can't afford to lose time so near to your exams. We will continue in the library," Miss Spruce announced. "Come along." They trudged their way up the long flight of steps by the office, filed into the library, and seated themselves around the tables. Rebekah saw Roger Peterson slumped, not looking at anyone. *I hope he has a blinding headache*, she thought. *I hit him hard enough.*

"Now we've talked about moral confusion in *Macbeth*," Miss Spruce was saying, "and about how appearances can be very deceiving: '…bear welcome in your eye, your hand, your tongue; look like the innocent flower, but be the serpent under't,' Lady Macbeth advised. One of the strong ideas of the play is that evil can appear very attractive."

John's likeable face loomed into Rebekah's vision – was he evil? Could he possibly have killed the Governor? And then her mind shifted to the slave girl's face and her urgent expression. What had Mr. Stowe said in his letter? "I suspect there will be little activity until my return." And he had been right, until that day John had taken her to Admiralty Park. Why had the girl appeared then? *Was she concerned about me? But why? Did she come to warn me about John?*

"Now students, I want you to consider another issue," Miss Spruce was saying, "I want you to think carefully about who was most responsible for the murder of King Duncan."

Juan quietly pointed out that given Macbeth had stabbed the king with daggers it had to be his fault.

Rebekah put up her hand.

"Yes, Rebekah?" Miss Spruce looked delighted.

"If someone persuades you to do something bad, isn't that person to blame as well?"

"That's an interesting question. Can you give us an example to support that idea?"

"Well," she said, "suppose a slave mistress takes poison from a slave to kill her husband because he is cruel? And the slave gives it to her to save her granddaughter from him? Is the slave to blame or is the slave mistress to blame? Or is the slave master to blame?"

Miss Spruce's face creased into puzzlement. "Rebekah, what has this to do with *Macbeth*?"

Rebekah shrugged her shoulders. "I was just thinking."

Juan leaped in. "You were thinking about Lady Macbeth, weren't you, Rebekah? Because that's what she did – she persuaded Macbeth to murder the king."

A lively discussion ensued but Rebekah was far away, images of the girl and the old woman, who was surely her grandmother, invading her mind. On her lap, discreetly hidden, was her folder which held her loose drawings and her sketchbook. With Miss Spruce distracted by the oddity of having her entire class engaged, almost, Rebekah opened her pad and looked again at the girl standing by the cove at Admiralty House with her baby bump protruding; standing that Christmas afternoon by the dining table where the white couple sat; and then gazing down at Nancy – so ill on the kitchen floor. And she remembered the white woman with her terrible eyes sitting silently at the table and eating the bird meat. *What happened, Rebekah wondered. What really happened?*

"Now, class," Miss Spruce was saying, "we've considered Macbeth himself and we've talked about the role of his wife. Is anyone else responsible for the murder, do you think?"

"The witches," one girl said. "They were tricky."

"Indeed," agreed Miss Spruce. "Do you think they're real witches or just spiteful old women? Are they evil? Because if they are, if their spells really work, is it possible Macbeth and Lady Macbeth could have had no control over their actions?"

The mention of evil nudged Rebekah into seeing again the fruits in the basket and the glistening, white toad. She picked up her pencil and started to draw. And there coming into view on the page was the horrible old woman who had carried the basket. The grandmother. *She looks like a witch*, Rebekah thought, as she drew the old crone's face – the eyes fierce and fanatical, the mouth tight and determined.

The scene changed to a room where there was a cedar four poster bed. Lying on the bed was the white man, a sheen of sweat on his ashen face. *He's really sick*, Rebekah observed. She saw her young girl, no, woman now, enter the room with water in a glass and saw him painfully raise himself to take the glass from her hand. The scene dimmed out. After Rebekah finished drawing him, she moved to another page, drawing another room – a small room with several wooden chairs that she knew Papa Malachi would like. The room filled with people she hadn't seen before but who were dressed as strangely as the white couple. Rebekah's eyes focused on the white woman who looked sickly and was slumped in her chair. A red-haired woman seated next to her was talking rapidly. Rebekah drew them. Then she drew them again, their faces looking up towards the doorway as Bek entered the room. The mistress pointed to Bek and the red haired woman shot out of her chair and grabbed her shoulders. Rebekah found herself drawing the woman with the red hair again, this time shaking Bek, her mouth moving rapidly as if she was shouting although Rebekah could not hear the words.

"Rebekah, what do you think?" Miss Spruce's voice jerked her back to the class.

"I dunno." A thought came to her. "Miss Spruce?"

"Yes?"

"Did Lady Macbeth get pregnant?"

"Why, yes. Remember she tells Macbeth she has had babies? We don't know what happened to them, though. They probably died."

"Oh," said Rebekah. She had completely forgotten.

"So, what do you think about the witches? Are they responsible?"

"I'm not sure." Another thought came to her which seemed very important though she could not tell why. "Do you think the witches got beaten up?"

"What an extraordinary question to ask, Rebekah! What made you think of it?"

The scars on the young woman's back I saw in Mr. Stowe's garden, she thought. *But I can't mention those.*

After the lesson was over, Miss Spruce came up to Rebekah smiling ruefully. "Honestly, I don't know sometimes where your mind goes. You're very perceptive one minute and way off the next."

"Oh."

"Never mind, I'm sure you'll do well in your exams. Rebekah, would you mind carrying these books to the office for me."

Rebekah took the books and they both walked down the stairs. Once she'd left the books in the office, she went back up the stairs, and opened the library door. Her eyes widened. The red door with the silver knocker was wide open. And there at the library table where she had sat, was a small lady bent over her folder, flipping the pages of her sketchbook and the loose drawings one by one. She turned at the sound of Rebekah's footsteps, and Rebekah could see she was wearing a neat cherry red, double breasted suit with two rows of black buttons, and a black beret upon her thick, straightened, white hair cut to frame her face.

Rebekah pondered what reds she would use to create the suit and how she would capture the lady's bright, dark eyes – show how they dominated her face and made her seem much younger than she was. Even her face and hands told the lie, uncreased and unwrinkled. She must be old, Rebekah thought, real old, but not ugly to look at. Not at all. Wanda had been wrong about that.

Dr. Delacroix – for it was obviously Dr. Delacroix, finally – filled the room with the scent of jasmine. She gazed steadily into Rebekah's eyes and then said in a clear, musical voice, "I believe it is time we were introduced. You are Miss Rebekah Eve, are you not?"

Rebekah nodded.

The old lady held out her tiny unwrinkled hand. "And I am Dr. Ella Bien-Aimée Delacroix, sometimes known as the Lady of the Library."

Chapter 23

The Meridian apartment was much bigger than Rebekah had imagined. Dr. Delacroix seemed to sense her surprise. "Once I taught 45 children in this classroom," she said. "Then it became converted into my apartment. I have devoted my life to the Meridian so you could say the school owed me this conversion. Sit down on the sofa, Rebekah."

Rebekah did as she was told. The sofa, placed well away from one of the walls, was old fashioned – wing-backed and covered with the red velvety material she had seen through the peephole. Behind it was a very old, four-legged electric stove made of enamel. *Mama would hate it*, Rebekah thought, but to her it was so old it was cute. Two of the walls were lined with books. *Why*, she thought, *Dr. Delacroix has more books than Mr. Stowe.*

Her eyes rested on the archway in the middle of the wall opposite her. It led to another room that had to be Dr. Delacroix's bedroom. She was tempted to get up and see what it was like but that, she told herself, would be rude. Facing her was the bedroom's large window under which was some odd-looking instrument. It looked like a strange tube with a handle. Next to it was a large ear trumpet that seemed to fit into a hole in the wall.

She turned her eyes back to the room in which they were sitting. A writing desk with drawers next to the door caught her attention, because placed on it was a cedar writing box opened and ready for use. She let out a little gasp of recognition.

"Is that the box my great-grandfather made?"

"Certainly, it is," she replied. "Jacob Malachi Eve was a very gifted man."

She sat down on the most extraordinary rocking chair Rebekah had ever seen. Made of wood, it had two gigantic ear trumpets stretching up from each armrest to the top of its back. The Lady carefully turned each trumpet away from her ears.

"I can hear you perfectly well, Rebekah, but I am a little hard of hearing when it comes to listening to the children in the library or the headmistress in school assembly."

She pointed to a square, glass window embedded in the wooden floor. Fascinated, Rebekah looked down and saw it had a hinge allowing it to be lifted up. Getting up to look through it, she saw the raised platform in the school hall directly below and remembered how she had first noticed the window in the assembly hall ceiling at the beginning of the spring term. *Dr. Delacroix's like a spy*, Rebekah thought. *She wants to see everything. And hear everything.* She looked again at the ear trumpet near the bedroom window and the strange instrument. *It's a periscope*, she realised, remembering one she had seen in a movie about submarines. *So that's how she's able to know everything. She can see the playing fields and the inside of the art room all without anybody seeing her at the window.*

"Now then," said Dr. Delacroix once Rebekah had sat down again, "your father is well?"

"Yes, thank you."

"I taught him, you know. A very bright young man. And a very sincere young man. And your mother, she is well?"

"She's fine."

"I believe she is in a relationship with a Mr. Thomas Forrest?"

Rebekah's cheeks burned with a mixture of fury and embarrassment at the Lady's intrusiveness.

"I don't like to intrude into people's private affairs," Dr. Delacroix said, her back bolt upright and her head poised like a queen's.

Excuse me, thought Rebekah, remembering the letter the Lady of the Library had written to her father all those years ago, and letting her eyes turn to the bedroom entrance and the periscope.

"But in this case it is an important question. Is she?"

"Yes," said Rebekah.

"He is a lawyer, is he not?"

"Yes."

Rebekah made up her mind she wasn't going to say one word more about it.

"Thank you, Rebekah." Dr. Delacroix rocked in the chair for a few seconds. "You may be wondering why I want to see you. There are several important reasons. But first you must understand that I do not make myself known to all and sundry. I, therefore, request that you do not discuss our meeting with any of your friends. Discretion, Rebekah, is the better part of valour. Do you understand?"

Rebekah was not sure she did but she nodded anyway.

"So where shall we begin?" She got up from the chair, went to the writing box and took from the drawer a piece of paper which she gave to Rebekah. Looking at it, Rebekah saw a list of women's names. "I don't understand."

"Whatever anyone tells you to the contrary, Rebekah, it is possible for a woman of colour to be a great artist," the Lady of the Library said firmly. Her eyes were both dark and bright, intense, as she continued. "Juan Symonds is quite right. In your case, it is not only possible; it is inevitable. It is your destiny." She handed over a list. "These are names of female artists and sculptors of colour who have achieved much. I am sure Mrs. Chatterjee will be happy to order them for the library. Now do you understand me?"

Rebekah found her face relaxing into a huge smile and the muscles in her stomach relaxing. She hadn't realised how tense she still was after her conversation with Mr. Fenwick. *She must have been listening in. With that ear trumpet next to the periscope.*

The Lady of the Library wasn't done. "You will not let anyone, not even an art teacher deter you, are we agreed?"

Rebekah nodded happily, totally ready to forgive her for asking about her mama and that man. "Another reason I wanted to see you has to do with recent events." A hint of a smile crossed Dr. Delacroix's face. "You have had an eventful day," she said. "I congratulate you on the accuracy of your aim."

Rebekah's eyes swivelled to the glass window in the floor. So Dr. Delacroix had seen her hit Roger with her school bag in the assembly room. She must have witnessed the whole thing.

"The question is," Dr. Delacroix said quietly, "what is it that made Roger Peterson attack Wanda Lambert?"

Rebekah stared at her feet. She could feel Dr. Delacroix's eyes on her. "I don't know," she muttered, her cheeks burning. She hated lying, she really hated it. But she had promised Wanda. She remembered Wanda's fear that John Peterson would hurt her family. *He wouldn't hurt the twins ... would he?* The smallest chance that he might was another reason not to tell anyone about the gun. "You are loyal to your friends, I see."

Rebekah raised her chin. "Yes. Wanda is my best friend."

Dr. Delcroix allowed herself an approving smile. "I admire loyalty to friends. There is not enough of it, I fear, in today's selfish society." She looked down at Rebekah's folder on her lap, opened the sketchbook inside and gazed steadily at one of the drawings.

It was a relief for Rebekah to look up from her shoes. *Nervy. You shouldn't have taken my folder without my permission,* she thought. But she decided to excuse the Lady of the Library because of what she had said about her art.

"I saw you drawing during Miss Spruce's Shakespeare class," Dr. Delacroix said at last.

Course you did, Rebekah thought.

"Rebekah, Mr. Stowe has told me about your drawings of the past. You started with this young lady, did you not?" She showed it to Rebekah – the drawing of Bek with her swollen stomach standing on the beach at Admiralty Park.

"Yes," said Rebekah. "But I first drew her when she was much younger, just a child."

"So Mr. Stowe told me. Do you know who she is?"

"She's Sally Bassett's granddaughter. She's the slave who was supposed to have poisoned her owners. Grandma Kezia told me that story ages ago. But she didn't do it. I'm sure she didn't do it! Sally didn't give the poison to her."

She could hear her voice rising higher and higher, insistent on Bek's innocence. When had she come to care so much?

"I want you to slow down a little, Rebekah, and guide me through this step by step. First of all, do you know her name?"

"I didn't at first. I asked her name and, when she answered, I thought she was calling out my name, the special name my daddy calls me – Bek. But her name *is* Bek."

"You are right. However, strictly speaking it wasn't exactly your name because it was spelled B-e-c-k."

"How do you know?"

The Lady smiled. "I am relieved to observe you have a questioning mind. I know because her name is in the records of Bermuda's Assizes, of the courts, in 1730. She was, as you have said, a slave and her full name was never written down as Rebekah, or indeed Rebecca. She was known only as Beck."

"It's funny she has nearly the same name as me, isn't it?

"Does that bother you?"

"Mama thinks she looks like me. So did Grandma Kezia at first. And once, when I looked at myself in the mirror, I saw her instead. But I don't think she's me – I don't think she looks like me. But I can't show you the drawings of her when she was little because . . ."

"You have not been able to keep them. Mr. Stowe explained that as well. We were both astonished by the fire in the library. Tell me, did she ever speak to you?"

Rebekah explained about how the child had on several occasions asked her to draw her and how she had touched her gold earrings. "I thought she said, 'No finery.' It was very strange."

"I can certainly explain that, Rebekah. You see, a law was introduced so that slaves were not allowed to wear fine clothes or adornments of any kind on pain of severe punishment. They could be whipped, branded or have their noses slit."

Rebekah flinched.

"How did she look when she was little?" Dr. Delacroix asked

"She was very pretty, and she looked happy – at least I think she did When she was older, she looked sad."

"That is understandable. The life of a slave could never be a happy one."

"No," agreed Rebekah, remembering the pictures she had drawn of the older slave, Nancy.

As if picking up on her thought, the Lady of the Library said, "But you have drawn other people, have you not?" She pointed to the loose drawings of Nancy in the kitchen and then of the slave master whipping her. "Do you know who this woman is?"

"I thought I heard someone call her Nancy."

Dr. Delacroix inhaled sharply, nodded in apparent

satisfaction, then said, almost to herself, "Her name was spelled N-a-n-c-e-y." She was silent for a moment. "That was a terrible scene to see, Rebekah. Are you sure it was her master?"

"He is the only man I've seen. It's all there in the folder, you know. But sometimes he looked at Nancey as if he, as if he . . ."

"Wanted her?"

Rebekah felt herself flush. It didn't seem right to talk about such things. She nodded. "But Dr. Delacroix, the white woman, the wife, she hated Nancey, I could tell. And Nancey hated her right back."

"And what do you think the mistress thought of Beck?"

"She liked her. I'm sure she did. At first, anyway." Rebekah reached for sketchbook and showed the Lady of the Library the picture of the child smiling at the woman while she was chopping vegetables in the kitchen. "See?"

"Interesting," said Dr. Delacroix, taking back the sketchbook, "very interesting. And most unexpected."

"But then Beck began wearing Nancey's dress and I didn't like that at all. She looked terrified."

Dr. Delacroix sighed. "She would have been terrified, the poor child. Do you know the names of the slave owners, Rebekah?"

She shook her head. "Mr. Stowe never told me."

"They were named Thomas and Sarah Forster."

"Are their names in the records as well? Is that how you know?"

Dr. Delacroix gave her a nod of approval. "You have the makings of a historian, Rebekah. Yes, indeed. Thomas Forster was a mariner and a slave trader. He was also a grandson of the Governor. His wife, Sarah, was the daughter of a white landowner called John Jennings, a man who as you will see could be very important in the story."

But Rebekah's mind couldn't focus on Jennings or the wife. She was remembering how she had called Mr. Forrest Forster by mistake. *He is a descendent,* she thought, *he has to be. That's why he looks so like the husband.* Rebekah looked up to meet the Lady of the Library's steady gaze.

"Do you think Forrest and Forster could refer to the same person? Like somebody mixed them up?"

"Sometimes names were given different versions," said Dr. Delacroix, gently, "For example, the Forsters were also called Fosters. Forrest would not be an impossible variant."

She turned to another image in the sketch book.

"But now, Rebekah, I want you to tell me about Sally Bassett. When did you first see her? Do you remember?"

Rebekah explained about the old woman she had seen on the fire truck the night of the Christmas parade. "I'm not absolutely sure but I think that was Sally Bassett."

"You look worried, Rebekah. What is it?"

"It was a strange thing to see – Santa turning into a horrible old woman on top of a fire engine. I thought I was going crazy."

"Vision is a wonderful gift, Rebekah. Do not fear it. Did you ever see the old lady as a young woman?"

Rebekah thought about it, remembered the lattice and roses in Mr. Stowe's garden and the awful vision they had unlocked. "I might have but if I did, I didn't see her face. I saw her back covered with terrible scars."

"Show me," the Lady said, and Rebekah flipped through her sketchbook to point out the drawing. The Lady's breath drew in sharply at the sight of savagery burnt into the young woman's back.

"It mightn't have been her. It might have been Nancey."

"No," said Dr. Delacroix adamantly. "It was not Nancey."

Rebekah felt a stab of anxiety. "I hope it wasn't Beck."

"No. It was Sally at a much younger age."

"How do you know?"

"I can't know with certainty but given the depth of the

scarring," the Lady of the Library shut her eyes for a second to block the sight, then looked directly at Rebekah, "and given all your drawings seem connected to a specific story, she is the most likely of the three enslaved women in that story because of what had happened to her when she was a much younger woman. She lived in Southampton Parish – they called it Southampton Tribe in those days – but it was much the same length it is today. This was in 1712 so we are going back even further in time. She was accused of swearing and of threatening that something bad would happen to John Jennings, the father of Sarah, Forster's wife, on the 26th January. Sure enough on that day damage was done to his property and she was punished for it five days afterwards."

"She was whipped?"

"Oh yes. John Jennings was also a Justice of the Peace and he ordered her to be publicly whipped the length of Southampton. The court ordered – I have the words by heart – 'She receiving three lashes well laid on her naked back at the end of thirty paces from the West End of the said Tribe to the East End of the same.' That, Rebekah, would mean she received at least a hundred lashes."

Rebekah imagined the horror of the scene – being made to walk thirty paces, another thirty paces, another thirty paces, another thirty paces; the lash cutting her naked back all the while.

"Couldn't Sally have run away?"

"No, Rebekah," said Dr. Delacroix, still gently rocking in her chair. "She would have been leashed like a dog and pulled to her feet every time she fell."

"And she survived that?" Rebekah asked.

"Well, you know the answer to that. You saw her in Mr. Stowe's garden as a younger woman with terrible scars and you saw her as an old woman with her basket of poisons. So, she certainly survived the whipping. Tell me, these are all of the drawings you have done of Sally Bassett?"

"Yes."

"All your drawings are important, Rebekah, very important. But it is this one that is astonishing." She took out the drawing of Sally Bassett visiting the Forsters' cottage and the white woman whom she now knew to be Sarah Forster.

"Yes," Rebekah said. "Sally didn't give the poison to Beck, the way people say she did. She gave it to . . ."

"Mrs. Forster. You are certain of that?"

"That's what I saw. Beck was standing away from the house on the pathway. I think she was told to keep watch. Sally Bassett pointed to her and then looked at Mrs. Forster as if, as if–"

"They were agreeing on something?"

"Yes."

"Beck was approaching, if not already at, the age of childbearing. If Thomas died, she would escape his cruelty. You see, Rebekah, it has always been thought that Sally Bassett's part in this poison plot had much to do with Beck, her granddaughter. But your revelation suggests that Sarah Forster hated her husband and wanted him dead. What you saw could mean that perhaps they were agreeing if Sally gave Mrs. Forster the poisons and told her how to use them, Beck would gain her manumission."

Rebekah looked puzzled. "What is manumission?"

"Her release from slavery, her freedom."

"But why poison Nancey?"

"I don't know whether we'll ever know the truth of that, Rebekah," Dr. Delacroix said. "Some people think Nancey was poisoned by accident, some don't. Perhaps Sarah did mean to poison Nancey. It wasn't unusual in those days for a mistress to blame the enslaved woman who caught her husband's eye."

"Do you think Mrs. Forster poisoned herself?" Rebekah took back the sketch book and flipped the pages until she reached the painting she had drawn of the white husband and his wife sitting at opposite ends of their table on Christmas day, their pale faces even paler, as Beck waited on them with dull eyes. "There she is. The white lady had this scarf around her dress . . ."

"A fichu," the Lady of the Library said looking gravely at the sketch. "I agree Mrs. Forster looks sickly as well. Perhaps she put a little poison in her own food so that suspicion would not fall on her. From her point of view, it was as well she did, because the poison plot came to light. It might not have done, you know. Thomas Forster could have died with no one thinking anything about it."

"And Beck," said Rebekah sadly, "would have been all right and nobody would have blamed her. I wonder how it was found out that Mr. Forster and Nancey had been poisoned."

"It was because of another poisoning that had happened three years previously but was only discovered at the time Sally was arrested. Two slaves were found guilty of poisoning their owner ... at one stage the wife was also implicated. However, she was never brought to trial."

Rebekah thought of the scenes she had just drawn of that red haired woman talking to Mrs. Forster and of the mistress pointing to Beck.

"Something made Mrs. Forster's feelings about Beck change. People gossip a lot in Bermuda," she said. "Maybe people started to gossip about Mrs. Forster, so she had to put the blame on Beck."

Dr. Delacroix paused, considering this. "Perhaps." She took back the sketch book and gravely examined the drawing Rebekah had done of Beck when she had been at Admiralty House. "Rebekah, can you tell me why you have drawn her in this condition?"

"Because that's how she looked."

Dr. Delacroix was silent for a moment. She placed the sketchbook and the drawings on a small cedar coffee table in front of her. Then she asked, "Where did you see her?"

Rebekah had been so anxious to catch the likeness before the girl disappeared, she had hardly sketched in the background.

"At Admiralty House. By the cove, you know?"

Dr. Delacroix's face took on a grim expression. "I have never been to Admiralty House."

When Rebekah looked surprised, she continued, "During the Second World War and afterwards, black women or black men, for that matter, were never invited to visit the home of the Admirals of England unless they went there to clean. After the British left in the 1950s, I hadn't the slightest desire to go there. I am told the house was built so that the Admirals could look out to Dockyard and see the ships coming in along the North Shore."

Then Rebekah remembered looking out to the west from the jetty near the cove. "Yes. But when I saw the girl, all the Dockyard buildings disappeared."

Dr. Delacroix nodded. "That makes sense...the fortifications would've been added later. Are there trees on the property?"

"Yes," Rebekah said, "but they changed. At first there were poincianas. When the girl appeared, they vanished. There were just cedars and palmettos – maybe other trees I didn't recognise."

"Many of Bermuda's exotic, ornamental trees did not arrive on our island until the later 18th and 19th centuries. Beck would not have seen them. This means your vision has integrity."

Rebekah remembered Mr. Stowe using that same odd choice of word, "integrity". She hadn't been sure about the word "integrity". Now she thought she understood.

"You mean what I saw was true?"

"Yes, that is what I mean."

She remembered the frangipani tree fading away from her drawing of the cove near Building's Bay, and...

"The kiskadees disappeared, too. At least, I couldn't hear them."

"That, too, is to be expected. The Great Kiskadee did not

arrive in Bermuda until 1957."

Rebekah glanced around again at the books on Dr. Delacroix's shelves, a fair amount of them on botany and zoology. *She's like my daddy*, she thought, *and like Mr. Stowe. She knows stuff.*

"So, Beck was pregnant," Dr. Delacroix was saying, eyes still on the drawing. "In all likelihood with Thomas Forster's child, another slave to add to his estate. Both Sarah and Sally were too late to save her from that. And perhaps the pregnancy was another reason for Sarah to blame her."

The Lady of the Library fell silent and Rebekah wondered whether she should leave. But one worry still nagged at her.

"Dr. Delacroix . . ."

She looked up at Rebekah. "Yes?"

"I'm the only one Beck comes to. It's as if, as if . . ."

She couldn't find the words. Dr. Delacroix waited patiently.

"It's as if I'm special to her."

"I am sure you are, child."

"Because she's me?" Rebekah asked in a small voice. "Do you think I've been reincarnated like the *On a Clear Day* movie?"

"Not at all, my dear. You have your own identity." Dr. Delacroix bent to pick up the painting of the girl by the cove. "As you so rightly pointed out, she does not look like you. She is *not* you. You are special to her, Rebekah, because she trusts you with her story. If she had told it then, who would have believed her?"

"I'm glad she didn't poison anybody."

"Because she was young and pretty?"

"No ... just ..."

And as she struggled to articulate her thoughts, she remembered the first time she saw the girl she now knew was Beck – her guileless face, her playful spirit. Just a girl, who, as Rebekah had since learned, was forced to grow up in a cruel, cruel world.

"No. Because she was so innocent. Even if she had poisoned the Forsters, I don't think she would have been as guilty as . . ."

"As Sally Bassett? Certainly, it is easier to think badly of Sally Bassett," Dr. Delacroix said. "It is one reason she has always had my sympathy. Like many freedom fighters, she has been vilified."

Rebekah inwardly started at the word, "freedom fighter". That was what Roger had called his brother.

Is the Lady of the Library saying it's a good thing to be a freedom fighter?

She didn't dare ask. So, she turned her thoughts to the discussion about guilt in class "I think Beck was completely innocent," she said now, "because she didn't do anything. Sally had the poisons. So wasn't she a bit to blame? Or Mrs. Forster because she used them? Or is Mr. Forster to blame because he was so cruel?"

"All very good questions, Rebekah. But we could argue that the evils of slavery and racism were to blame. Poison was not only a method; it was a metaphor. We could argue the system of slavery men like Thomas Forster perpetrated in Bermuda poisoned everyone ... as it has our society until this day."

Dr. Delacroix suddenly changed the subject. "You are enjoying your classes with Mr. Everard Leopold Stowe, Rebekah?"

"The classes are wonderful. But he's away, you know, and I really miss him." The words out of her mouth, she was startled to hear a smart rap of the knocker against the door.

Dr. Delacroix seemed suddenly exhausted. She made no effort to rise from her chair. "I am not sure I am available for callers. Rebekah, would you be so kind as to see who it is? You may look through the peephole." She gave a slight ironic smile. "I believe you know where it is."

Guiltily, Rebekah remembered looking through the peephole from the other side of the door and seeing the Lady of the Library's dark eye. She got up from her seat and went to the eyehole to the right of the door. Peering through it, she realised she could see the whole library – no wonder Dr. Delacroix had been able to see her drawing the pictures of Beck. But there did not appear to be anyone at the knocker. She turned around to go back to the sofa when the knocker tapped again against the door.

"Look again, Rebekah."

Obeying, once again she pressed her eye to the lens in the hole and saw part of a face that appeared huge and distorted. With delight, she recognised the lopsided eyes and the crooked nose. "Oh," she exclaimed, beaming with more pleasure than she'd felt for months, "it's Mr. Stowe."

"Well, I suppose we should let him in," But Rebekah could tell from her eyes that she was equally delighted by Mr. Stowe's appearance. "Open the door, Rebekah."

Struggling with the complicated bolt, she finally managed to open the door and there he was smiling at her.

"It isn't June yet!"

"It will be by the weekend," he pointed out. "Besides, Mrs. Stowe's sister has recovered nicely, and we are both very pleased to be home. Good afternoon, Dr. Delacroix, and how are you? Please don't get up. It is a pleasure to see you and Rebekah are now properly acquainted. And how are you Rebekah? Have you been drawing and painting as I advised you to do? But of course I needn't ask."

Rebekah opened her mouth to tell him about all the drawings she had done of the girl and how none of them had disappeared; however, before she could get a word out, Dr. Delacroix cut in. "I am looking forward to hearing about your travels, Mr. Stowe."

"I certainly have much to tell you. In recent months I have had the pleasure of visiting your part of the world."

The Lady of the Library gave him a broad smile, her eyes alight. "I am very happy to hear it. Now Rebekah, it is time for you to go home. We do not want your mother to be concerned about your whereabouts."

Furious, Rebekah picked up her bag and her sketchbook. *Dr. Delacroix just wants Mr. Stowe all to herself. It's not fair.* She could see that Mr. Stowe caught her glare, but he didn't seem angry.

"Rebekah?" Dr. Delacroix raised her hand.

"Yes, Dr. Delacroix?"

"Remember not to discuss our meeting with any of your friends. Do you promise?"

She nodded, trying to swallow her resentment. It helped that Mr. Stowe was smiling at her, clearly pleased to see her again. Then, in one sentence, he turned her mood to sunshine.

"I hope we will have our lesson together this Sunday, at the normal time?"

"Oh yes! Yes, please."

"Bring everything you have done – don't forget now."

As if she could.

Chapter 26

Outside the rain had stopped, and the hot sun made steam rise from the many puddles in the school yard. Instead of taking the bus home, Rebekah thought she would walk to Grandma Violet's apartment in the back of town. Ever since Christmas, she'd felt differently about visiting her grandmother. Before she had never thought of dropping by – the only time she had seen her was when her mama invited her over, which wasn't very often. But now, she far preferred to see Grandma Violet in her own home. There, Grandma Violet was amusing, quite different from the sad, little, old lady she became when she visited Mama.

"I feel really sorry for the Peterson family," Grandma Violet said as she and Rebekah sat at the kitchen table drinking fruit punch.

Rebekah spluttered on her drink. "Why?"

"Apparently, the police have brought the older boy – what's his name? John – in for questioning over them murders. They went to his apartment early this morning and arrested him."

No wonder Roger was so upset. He must think Wanda reported John's gun to the police. But she wouldn't do that – I'm sure she wouldn't . . .

"The younger brother's in your class, Rebekah, isn't he?

Roger?

"Yes," Rebekah said. She was desperately trying for a casual tone. "Why do the police think John Peterson had anything to do with it?"

"I don't know for sure. But somebody told me they suspect him of being one of them Black Beret Cadre members. They've questioned other members as well. Seems to me the police target young black men. It's no wonder some of them want to join the Black Berets."

Black Berets. She remembered Uncle Gabriel talking about them at Christmas and how he thought they had a point.

"Do you agree with the Black Berets, Grandma?"

Grandma Violet shrugged. "I dunno. I don't hold with politics myself. Never have. Life to me's about putting bread on the table. Don't hold with no violence neither. But I feel bad sometimes for our young men. And I feel bad for Mrs. Peterson. She's a nice woman. Was Roger in school today, Rebekah?"

"Yes."

"Did he look upset?"

She remembered the thud of her bag as it hit his head. "I dunno. I've got to go now. I've got lots of homework."

Rebekah found conversation at dinner that evening especially difficult, particularly as the dog kept trying to lick her.

"Jasper sure likes you," Mr. Forrest said, still too eager for her to like him – his mouth grinning, showing his crooked, yellow teeth.

"I wish he didn't," she muttered. Fortunately, Mama seemed to wish the same thing. "I want the dog outside, Thomas, *now*."

"All right, all right." Mr. Forrest got up. "Poor old Jasper. Come on then." He took the dog out.

Coming back into the kitchen, he grinned amiably at

Rebekah. "Done any drawings of slave masters lately?"

Rebekah felt a spasm of apprehension. Suppose he insisted on looking at her folder? She smiled weakly but didn't answer.

"Just kidding." he laughed. "There's no need to look so worried."

"I'm not worried," she said, thinking about the picture she had drawn of the Forsters slowly being poisoned.

"Have some more meat, Rebekah? No?" He leaned back in his chair. "I've sure had an interesting day. Hey Patricia, did you hear the police have arrested a guy for the assassinations? Apparently he needs legal aid. I've been given his case. Apparently, someone requested yours truly take the case."

"Who have they arrested, Thomas?"

Rebekah held her breath.

"A young man called John Peterson," he said. "A Black Beret Cadre member. Do you know him, Rebekah?"

"No." She felt her cheeks flush with heat. *The Lady of the Library must have asked for Mr. Forrest's help. So that's why she was being poky about Mama's boyfriend.*

"You know, his brother Roger's in your class," Mama pointed out.

As if I don't know that.

"John's a lot older, of course – he must be 19 at least. How come they arrested him, Thomas?"

"They've got evidence."

"That he's Black Beret? That's not a crime, not yet. Poor Mrs. Peterson. She goes to my church, you know. She must be real upset. Once the police have a black suspect, they never let go. Specially when he's male."

"That's nonsense, Patricia. They have to have evidence to prosecute. And if they do, the young man will have a fair trial."

"Are you serious, Thomas?" Mama's voice got louder. "I forget – you've lived your whole life in Canada – that's why you're so naïve. You think a young black man on this island gets *justice?*"

"Patricia, I will make sure that he does. That's all I can say because of lawyer/client confidentiality."

Rebekah thought anxiously about the gun Wanda had told her about. *Is that the evidence?* she wondered.

The word "justice" reverberated in Rebekah's head. She got up from the table. "I'm going to my room to do some homework," she announced.

She lay on her bed so exhausted she thought she might nap for a while. But instead she found herself staring at some steps leading up to a large, grey stone building. Her eyes were drawn to two narrow cross-slatted windows at the top of the arched entrance and then to the doorway itself. *It's the State House,* she realised, *the State House in St. George's overlooking the square. But it looks different somehow, it's not painted white and the roof looks different.* This was the point at which she'd usually be reaching for her sketch book. But she felt compelled just to watch. She saw crowds of people, pushing, pushing into the building itself, into the main chamber. At first the chamber was so dark she could hardly see but slowly it lightened. She saw a row of men and women, dressed in old fashioned clothes like the ones she had painted the Forsters wearing, sitting on a bench. She looked ahead, and, in front of her, was an old woman standing, her hands and feet manacled. Her back was to Rebekah but sometimes the woman turned to glare wildly at the spectators, who stared back placidly at her contorted face. It was Sally Bassett. Then Rebekah's eyes took in a raised platform at the back of the room. She saw a row of people sitting on a bench to the platform's left and gasped because one of them was Beck, she was sure of it, and next to her was Mrs. Forster. Rebekah could just see the dull, yellow hair scraped back from that long, melancholy face. To the right of the platform she saw two rows of empty seats. Rebekah's brain cleared.

It's a courthouse. Of course, it is! Miss Spruce told us the Assizes, the court of justice, used to be held here. Sally Bassett is going to be tried and those seats are for the jury and the platform is for the judge.

Just as that insight came to her, the jury members, all white men, slowly filed in. Next entered the white judge in a long, black robe and everyone stood up.

The judge started to speak, but Rebekah could not hear what he was saying – all she could see was his mouth moving. A man walked to the witness stand which was next to the clerk. The man's mouth moved and so sometimes did his hands. The clerk wrote everything down. When the first witness finished, another man took his place and after him, a woman. *It's the red haired woman I drew sitting with Mrs. Forster in the cottage after the poisonings, the one who shook Beck,* Rebekah realised. As their lips moved, there were times Rebekah could tell when some people interrupted. The lawyer would stand up and his mouth would shape something, and then the jury members would mutter to each other. After the woman stepped down, Mrs. Forster took her place. In contrast, her mouth scarcely moved at all, nor did her hands. Yet, Rebekah could tell, everyone in the courtroom was transfixed by what she was saying. Though her lips barely parted – the lawyer, the judge, the jury, and the spectators were all visibly mesmerised. And then, it was Beck's turn but instead of walking directly to the stand, she half ran towards Rebekah, and stood directly before her.

"Don't draw me now," Rebekah knew she was pleading. "Not now. Don't draw me now."

And then Beck took the stand.

Because Rebekah had not visited Mr. Stowe since just before Christmas, when she arrived that Sunday for her lesson, the garden came as a surprise. It was lush and trees she hadn't noticed because they had been practically bare of leaves were now rich with blossom. "Summer is certainly here," he said, pointing to the clusters of vivid, red flowers cascading in all their June glory from the boughs of his royal poinciana tree.

"They're so bright, they look like they're on fire," she said.

"You're right. That's why some folks in other countries call it a flame tree although we call it a royal poinciana. But I have a different kind of flame species." He led the way to another tree, leafless, but covered with so many scarlet bells they seemed to burn into the sky. "Do you like it?"

She nodded, trying to imagine how she could possibly paint it.

"Now that is the Illawarra flame tree. I saw many of them in Australia. In Bermuda June is the month for the flame trees to start blossoming," he said a little sadly. "It's almost as if they know . . ." He beckoned her to the studio. "I think we'll work inside today. It's too hot outside this afternoon. Besides, I want to look at the pictures you've done while I was away."

She spread some of them out on his table and pointed to the one of the lily, explaining how painting it had frustrated her.

He looked at it carefully. "Well tried, Rebekah, but the problem was you started too light. Remember going dark to light, even when you are painting a white flower, will give you that luminosity. Now have you painted more pictures of the child?"

"Yes. She's grown up now. And it's as you told me in your letter – the pictures of her haven't faded at all. How did you know?"

"Let me see them." She handed him the sketchbooks containing the pictures of Beck, Nancey and the Forsters at Christmas, as well as the ones of Beck she had drawn on the Admiralty House grounds and in the library. Then she explained how Dr. Delacroix had told her their names. "But the girl's name is spelled differently to mine."

"Yes," he said. "Are there any more?"

"No but . . ." She hesitated, remembering the vision she had of Beck in the State House.

"What is it, Rebekah?"

She explained how she had seen the trial in the State House and the old woman in the dock and how the witnesses had given evidence.

"Could you hear what they said?"

She shook her head. "I could just see their lips moving."

"Did you draw all this, Rebekah?"

"No. Somehow I didn't feel like it. And then Beck appeared. She begged me not to draw her. Her voice was very faint but I'm sure that's what I heard. She didn't want me to draw her giving evidence against Sally."

"I see," said Mr. Stowe. "The poor child."

"I feel terrible about it," Rebekah blurted out. "I *saw* what happened. Mrs. Forster blamed Beck because people were starting to talk. Like this woman who visited her." She pointed to the drawings of the red-haired woman talking to Mrs. Forster after the poisonings, of the mistress pointing to her, and lastly of the red haired woman shaking Beck. They forced Beck to tell the court her grandmother made her do it. I know they did."

"I am sure you are right, Rebekah," Mr. Stowe said. "I am sure she was told that if she gave evidence she would not be punished."

"But Beck didn't do it! Mrs. Forster did it. It wasn't fair."

He sighed. "There are so many unfair things in this world. Sometimes we can only do our best in the best way we can."

Then he changed the subject. "Tell me, Rebekah, how is art at school these days?"

She shrugged. "We're having our art exam in two weeks."

"A still life?"

"Mr. Fenwick says he's going to write a word on the board

and we're to paint what it makes us think of. But he says we must still pay attention to proportion. I just hope he don't choose something too, too English."

Mr. Stowe laughed. "Like what?"

"Like a tube of dopey polo mints!"

The word Mr. Fenwick did choose was unexpected. 'FIRE', he printed carefully in white chalk on the art room's blackboard. The students let out a chorus of protest. "That's too difficult, Mr. Fenwick. It's not fair."

"Remember you don't have to paint the thing itself, if you don't want to, just what it makes you think of. You have been given several pieces of paper. For half an hour I suggest you experiment with your ideas. It's hot enough today," Mr. Fenwick added. "I'm sure you'll think of something."

It was true, the day was unusually hot for June – nearly 86°F. Three ceiling fans whirred over them at their fastest speeds.

Rebekah shut her eyes, her mind for the moment totally blank. *Fire*, she kept telling herself. *Fire. What can I do?*

The memory of the flame trees in Mr. Stowe's garden came back to her. But she wouldn't draw them there; she'd draw the poinciana trees in Admiralty House grounds where she had seen Beck standing by the shoreline, her body swollen with child. She sketched them in with charcoal, conjuring in her imagination the overall shapes of the trees, the dark, the light and the half lights of the green lacy leaves, and the burning blossom. From charcoal to paint, the poincianas sprung out of her paper, their flowers blazing in vivid vermilion. But there were two hours to go. What else could she draw about fire? Again, she shut her eyes.

She saw crowds of people jostling and half running along a beaten pathway. They were dirty and ugly, their toothy mouths contorted into grimaces of jeering laughter though the whole scene was eerily silent. The women were in long skirts, the men in long shirts and breeches. In the distance a tiny figure shuffled along the middle of the pathway until finally she came into Rebekah's view. She was old and bent and though her hands were tightly bound at the wrists with palmetto twine, she clenched them into fists, shaking them all the while at the mocking mob, who, instead of waiting for her, were rushing past her. Her face was contorted too, yelling silent words at the people as they hurried towards the harbour.

It was Sally Bassett.

Watching the mob wait and thinking about what was to happen made Rebekah's heart beat so fast and her head spin, she had to make herself draw to relieve the tension. Taking another piece of paper, she picked up her charcoal and found herself drawing first a tall, tall pile of wooden sticks and logs against what she knew would be a blue, blue sky. Next, she drew in Sally, bound to the stake she had sketched in its centre. *Don't let Beck be here*, she prayed. *Don't let her see this.* But, even as she prayed, Beck showed up, blocking her vision of the fire. Her stomach was even larger now, and she was standing among the crowd by the water. Two white men grabbed her by the arms and shoved her in front of the pile of sticks so that she was facing her grandmother. Rebekah watched the two women's desperate eyes meet. One man held a knife to Beck's throat; the other thrust a flaming torch into her hand. Rebekah gasped as she understood. Beck was to light the fire. That was her punishment. There was nothing Rebekah could do, nothing she could do to stop it. Beck had to light it. And Rebekah had to paint it. She knew that without a shadow of doubt. There was no avoiding it. It was – it was *required* of her to paint the fire. Rebekah chose her pastels – reds, yellows, blues, and violets – looked at the high pile of sticks and watched as the two men dropped their hold of Beck, though one still held the knife. *Run, Beck, run, run, run*, she pleaded, though she knew it was impossible. She held her breath. Beck slowly bent towards the bundles and held the torch against the sticks.

I can't paint Beck lighting the fire, her mind screamed. *I can't. I won't.*

It was only when Beck moved back from the fire that she could begin to paint. Once the flames took hold, Rebekah wove her pastels through the bundles, letting the flames go higher and higher, licking Sally's arms, her shoulders, her neck, her screaming, agonised mouth. And it seemed to her that Beck was at her shoulder, watching, watching as she painted. The flames blazed through Sally's long braids, consumed them, consumed her whole body, coughing out a shower of sparks.

However, it wasn't over yet.

Rebekah took another piece of paper. Using more pastels, she created a soft, solitary pile of ash, again against that blue, blue sky, the people all gone because the fun was over.

Just one more thing to paint.

She began at the base of the ash, a clump of darkish thin green leaves blooming into view, on the page, and out of it, one purple Bermudiana iris.

"Some say that's when it first grew in Bermuda," her papa had said.

Rebekah burst into tears.

Chapter 25

Wanda tapped her on the shoulder. "Why are you crying, Rebekah?" she whispered. "What is wrong?"

Mr. Fenwick strode up to their desks. "Wanda Lambert, how dare you talk in an exam? Do you want to be disqualified?" Then he noticed Rebekah's heaving shoulders and tears. "Are you ill, Rebekah?"

He looked at her painting of the trees. "This is very competent. There's no need to cry, Rebekah."

He didn't appear to notice the ones of the old lady and the fire and the ash. *Just as well*, she thought, *because they'd make you very angry.*

She heard the classroom door click and open. "Mr. Fenwick." It was Mrs. Drinkwater. Some students struggled to their feet as was required when the principal entered the room, but she waved them back to their seats and made her way to Rebekah's seat. "You poor child," she said, looking at the painting of Sally Bassett consumed by fire. "You poor child. Mr. Fenwick, I need you to excuse Rebekah from your class."

He nodded. "She has certainly completed her examination to my satisfaction. The trees are very well executed."

"Now, Rebekah, come with me and bring all your paintings

with you. We will return them to you for grading," Mrs. Drinkwater told Mr. Fenwick as he started to object. "You need not be concerned about that."

Wiping the tears from her eyes, Rebekah obediently got to her feet and tried not to notice the curious stares of the other students in the class. It was such a relief to escape the art room. She followed Mrs. Drinkwater outside, across the road and the school yard, and into the main building. "We are going to the library," Mrs. Drinkwater said. "Dr. Delacroix is most concerned about you."

"How did she know something was wrong?" Rebekah asked but then she remembered the periscope. Dr. Delacroix must have been watching the art examination from her bedroom window.

"She telephoned me, requesting your presence immediately. Come along now."

They made their way up the steps to the tower. The library was open. Mrs. Chatterjee was tidying some shelves. Ignoring her, Mrs. Drinkwater rapped the silver knocker smartly on the red door and immediately it opened. There to Rebekah's surprise and delight was Mr. Stowe. Behind him, Dr. Delacroix was sitting in her rocking chair. She was wearing a silk purple dress with jade buttons. After an exchange of greetings, Mr. Stowe took the paintings from her and, placing them on the table in front of Dr. Delacroix, beckoned Rebekah to the red sofa. Propped against the sofa was a parcel wrapped in birthday paper. And next to it a closed wicker picnic basket.

"I know I am leaving this young lady in safe hands," Mrs. Drinkwater said. "I cannot remain. I have a school governors' meeting in half an hour."

Dr. Delacroix's lip curled slightly causing Rebekah to remember another Christmas revelation – she had never been appointed headmistress. But after Mrs. Drinkwater left, Dr. Delacroix smiled at her and then at Mr. Stowe. "I think, Mr.

Stowe, a little restorative is in order. Do you agree?"

"I do indeed, Dr. Delacroix." He went to the cabinet on the wall above the enamel cooker and took out a bottle of cordial and three crystal glasses. After pouring a little of the red liquid into each glass, he handed one to Dr. Delacroix and one to Rebekah.

She looked at the cordial doubtfully. It was thick, like cough medicine.

"Drink it, Rebekah, it will do you good." Then he sat down in the arm chair next to Dr. Delacroix's rocking chair, his own glass in hand, and they both examined Rebekah's paintings with great seriousness.

Rebekah sipped the cordial. It was rather sticky and sweet, but it did make her feel better. The sick and shaky feeling that had come over her began to recede.

"I think in her art examination Rebekah has acquitted herself to the highest standard. Would you agree, Mr. Stowe?"

"I would, indeed, Dr. Delacroix."

"Tell me, Rebekah, did you hear what Sally Bassett said?"

She shook her head. "There was no sound. But I thought I could see her shouting something to the crowd of people."

"You were quite right. It is said that she told them, 'No use you hurrying, folks. There'll be no fun till I get there.'"

"I heard her say that on the fire truck," Rebekah said. "At least, I think I did. I kind of heard it in my head."

Dr. Delacroix nodded. "You see, she knew the burning of a black woman was not only a deterrent against escaping or fighting against slavery, it was also for the crowds an event of sheer entertainment."

"I didn't see the Forsters there," Rebekah said.

"Thomas was probably still far too sick."

"Yes," agreed Rebekah. "But Mrs. Forster could have come. She came to the trial. Maybe she felt sorry . . ."

"I doubt it," said Dr. Delacroix. "I'm sure she was relieved the woman who knew what she had done was well and truly dead."

"I think Rebekah could be right," Mr. Stowe said quietly. "Perhaps Mrs. Forster could not face the terrible consequences of what she had done. Perhaps watching the fire was too much for her."

"She didn't find watching her husband slowly dying of poison too much to watch, did she?" The Lady of the Library started to rock in her chair.

Mr. Stowe nodded at the truth of this. "But she did not hate Beck, as Rebekah's picture shows us."

Dr. Delacroix leaned forward, "Tell me, Rebekah, Beck is also missing from your pictures, is she not?"

Rebekah stayed silent, hot tears prickling her eyelids.

Mr. Stowe looked at her with sympathetic eyes. "Did something happen that you have chosen not to paint, Rebekah? It is your choice, of course. But if it is very painful, it would be better for you to confide it. It would relieve you."

"Mr. Stowe is quite right," agreed Dr. Delacroix, "although what could be more painful than the burning of Sally Bassett I can't imagine."

Tears streamed down Rebekah's face as the vision of the men grabbing Beck came back to her. "I couldn't paint it," she sobbed, "I just couldn't."

"What couldn't you paint, child?" Dr. Delacroix's voice softened. "What was it?"

"Beck lit the fire," she whispered.

Mr. Stowe walked to her and handed her from his pocket a very clean, white cotton handkerchief. She wiped her eyes and her nose. "They made her do it. Two white men grabbed her – one held a knife to her throat and the other gave her the torch."

There was a heavy silence as Dr. Delacroix and Mr. Stowe thought about this revelation.

"The ultimate evil," Mr. Stowe said finally. "The ultimate destruction of a child's innocence."

"Yes," the Lady of the Library said eventually. "But harsh though this may sound, Beck shouldn't have given that evidence when she knew it wasn't true. And she shouldn't have lit that fire."

"She was terrified," Rebekah pleaded. "I know she was. And she was so young. She could have been burned, too."

"No, Rebekah, she would never have been burned, precisely because of her youth."

"What do you mean?"

"She was of child bearing age – she had auction block value. She would have been worth £20, maybe more. When the foreman announced the verdict at Sally Bassett's trial, he said, 'Guilty and we value her at one pound four shillings and sixpence.' Sally Bassett was so old, she was not worth keeping. And burning her made an example to other slaves who might be considering a similar solution."

"I never realised," Rebekah started, "I never thought of people being worth money."

"They were *slaves* and as such considered not human but property – like sticks of furniture."

"Yes," agreed Mr. Stowe quietly. "But we must grant, Dr. Delacroix, that's a very harsh reality for a young lady like Rebekah to take in."

"It is a reality many young people of our race had to accept from a very young age," Dr. Delacroix said quietly. "Sally Bassett was probably born a slave."

"And Beck," Rebekah put in quickly.

"Yes, indeed, child. And also Beck's mother."

"Who was that?"

"Sally Bassett's daughter. It is likely that she was raped by Thomas Forster."

Rebekah flinched.

"Beck would have been the result."

"What happened to her, to Beck's mother?" Rebekah hadn't even thought about Beck's mama although she realised she should have. Everyone has a mama.

"We don't know." Dr. Delacroix sipped her cordial. "She probably died in childbirth. So many women did. Or perhaps she was sold and sent abroad. As I told you, Rebekah, I believe Sally Bassett wanted to protect her granddaughter from the same fate. When her granddaughter became sexually of age, Sally Bassett knew what Mr. Forster might do to Beck. Until your drawing showed us otherwise, we thought she tried to prevent it by killing the whole family. From your paintings in Admiralty House, we now know she was too late to save Beck from rape."

"I wish Mr. Forster had died," Rebekah blurted out. "If the poison had worked, then everyone would have been all right." *And*, she thought to herself, *Mr. Forrest might never have been born. He's not evil but he sure is irritating.*

"Not everybody," the Lady of the Library pointed out. "What about Nancey? She would have died too. Do you think she deserved to die?"

Rebekah sighed. "I never thought about that. No, of course not, because Mr. Forster was so cruel to her as well. It's so – it's so confusing. I wish he had died but it's never right to kill, is it?"

Dr. Delacroix sighed. "That is a very difficult question, child. Dr. Martin Luther King was against it but not all civil rights activists agreed with him. However, killing, any kind of violence should certainly be the very last resort. But people like Sally Bassett are trapped by an evil system."

Rebekah thought about John Peterson. *Had he felt trapped? Was that why he had a gun?*

"And Mrs. Forster, too," said Mr. Stowe. "Although she was white, she too was trapped in her marriage."

Dr. Delacroix sniffed. Rebekah could see that she had no

sympathy for Sarah Forster. "The most important point," the Lady of the Library said firmly, "is that people who say they fight for justice *do* fight for justice and not for their own selfish reasons."

There was a tight little silence which Rebekah found so agonising, afraid she might blurt something out about John. She could feel Dr. Delacroix's eyes drilling into her. The woman is like a witch, she thought. The word "witch" in her mind made her think back to the fire and the awful realisation that Beck had lit it. "I wish I didn't see these things," she said with heartfelt emotion, "I wish I could just draw normal stuff."

Mr. Stowe shook his head, "Never wish that, young lady. I believe, Rebekah Eve, that you are someone we have needed for a very long time."

She looked at him. *Is he teasing? But, no, that's not like him.* Mr. Stowe was sometimes funny, but he never used humour to make her feel foolish. She opened her mouth to ask him what he meant but then he continued.

"I think you are a kind of griot, a teller of history. In Africa griots are revered for their knowledge of history. Sometimes they tell their historical accounts, sometimes they sing them."

"But I don't tell stories." she objected. "And I can't sing either."

"It doesn't matter. The principle is the same. Griots use their art – in their case their poetry and their music – to reveal the truth. Instead of words and song, you have used your vision and your painting to disclose secrets long since hidden, the secrets of history."

"Yes," agreed Dr. Delacroix. "If it weren't for you, we wouldn't know that Sarah Forster colluded with Sally Bassett; we wouldn't know that Beck had nothing to do with the poison. It may seem to you a burden, but you have a gift for revelation."

Mr. Stowe gazed at Rebekah steadily. "What you are doing is so important."

"Why?"

It was Dr. Delacroix who answered. "For black people in Bermuda, our history has so often been what white people wanted it to be. For over 200 years, our people were listed in bills of sale and wills and court records as mere pieces of property without face or voice. Our hopes, our feelings, our dreams, let alone our achievements, were rarely recorded. Your paintings have the power to change that – to let us be seen and understood – as equals."

"But how do we know I'm not imagining stuff?" Rebekah asked. "I could be crazy, you know."

"You are perfectly sane, Rebekah, never worry about that," Mr. Stowe said. "You have been given a gift. Remember that and never turn your back on it. Dr. Delacroix and I believe Beck's spirit sought you out to tell her story because she knew she could trust you. And she was right."

"Beck kept fading," she reminded them. "I still don't know why."

"Think carefully," Dr. Delacroix said. "At what point did your drawings *not* fade?"

"On Christmas Day when I did the drawing of her face in the mirror," she said promptly. "And before that when I drew the Forsters and Beck waiting on them. But when I drew Beck as a young girl, I couldn't keep her."

"That makes sense. Doesn't it?"

Her brain ached with the effort of figuring it out and then she understood. "Everybody knows about Beck and the poison, or think they know, because of the court records. But they don't know her as a little girl because nobody wrote down what she was like."

Dr. Delacroix and Mr. Stowe smiled at her approvingly.

"Exactly," Mr. Stowe said. "When you first saw her, she was a child, an innocent child whose life was never recorded either in words or in pictures. It is possible at that point she did not understand what being a slave meant – perhaps she did not even realise she was a slave."

"I don't know," said Rebekah, "I think she knew she was a slave early on because she said 'No finery.' But she was innocent. She was so cute."

"Yes. And then, cruelly, she was forced to grow up."

Rebekah thought about growing up and how it means you don't necessarily have a happy ending the way you do in stories. She remembered the time she and her daddy had gone fishing at Hog Bay and how cold she had felt when she knew he wouldn't live with them anymore. And how your daddy so busy in the fields there's never time to talk about important stuff or if there is, it's not the right time. And how the stars when you look at them make you feel so lonely that sometimes it's better not to look at them at all. Beck had seen those same stars, Rebekah realised. How much worse it must have been for her, an orphan slave. She didn't have anybody. She just had a grandma, an old woman crazed with hate, and an owner who had raped her mama and then Beck herself.

"Until you saw Beck," Mr Stowe continued, "she was only a named witness in the court records. When she was asking you to draw her, she was asking you to give her back her identity."

"But I couldn't do it. Because the drawings I did of her when she was little kept fading. And then there was the explosion in the library, remember?"

"Dr. Delacroix has an interesting theory about that," said Mr. Stowe. "May we hear it, please?"

"Certainly. I am convinced that Mrs. Forster's spirit was the force behind the fadings and the fire. Of all the people, she would be the one who would most want the truth to be kept secret. To have you reveal her as the murderess would be intolerable for her. As for Sally Bassett – her story has not been hidden exactly. It has been orally passed down the generations. But your paintings show us her pain and her spirit. They have not demeaned her. Even in this century there have been people who wanted to trivialise the fate of Sally Bassett."

"I don't understand."

"Mr. Stowe, would you be so kind as to take the dinner bell from the third drawer of my writing desk?"

Rebekah couldn't fathom what a dinner bell had to do with Sally Bassett or indeed what a dinner bell was. But she could see Mr. Stowe was not surprised by the request. He calmly went to the Lady of the Library's desk and removed what looked like a brass doll with a full, long, jagged skirt and a turban on her head and handed it to Dr. Delacroix. The look on her face as she held the doll-like thing in her hand was utter disgust. "This, Rebekah, was a Bermuda souvenir, a dinner bell made for tourists coming to our island. Rich people would ring it to summon their slaves, and later when slavery was over, their maids, to serve them their meals. This one is meant to be Sally Bassett so that cast in brass, the poisoner is still the obedient slave serving food." Dr. Delacroix shook it and Rebekah could see that the doll's feet under the skirt were the clappers. She shuddered at the tinkle of the bell and felt the Lady of the Library's eyes upon her.

"Yes, my dear, it is evil, is it not?"

Rebekah nodded. "But why do you keep it?"

"That is a very good question. I could throw this away, but if I do, I throw away a piece of evidence of how our history has been misrepresented. At present we have no place in Bermuda where the truth about our people is shown through artefacts and pictures. One day I hope there will be a museum on our island where this object can safely be kept and seen for the insult it is. Do you understand?"

"Yes," said Rebekah, "that makes sense." And it did. She began to see how pictures could change people's opinions for good or for bad. Then she thought regretfully of the times she had seen Beck as a child. "I wish my drawings of Beck when she was young had lasted," she said.

Dr. Delacroix snorted. "Youth! It lasts for such a little moment. I know. There is nothing permanent about youth. There is only permanence in character. Remember that, Rebekah. Try to avoid being young and foolish."

Rebekah thought somehow this was very sad advice.

"Better still," said Mr. Stowe, "be young and joyful. Rebekah, today is Dr. Delacroix's birthday."

"It is?"

"Yes," said Dr. Delacroix with satisfaction.

"Happy birthday, Dr. Delacroix."

"Thank you. A significant birthday. Mr. Stowe has kindly brought me a special lunch." The Lady of the Library pointed to the picnic basket. Rebekah rose to her feet.

"One minute, Rebekah," Mr. Stowe got up too. "It is thanks to Rebekah that I believe I have the perfect present for you, Dr. Delacroix."

"I noticed the parcel by my sofa," she said, her eyes gleaming. "What is it?"

"It is only right that Rebekah should unwrap it for you."

Rebekah was puzzled. "I don't understand."

"You will. Would you unwrap it please?" He handed it to her.

Carefully she did as she was told and there before her was the painting Rebekah had done of the young woman, the one Mr. Stowe had liked so much he asked her if he could keep it. She looked at her subject's eyes, and suddenly she understood.

"Oh!" she exclaimed. "Oh!"

"Let me see," Dr. Delacroix demanded tetchily. "It's supposed to be my present."

Mr. Stowe stepped forward to help Rebekah hold the

picture before her.

Looking at it, the Lady was mesmerised into silence. Rebekah could swear there were tears in her eyes.

"Be young and joyful," she said at last. "I was, you know."

"Yes," Mr. Stowe said, "you were."

Chapter 26

The end of year examinations came and went with Rebekah doing well enough in them to appease her mother, especially as she received A's for history, literature and, much to her surprise, art.

Summer break gave her lots of time to think about Beck and what had happened to her after the burning. Mr. Stowe had told her when she asked him about it that Dr. Delacroix was certain Beck had been sold and shipped abroad. "Dr. Delacroix looked at Thomas Forster's will and there was no mention of Beck though other slaves were listed."

"Maybe," said Rebekah hopefully, "Mrs. Forster kept her promise and freed her."

"I doubt it, Rebekah. Mr. Forster was told Beck was responsible, remember. Perhaps he thought she might try to poison them again. And Mrs. Forster would not want a constant reminder of her guilt in the house. It's likely Mr. Forster would continue his assault on Beck, as his wife well knew. Suppose Beck told him and he believed her?"

"I wonder if I will see her again."

"That too I doubt. Because now you have told her story. But time will tell."

Sometimes Rebekah tried drawing Beck standing on the deck of a sailing ship, a little girl beside her, but the drawing of them never looked right. One day while she was sketching in the kitchen, she drew Beck with a little boy beside her, waiting on the edge of a harbour and watching a ship with billowing sails as it came in to anchor.

"Who's that?" Mr. Forrest asked her, peering over her shoulder. Her mama was sitting at the counter reading the paper.

If you only knew, Rebekah thought. "I dunno," she answered. "Just someone I made up."

"That figures," he said. "She doesn't look as real as some of your other drawings of people."

She couldn't argue with this. *She doesn't look real because she's not appearing to me anymore; I really am making her up.* Rebekah sometimes had to concede that maybe Mr. Forrest wasn't as foolish as he looked. "That little boy next to her looks real though," Mr. Forrest continued. "His eyes are so striking, an unusual green."

Startled, she looked at the face of the child she had drawn. He did look familiar – but she couldn't think why.

"Let me see," said Mama, looking up from her paper. "Is it Troy or Trey?"

Rebekah shook her head. "I would never draw one twin without the other. It wouldn't be right. It's just someone I made up."

"Well, let me see."

Rebekah took her sketchbook over to her mama, who looked intently at the drawing. "Why, Rebekah, that looks just like Mr. Peterson when he was little."

"Are you serious?"

"Of course. I should know. I grew up with him. Besides, he has those exact same green eyes."

Is that why he looks so familiar? Because he's John's ancestor?

Mama shut the sketchbook and handed it back to Rebekah.

"I feel so sorry for the Petersons right now."

"Well, you needn't," Mr. Forrest said. "John, or Zende, as he insists on being called, has been let go. There wasn't enough evidence to keep him. I'm glad of it but he wasn't easy, I have to say. As soon as we met, he looked at me as if I were a piece of scum even though I was doing my best to help him. Sometimes I wonder about this country. Is it my fault I'm white?"

"Hmm," said Mama, "I wonder how long he'll stay free."

"Patricia . . ."

"Are we going out to dinner or what? Rebekah, you want to come?"

"You're very welcome to come," said Mr. Forrest.

But she didn't want to go out. She wanted to think.

An hour or so later, the doorbell rang. Rebekah thought it might be Wanda, so she hurried to open the door.

"Rebekah."

She could feel her mouth drop open. "John? How do you know where I live?" Then she understood. "You're here to see your lawyer?"

He wrinkled his forehead "Why would you think I'm here to see my lawyer? Roger told me where you live. I just wanted to say goodbye."

"Why?" Rebekah asked bluntly.

"I'm leaving Bermuda tomorrow, for Canada."

"So?"

"So . . ." He shifted his feet awkwardly. "So – Rebekah, can I come in?"

She hesitated a minute. But he looked so harmless, and just as likeable as he had seemed when she had first met him at Kentucky Fried. Not fierce at all.

"All right."

She led the way to the kitchen at the end of the hallway and pointed to a seat at the counter. He sat on it while she sat on another, her paintings in front of her. His eyes fell on them and he picked up one of Beck, the one of her standing pregnant at Admiralty House.

"That is beautiful, so beautiful, Rebekah. That's sort of why I'm here. Your art."

"I don't understand."

"I can't stop thinking about your painting. I think you see the truth the way most folks don't. You see a truth more of us need to see but are too afraid to look at."

Mr. Stowe had said something similar. What had he called her? A griot, something like that. She looked at John's eyes, greener than ever in the fluorescent kitchen light, and then at the picture of Beck standing by the shore, and suddenly she could see him so clearly. *He really is a descendent of Beck and her little boy – he has to be.* She thought of the drawing she had just done of them both and how she had drawn the child's eyes – as innocent as Beck's had been and as defenceless. John's eyes were just as vulnerable now, she thought, but were they innocent?

"I was arrested, you know, thanks to that friend of yours."

"Wanda didn't do anything. She wouldn't and anyway . . ."

"Anyway?"

"Your brother attacked her, and she had no idea why. That wasn't nice. He had no business . . ." She could hear her voice rising in outrage.

"I'm sorry about that. Roger shouldn't have done that. But we both thought she'd told the police. I'm not a bad person, Rebekah, I want you to know that. I just want Bermuda to be a fairer place for all of us."

What about the gun? What about the assassinations? If she was so good at seeing the truth, she wondered, how come she couldn't be completely sure he was innocent? Just as she was gathering her nerve to ask him if he'd used the gun, Mr. Forrest's furious voice shouted, "John Peterson!"

Both of them jumped. Rebekah looked behind John to see that somehow Mr. Forrest had come into the house and down the hallway to the kitchen without either of them hearing, they were so wrapped up in their conversation. Rebekah looked behind him, but her mama wasn't there.

"What the hell are you doing here?" Mr. Forrest's face was flushed with rage. "You cannot just visit me like this just because I'm your lawyer."

John looked at Rebekah then back at Mr. Forrest. "I haven't come to visit you. I've come to see Rebekah." To Rebekah he said, "Why is Mr. Forrest in your house?"

"He lives here," she explained awkwardly, "at least some of the time."

"How do you know Rebekah? She is only thirteen … and you, you have no business being mixed up with her," Mr Forrest spluttered.

"You're her stepfather?" John looked down at the brutal painting of Forster and Nancey. "That must be tough on you, Rebekah. I recognised him at once, you know."

Mr. Forrest looked like his head was about to explode – his face was redder than she had ever seen it. And she could see that he wasn't just angry. He was hurt to the core. She almost felt sorry for him.

"No," she said. "He's not my stepfather and he's not a … the slave master."

"But he looks like him."

His eyes went meaningfully to the painting.

"It's just a coincidence. The slave master is someone from the past and his name is Forster. See?" She pointed to the title.

"The name is near enough. Thomas Forster? He must be an ancestor."

Rebekah suddenly felt weak with exhaustion.

It was all so complicated. "I think you should go now, John."

He nodded. "Can I have a drawing of yours, Rebekah, to take with me? I'd really like that."

She could feel Mr. Forrest's indignant eyes upon her, daring her to give him the one of the slave master and Nancey. She thought for a moment, went to her sketch book, and handed him the one of Beck and the little boy. John looked at it for what felt like a long time though just seconds went by. She could see him taking in the detail of the little boy's face and she wondered whether one day he would recognise himself as clearly as he recognised Mr. Forrest. Then it dawned on her that John actually hadn't recognised Mr. Forrest's true significance at all, just as Mr. Forrest hadn't recognised John's.

If Thomas Forster raped Beck and she gave birth to John's ancestor, then they are blood kin, she realised, *and what would they both think of that? Shall I tell them?* She decided against it. They were so angry with each other, it wasn't the right minute and maybe she wasn't the right person.

"Thank you," he said. "This is very special."

"Please go now," she said quietly.

"So you've known John Peterson all the time," Mr. Forrest said after John had left. "If your mother finds out ..."

"Mama knows the family. She grew up with Mr. Peterson. You heard her say so. Besides, Roger is in my class."

"That's different. His brother is far too old for you to be messing with ... And – he's a *criminal* ..."

"You said there was no evidence."

"Oh, Rebekah, that doesn't mean he's *innocent*. It just means the police don't have sufficient evidence to prove his guilt – yet." He searched her face. "Rebekah, has he told you anything I should know?"

She couldn't tell Mr. Forrest about the gun. Beck had suffered enough and John was Beck's family; Rebekah was certain of it. She just couldn't tell.

"Rebekah?"

"No. Except he's leaving Bermuda."

"He is? When?"

"Tomorrow."

He drew in a quick breath, let it out. "Tomorrow?"

"Yes."

His shoulders seemed to relax with relief. He walked towards her drawings. Stared down at the one he'd hated so much and took in the label. "Rebekah?"

"Yes?"

"The drawing you gave to John Peterson – the little boy was like him, wasn't he?"

She nodded. "An ancestor."

He sat down beside her at the kitchen counter. "Patricia dropped me off so that she could go see her mother. She'll be here soon."

"All right."

She shifted uncomfortably.

He looked again at her drawing. "Rebekah ... I ... I need you to tell me everything you know about this Thomas Forster," he said. "Who was he?"

So, she told him after all.

Chapter 27

All the Eve family could talk about was Aunty Gwen and Uncle Gabriel's baby – when it would arrive, what sex it would be, and what name it might have. It was irritating. Rebekah still fervently hoped they would have a boy, but her hopes were dashed when Grandma Kezia surprised her – and her mama – by calling on the telephone to give them the news. "It's a girl," she said, "seven pounds one ounce and the cutest baby you ever did see. They'll be home from the hospital tomorrow and here next weekend for a celebration. Your daddy will bring you here after your art lesson on Sunday so you can meet her."

Mama pursed her lips when Rebekah told her about the baby. "A girl, huh? Let's hope the Eves still pay you some mind."

Rebekah tried to hide her own lack of enthusiasm from her mama. But she felt annoyed when her daddy said, on their way down to St. George's, that the baby was a very pretty little thing. Even more annoying, he didn't appear to notice she was annoyed.

Grandma Kezia, who had made banana and gingerbread to celebrate the baby's homecoming, was bustling in the kitchen. "No, no, child," she said when Rebekah asked if she could help. "Aunty Gwen is in the living room with the baby. She's really looking forward to seeing you. Off you go."

Reluctantly, she did as she was told and found Aunty Gwen on the sofa, the baby in her arms. Uncle Gabriel was sitting in an arm chair smiling so widely, Rebekah thought he looked foolish. Aunty Gwen looked up.

"Hello, sweetie. How's my favourite niece?"

"Fine. Congratulations, Aunty Gwen."

"Why thank you, Bekah. Isn't she gorgeous? Come and sit down beside me so you can hold her. She won't break, you know," she laughed as she saw Rebekah's apprehensive expression. Gently, she placed the sleeping child in Rebekah's arms. "There," she said. "What do you think, sweetie?"

As Rebekah looked down, the baby's eyes opened, looking straight into hers; a tiny yawn escaped her bow of a mouth. It was the yawn that captivated her. How could a baby one week old be able to yawn like that? She let the little fingers curve round hers, enchanted by their pearly fingernails, and felt such a rush of love she couldn't believe it.

"She's beautiful, Aunty Gwen. Have you decided on a name yet?"

"We were thinking of Rebekah. What do you think?"

She felt deeply honoured but also resistant to the idea. "Don't you think it will be confusing?"

"That's what Gabriel says. Still, we were considering it because we want you to be very much part of our daughter's life, Bekah. You have so much to show and teach her."

"That's nice." She bent down to kiss the baby gently on her forehead.

"So, we'd like you to be godmother."

"You're serious?"

"Of course. We wouldn't joke about something that important."

A feeling of warmth swept through Rebekah's body, she was so pleased. "I would love to be her godmother," she said.

"Have you thought of any other names?"

"Well, we both like Raawiya. It's Arabic."

"Do you like it?" asked Uncle Gabriel. "You must like your goddaughter's name, you know! Not to mention your cousin's."

"Yes, I do," she said. "Raawiya. It's different."

"It means 'story teller'."

"How come you're smiling, Bekah? What are you thinking?"

"Oh nothing."

She heard Mr. Stowe's words in her head. *I think you are a kind of griot, a teller of history.* Would Raawiya become one too? In a way Rebekah hoped not. Seeing history so clearly could cause so much pain – hostility, too, when the reality was too harsh. Mr. Forrest's expression when she had told him about Thomas Forster came back to her – anguished, defensive. And though he tried to hide it, Rebekah could see he was angry with her for telling him a truth he did not want to face. He had asked but, even so, he wasn't ready. When she had finished, all he could say was, "My father wasn't like that, Rebekah. He was a good man." He couldn't even comment on the possibility he and John Peterson were related.

Now she looked down again at the baby, marvelling again at how complete she was with her cap of black hair and her perfectly shaped shell ears.

"I think it's a lovely name."

After tea Grandma Kezia presented Aunty Gwen and Uncle Gabriel with a soft package.

"I made this for Raawiya. I hope you like it."

Gwen opened it and there in the tissue was an exquisitely worked baby quilt in purples, pinks, greens and blues. "It's beautiful, Grandma Kezia. Too beautiful to use."

"All the pieces are cotton so it will wash. It's meant for using. The ones I made for my boys lasted years, you know. I still have them somewhere."

Rebekah admired the way the tiny pieces of cloth were

sewn together to form flowers and butterflies surrounding a crib. She remembered how Grandma had told her how she couldn't afford paints and how she had satisfied her love for colour by using fabric instead.

As if reading her mind, Grandma Kezia said, "I made a quilt for Dr. Delacroix once, you know. She said I was an artist."

"You are an artist, Grandma Kezia." Suddenly she remembered the beautiful sun hat Grandma Kezia had once made for her out of woven, dried palmetto, as well as all the quilts she had pieced.

"Don't know about that but I was always good at sewing and craft."

"What do you think of her, Bek?" her daddy asked. "I know you met her at last. Mr. Stowe told me."

"The Lady of the Library? I think she's a very poky, interfering woman."

They all laughed at that. "I don't see what's so funny," Rebekah objected. Which made them all laugh even harder. Even Raawiya started to gurgle. After a time, Rebekah couldn't help joining in. It felt good to laugh after everything she'd been through; it felt good to belong. She thought of all the ways the Lady of the Library had helped her, beginning with the art books and her introduction to Mr. Stowe. And her comforting conviction that Rebekah would be an artist.

"But ... it's a good kind of poky I suppose."

Epilogue

ebekah knew that her christening present to her goddaughter had to be a painting. But she didn't know what to paint until one day, sitting under Mr. Stowe's poinciana, she saw in her imagination a purple hillside. She saw it rise gently towards a blue horizon, its incline carpeted with fields and fields of Bermudiana irises. At the foot of the hill, a little girl was standing. The child pointed up to the sky and to four young, laughing women, dressed in white billowing dresses, sitting on the hill's peak. Grandma Kezia's brimmed palmetto hats were upon their heads. In the middle was a beautiful lady Rebekah could not at first identify because of her laughing eyes, her smiling lips. But then she saw the pride and strength in the sculpted face and knew it to be Sally Bassett. Next to her was the Lady of the Library as a young woman, familiar because of the vitality shining out of those dark, impish eyes. And in front sat Rebekah herself, older than thirteen but still young. The breeze picked up strands of her long black hair falling away from her hat. By her side, holding her hand, was a giggling Raawiya, definitely more child than baby now, her hair in two perky braids.

Rebekah looked again at the child at the base of the hill. It was Beck, her green eyes alight with mischief and joy, her tumble of tight curls tucked under a beautiful turban. Would Rebekah be able to keep her this time? She set out her paper, her charcoal and pastels.

I will put my mama in the picture, Rebekah thought, *my mama, Grandma Violet, Grandma Kezia, Aunty Gwen, all the women in my family. They all belong here.*

But she would not draw them just yet. She would start as her story, as all their stories had started, with Beck. And this time, she was sure, the painting would not fade. She picked up a pastel and started to paint.

The End

Author's Notes

The story of Sally Bassett can be found in a typed transcription of a précised court record held in the Bermuda Government Archives. It states that she was indicted and then tried for giving her granddaughter, Beck, poisons and for ordering her to use them to murder Thomas and Sarah Forster as well as their other slave, Nancey. Ten white people, including Sarah Forster, were witnesses against Sally but the crucial evidence in the trial was given by Beck. Found guilty, Sally Bassett was burned at the stake in June 1730.

A Dark Iris follows this account but differs in one important respect. Beck did not collude with Sally; she was innocent. I realised I wanted my work of fiction to focus on Beck, whose guilt I have always held in doubt, rather than on Sally. I wanted to show her entrapment in a vicious adult world. I also wanted Rebekah's revelation to be unexpected rather than one based on a known record.

A word about names – to give the novel an authentically Bermudian flavour, I have deliberately given many of my characters names that are familiar in Bermuda. However, none of my characters, other than those recorded in history, are known to me. They are the product of my imagination.

About the Author

Elizabeth J. Jones has lived and worked all her adult life in Bermuda. She is a graduate of the University of East Anglia and has had published history books and numerous articles about Bermuda for *The Bermudian* magazine. Her novel *A Dark Iris* was a finalist for the 2018 CODE Burt Award for Caribbean Young Adult Literature. Her story 'The Ceremony' appears in *New Worlds Old Ways*, an anthology of speculative fiction, edited by Karen Lord. Other stories and memoir are included in *The Stories We Tell*, edited by Tobias S. Buckell, *Take This Journey With Me*, edited by Rachel Manley, and *I Wish I could Tell You*, edited by Lynn Joseph.